# The Boss of Her

## By the Authors

**Julie Cannon**

Come and Get Me

Heart 2 Heart

Heartland

Uncharted Passage

Just Business

Power Play

Descent

Breakers Passion

Rescue Me

I Remember

Smoke and Fire

Because of You

Countdown

Capsized

Wishing on a Dream

Take Me There

**Aurora Rey**

***Cape End Romances:***

Winter's Harbor

Summer's Cove

Spring's Wake

Built to Last

Crescent City Confidential

**M. Ullrich**

Fortunate Sum

Life in Death

Fake It Till You Make It

Time Will Tell

# The Boss of Her

*by*

Julie Cannon
Aurora Rey
M. Ullrich

2018

**THE BOSS OF HER**



**ISBN 13: 978-1-63555-145-7**

This Trade Paperback Original Is Published By
Bold Strokes Books, Inc.
P.O. Box 249
Valley Falls, NY 12185

First Edition: April 2018



---

**Credits**
Editor: Ashley Bartlett
Production Design: Stacia Seaman
Cover Design by Tammy Seidick

# Contents

# Lead Counsel

*Aurora Rey*

# Chapter One

Elisa Gonzalez closed her eyes and wondered what karmic force she'd managed to piss off. She could think of no heinous act or ill will that would warrant the news she'd just received. Parker Jones was about to become her boss.

Parker Jones, who'd run off to New York the second she graduated. Who'd passed both the Louisiana and New York bar exams within a year and become the biggest of the big shots Tulane had put out in ages. Who'd flirted and had her way and—

"Gonzalez." Don Peterson, Elisa's least favorite managing partner at Blanchard & Breaux, glared at her.

From the look on his face, Elisa was pretty sure she'd just missed something really important. "I'm sorry. What did you say?"

"I said you've been selected to head up the local team. Although if you're going to flake out, it might not be such a good idea."

"No, no." Pride kicked in and she squared her shoulders. "My mind wandered for a moment. Won't happen again."

"See that it doesn't. Teaming up with Kenner and Associates could open a whole new area for us. According to their managing partners, Jones is the best. Bringing her on board is a big play and we don't want to fuck it up."

A thought occurred to her like a punch to the gut. "Wait. Who did the selecting?"

Don's eyes narrowed. "What selecting?"

"Me. Who selected me? Was it you?" Please let it be him.

"No, it was Jones. As lead, she got a say in the local team and she picked you as her second. You know her or something?"

Know her. Ha. That was one way of putting it. "We went to law school together."

Don nodded slowly. Elisa said a silent prayer that he would let it go at that. "Oh. Well, that's nice, I suppose. Make sure you're hospitable."

Elisa folded her arms. Don would deny his comment had anything to do with gender, but she could hardly imagine him saying it to a male associate. He probably didn't know Parker was a lesbian. Hell, he probably didn't know she was. Not because she was in the closet, but because he couldn't be bothered to get to know the people in the firm who weren't on his team. She sighed. Better than having him hit on her. "When is she coming?"

"Her flight gets in at nine tomorrow."

It took every ounce of self-control she had not to groan. That gave her exactly no time to mentally prepare. Much less to do any background research on the case. "Let me guess. She's coming right to the office."

Don shrugged. "She's not getting paid to go sightseeing."

"Do you want me to finish what I'm working on now or dive right into this?" She knew the answer but had to ask anyway.

"Give everything on the Brookings case to Manchac. He's got nothing better to do. It sounds like Jones wants to keep her team small and focused."

Of course she did. "Yes, sir. Anything else?"

Don looked her up and down with a slightly disinterested leer. "I don't know why, but Jones seems to think you're hot shit. Let's not disappoint her."

Elisa nodded. Then she turned on her heel and walked to her office without looking back. She glanced at the clock on the wall. If she wasn't teaching tonight, she'd be tempted to skip yoga in favor of trying to get up to speed, or as close to it as possible. The very fact of having that thought cross her mind made her mad. She indulged in a sigh that was part growl and clicked her laptop out of the docking station. She'd do some work at home, but she'd be damned if she let Parker get under her skin before she even showed her face.

She drove home, trying to find her Zen. She sort of wished she was simply going to yoga instead of teaching it. She could use the mindlessness that came with focusing solely on her breathing and the positions of her body. She shook her head. No, teaching would be even better. She'd have a dozen other people to focus on. That would be the best distraction of all.

She got home and changed, then walked to the yoga studio. She set up her mat and cued the low harp music she liked in the background. She greeted her regulars, introduced herself to the couple of newcomers, then started the vinyasa. Because it was a beginner class, and because she'd only been teaching for a few months, she kept things simple. In truth, she actually preferred to keep things uncomplicated—in yoga and life.

When the class ended, her friend Laura lingered. "Hey, girl. You want to grab a drink?"

Elisa sighed. "Yes, but I have to work."

Laura raised a brow. "Now?"

Elisa had to chuckle at her suspicion. From the moment they met in torts during their first year of law school, they'd banded together against the hypercompetitive, ambitious energy that seemed to surround all lawyers. Although they'd gone into different areas—Laura into patent law and Elisa into civil litigation—both resolutely refused to be part of the rat race. "You're not going to believe who I'm working for, starting tomorrow."

Laura's eyes got wide. "Who?"

"Parker Jones." She resisted inserting "fucking" as a middle name, so that was something.

Laura blinked dramatically. "Uh, how did that happen?"

Maybe she could use that drink after all. "You know what? Let's get a drink and I'll tell you all about it."

Fifteen minutes later, they sat on the patio at Cinco, margaritas in hand. Even at eight in the evening, the July air remained steamy. Elisa sipped her drink and willed her body to cool. Laura looked at her expectantly. "Tell me everything."

It didn't take all that long to relay the details of her day—the teacher pension case, partnering with a fancy New York firm, having their resident hotshot come in to handle discovery, Don telling her she'd been chosen for the team. And who'd be leading it.

"And it was Parker that requested you on her team? How did she even know you worked there?"

Elisa shook her head. "I'm hoping it's a coincidence. Like, they gave her a list and she decided to go with someone she knows."

"Is she going to be your boss?"

God. She'd been so focused on the idea of having to see Parker again, work with her, she hadn't given any real thought to the power dynamic that would come with it. "Fuck."

Laura made a sympathetic face. "Not really your boss. Lead counsel. That's different."

Elisa let out an annoyed breath. "Not that different."

Laura caught the eye of a passing waiter and, without bothering to consult Elisa, ordered a second round. "Do you think she took the job because of you?"

"No." Elisa's reply was instant and emphatic, before she gave it a second of thought. But even as she turned the possibility over in her mind, she grew more certain. "No."

Laura angled her head as she thought it through. "Are you sure?"

Parker had barely given her the time of day for most of their time in school. They were a year apart, so it wasn't like they had a lot of classes together. And the one time they'd talked at a party—talked and talked and kissed and almost a lot more—Parker blew it off the next day like it was no big deal. "Yes. The firms landed the case as co-counsel. That's above even her pay grade. There's also the chance that she doesn't remember me at all and picked my name at random." Even though Don had said otherwise.

"That seems unlikely. She may have been a jerk, but you're impossible to forget."

"Thanks." She appreciated the compliment, but it implied Parker did remember her, and that the memory made her think working together was a good idea.

"So, what are you going to do?"

Elisa squared her shoulders. "I'm going to spend tonight getting up to speed so I don't make an ass of myself. And then I'm going to work on this case just like any other."

"Diligently, thoroughly, but only during regular business hours?"

Elisa lifted her glass. "Exactly."

Parker sipped a martini and studied her closet. It would be hotter than balls in New Orleans. She'd almost turned down the case based on the fact it would force her to be in Louisiana for July and August. Almost.

The truth of the matter was that she'd been angling to go back. Between her mother becoming a widow and having two nieces and a nephew under the age of five, she'd found herself wanting to be home. And no matter how many years she might live in New York, no matter how much she loved her Park Slope apartment with views of the Manhattan skyline, New Orleans was home.

The opportunity hadn't been the first to come along. Headhunters loved lawyers admitted to the bars of multiple states and it seemed Louisiana and New York was a rare combination. And while many of those offers had been extremely lucrative, they'd been on the wrong side. She had no interest in defending financial institutions who treated clients' retirement accounts like their personal slush funds. And she sure as hell wasn't going to fight for the rights of petrochemical companies to continue decimating the fragile wetlands along the coast.

No, this offer was different. The Louisiana State Teachers' Association was suing a financial management firm over undisclosed and unlawful fees on their portfolio of pension funds. Her firm and one based in Louisiana had taken the case jointly, promising the client someone with Wall Street experience and a New Orleans pedigree. And Parker was that someone.

She might have taken the job based on that alone. Or the fact that it provided a chance to go home without having to give up her position or her life in New York. She still wasn't a hundred percent certain she wanted the move to be permanent. But what sealed the deal was Parker's research into the firm itself. Or, perhaps more precisely, one of its associates. Seeing Elisa's face and bio on the firm's website had sparked a trip down memory lane. One she'd love to take in person.

It wasn't uncommon for someone in her position to negotiate choosing her own team into the arrangement. So she did. And put Elisa at the top of the list.

This time tomorrow, she would see Elisa face-to-face for the first time since her graduation from Tulane Law. Based on the photo, the last eight years had been good to Elisa, at least physically. Parker would have expected her to be named partner by now, not still trudging along as an associate. But she remained as beautiful as ever, if not more so.

She scowled again at her closet. There really wasn't any way to make a suit suitable for a New Orleans summer. She'd just have to live with it. She selected half a dozen that weren't wool, along with some pants and a bunch of lightweight oxfords. She filled the remaining space in her suitcase with casual clothes and other essentials, figuring she could buy anything she forgot.

It was just after seven by the time she finished. She contemplated dinner, but decided she could squeeze in a run first. She wouldn't have time before her flight in the morning and she hated to miss a day. She changed and headed to the gym in her building. She picked her favorite interval program on the treadmill and cranked the music. She sped up and slowed down, sweating and appreciating the mindlessness of doing what the machine told her.

The machine stopped and, as always, she was surprised an hour had passed. She headed to the elevator and started planning her first day back in the great state of Louisiana. When she landed in the morning, she'd send her things to the apartment the firm had arranged on her behalf and head straight to the office. She'd meet her team, give them an overview of her strategy and her leadership style. Then they'd get to work. She should be able to get in close to a full day before heading to her mother's for dinner.

Back in her apartment, Parker showered and downed a protein shake. She looked around. The modern design was a far cry from the house off St. Charles where she grew up. She'd miss this, for sure, but she realized just how much she was looking forward to going home.

# Chapter Two

Parker accepted her suit jacket from the smiling flight attendant. She offered her thanks and stepped off the plane. Even on the jet bridge, the heat enveloped her. In the terminal, tourists and businesspeople of every age and race milled around. She slung her briefcase over her shoulder and tried to wind her way through the crowds of people who seemed in no hurry to get anywhere.

After getting her luggage, she found a guy who looked to be about seventy holding a small sign with her name on it. She followed him to the waiting car. Outside the heat was truly oppressive, the moist air filling her lungs and making it difficult to breathe. Was it worse than she remembered or had she simply forgotten?

Despite the man's diminutive stature, he hefted her suitcase into the trunk of the town car and opened the back door. "Ms. Jones."

"Thank you."

On the ride to the office, she checked her messages, including her new Blanchard email account. She'd half expected Elisa to reach out before she arrived. Maybe she didn't know Parker was already on the job. She tipped her driver generously and gave him the address to her apartment, then headed inside.

The cool air of the lobby welcomed her. She sighed. That was better. She took off her sunglasses and slid on her suit jacket. There was no security, so she headed to the bank of elevators.

A pair of women in pastel dresses and pearls got on with her. Even in professional settings, it seemed, some aspects of New Orleans never changed. They got off at six and she rode the rest of the way alone.

The offices of Blanchard & Breaux, LLP occupied the entire ninth floor and part of the tenth. A large oak desk dominated the reception area. The woman behind it, who reminded Parker of her Aunt Beulah, greeted her with a smile. "You're Ms. Jones, aren't you? We've been expecting you."

"Please, call me Parker." Parker extended a hand.

The woman blushed, but her smile didn't falter. "Yes, ma'am."

She couldn't fault the woman for her manners, but Parker had to fight the urge to wince. In that single, ten-second interaction, she was reminded of why she moved to New York in the first place. "Do you know which way my office is?"

"Oh, of course." The woman jumped up. "I'll take you there. Then I'll let Mr. Peterson know you're here."

"That would be great…" Parker trailed off, realizing she hadn't gotten the woman's name.

"I'm Bernice, but everyone calls me Niecy."

"It's nice to meet you, Niecy. Thank you for the warm welcome."

Niecy opened a door that already had Parker's name on it. The room was huge, with towering bookcases and wide windows. The large desk had a matching credenza behind it and a pair of matching chairs in front. Parker smiled. Although she had Manhattan experience, she'd never been on the side of big money. This office was officially the nicest one she'd ever had.

"Will it do, Ms. Jones?" Niecy sounded nervous.

"Parker." The correction came before she could stop herself. She made a point of smiling. "And it's perfect. Thank you."

Parker walked into her office. She set down her bag and eyed the computer sitting on the desk. It would certainly do.

"Parker. So glad you made it in. Flight uneventful, I hope?"

Parker turned. Niecy was gone, and in her place stood Don Peterson. Although they hadn't met, she recognized him from his online bio, as well as some of the additional research she'd done on him. "It was. Thank you."

"Your team is on standby whenever you want them, but feel free to take some time to settle in. You've got all the standard-issue equipment here, but we're happy to get you whatever else you need."

"This looks fine." And as much as she might like to get a feel for things, she hated to keep people waiting. "I'd love to meet the team."

"There's a conference room across the hall. I'll have everyone there for you in fifteen minutes."

"Great. Thank you."

Parker used the few minutes to text her mother and to review the bios of the team she'd selected from the firm's staff. She'd made her career on details, and that extended far beyond the case at hand. She spent a minute longer than she needed studying Elisa's bio.

They'd not been especially close in law school, but Parker had liked her enough. Elisa had been a serious student, but not uptight. She'd started at Tulane because she'd followed a woman, someone in Parker's class, to New Orleans. But from what she'd gathered, the relationship didn't last past her first year. She'd seen Elisa around, they'd been on law review together, but not worked on any of the same articles.

And then one night, spring of her third year, they'd been at the same party. She'd had probably one too many vodka sodas, thinking it might be the last time she'd have fun before buckling down to study for the bar. They'd chatted, then gone outside to get away from the noise and the press of people. They ended up on a wide lounge chair near the pool, alone. Parker hadn't planned on kissing her, but once she started, she didn't want to stop.

But then one of Parker's friends came out and called her name. Elisa waved her off, acting like it was no big deal. By the next morning, Parker's mind was back on school and she'd not given it a second thought. No, that wasn't fair. She'd given Elisa—the smell of her hair and the taste of her mouth and the gorgeous curves of her body—plenty of thought. But she had her priorities, and taking her eye off the prize hadn't been one of them. And since Elisa had played it cool the next time she saw her, Parker figured the feeling was mutual.

So why was she angling to cross paths with her now? Parker hadn't thought that part of it through. Not that she needed to. The case would keep them plenty busy. And Elisa was a perk of this job, not the reason for it. If something else came of it, well, she'd see how it played out.

In the conference room, half a dozen people sat around the big table. Elisa had taken the seat closest to the head and didn't waste a second making eye contact. Parker liked that about her—direct, confident, and by extension, sexy as hell.

The other four members of her team looked equally attentive, if not as appealing. Don Peterson was there, too. He wouldn't be working the case, but she imagined he wanted to see her in action. Make sure he was getting his money's worth.

Parker opened the meeting with introductions. She wanted to set a friendly tone, but efficient. She outlined the case and the timeline she wanted to keep for filing motions and briefs. "If all goes well, we'll be able to reach a settlement before the trial actually begins."

Drake Shelby raised a hand. "Is that what happened when you did this in New York?"

"It is." At the time, she'd wanted to go to court. Her idealism wanted to make a spectacle of financial managers who slid exorbitant fees into their fine print. But at the end of the day, settling meant more money back into the pension system and less on legal fees. "The goal is recouping money for our clients and creating a disincentive for having it happen again. If we do our jobs well, that shouldn't be a problem."

Don stood. "This is a new kind of case for our firm. We're partnering with Kenner now, but if we can be successful, while keeping the time and expenses down, it will generate a whole new specialization area for us."

Parker nodded. "Which is why I'm here. My goal is to create the in-house expertise moving forward. I'm here to lead and to coach, not to have you running around like a bunch of 2L interns."

The comment earned her a chuckle. She gave out initial assignments and made a point of making eye contact with each person. Other than one guy—Kyle Babin—she got the sense that everyone respected her role and was eager to get to work. Kyle seemed more resentful than anything else. She'd have to sort out whether it was his personality or had something specific to do with her. When the meeting ended, Parker turned to Elisa. "Ms. Gonzalez, do you mind coming back to my office for a moment?"

Elisa stood. She'd been wondering if Parker would single her out. She couldn't decide if she was annoyed or relieved to get it over with. "Of course."

Elisa followed Parker to her office, but at the door, Parked turned and gestured for her to go first. It was the kind of butch chivalry she'd usually find charming. Usually. "After you."

Elisa entered. It was bigger than hers, and had a better view. Not that she cared. "You don't need to call me Ms. Gonzalez."

Parker flashed a smile that gave Elisa a flutter in spite of herself. "Elisa, it's good to see you."

Elisa folded her arms, not ready to trade niceties. Even if Parker was better looking than she remembered and Elisa couldn't seem to stop herself from being attracted to her. "Why are you here?"

Parker's posture was relaxed. "I thought we'd just gone over that in the conference room."

"I understand the case. What I don't understand is why you're here, in New Orleans, in my law firm?" Despite what she'd said to Laura, she needed to make sure it had nothing to do with her.

"My father passed away last year and I've been angling to come back to be closer to my mom."

Much of Elisa's annoyance dissolved. She'd been so focused on her own reaction to Parker's return, she'd not given any thought to what might have motivated it. She also realized just how little she knew about Parker's life, before or now. "I'm sorry to hear that."

A muscle in Parker's jaw twitched. "Don't be. He was an asshole, and the world—my mother included—is better off without him."

She studied Parker's face, trying to discern whether grief undercut the ready dismissal. Either Parker was an excellent liar or she really didn't mourn his death. If anything, it seemed like Parker was, if not glad, relieved. "Oh."

Parker blinked a few times and focused her gaze on Elisa. "Sorry. I didn't mean to be so terse about it."

Elisa lifted both hands. "No apologies necessary. If you're glad, and happy to be back, then I'm glad it's worked out for you."

"I get the distinct impression you aren't glad." Parker folded her arms and leaned back against the credenza.

"About your father? I wouldn't assume to feel one way or the other."

"No." Parker looked at her in a way that made her feel exposed. "Glad that I'm back. Here. Working with you."

Shit. Elisa did not have words to describe the extent to which she didn't want to go there. She took a deep breath. Tread lightly. "Technically, I believe I work for you. Which is fine. I have no desire to be lead counsel."

Parker continued to study her. Her ability to be still made Elisa nervous, which, in turn, irritated her. "Why not? I'm only a year older than you and I made partner three years ago. You were just as smart as me."

Elisa took a deep breath and willed herself to remain calm. "It's not about being smart."

Parker moved her hands to her hips. And, God, what glorious hips they were. Of course, her pants probably cost six hundred dollars. That didn't help matters. "Please don't tell me this firm is riddled with misogynist bullshit. I'm so beyond dealing with that."

"No." Elisa found herself feeling oddly protective of her firm, and her role in it. "I opted not to pursue the partner route. I like my work, but I like my life, too. I chose balance over ambition."

Parker nodded slowly. She couldn't tell if Parker agreed with her or was merely filing that fact away. "I guess I never thought of it as an either/or thing. Work hard, play hard. You know?"

Elisa shook her head. "To me, that sounds exhausting."

"Oh, I sleep pretty hard, too. Especially after playing. It all works out."

And there it was. That cocky demeanor that had, after a few beers, seemed so fucking sexy. The underlying arrogance that felt so crushing the next day. Good thing she'd grown up since then. She no longer found it desirable or devastating. Even if she had to remind herself she was immune. Elisa smiled, refusing to give anything away. "I'm sure it does."

Parker looked at her in a way she couldn't quite decipher. "I hope you aren't sincerely upset that I'm here. I would have reconsidered the offer had I believed that to be true."

Elisa didn't know whether to believe her, but she supposed the statement itself counted for something. "I'm not upset."

"Good. Because I'm very much looking forward to it."

"Is there anything else?"

"Actually, I was hoping for a rundown of the rest of the team. I got a sense of subject matter expertise from their bios, but I'd like to get a feel for personalities—who has what strengths, who works well together. I thought you'd be the best person for that."

"Oh." Why did the request surprise her?

"It doesn't have to be today. I know not everyone is on your team usually."

"No, no. We're a small enough firm that we know each other pretty well."

"Perfect." Parker picked up a legal pad and a pen. "Shoot."

It was hard to know if Parker's waste-no-time attitude stemmed from her personality or her years in New York. Either way, Elisa made a mental note to stay on her toes. She might not operate that way, but she'd be damned if she let Parker think she couldn't keep up. She spent a few minutes describing the other members of the team. Parker nodded and scribbled notes.

"And what about Babin? Kyle."

Elisa quirked a brow. Even if she wasn't looking to ally herself with Parker, she had no loyalty to him. "He's arrogant, sexist. Not a bad lawyer, but not good enough to warrant his ego."

Parker tapped her pen against the pad. "I got the same feeling myself, so I'm thinking I'm going to agree with your other assessments. Thank you for taking the time."

"Of course." Elisa nodded. "Is that all?"

"I'd like to do team meetings each day at ten and four. They probably won't be more than twenty minutes, but I want to make sure we all stay on the same page."

"I'll add it to everyone's calendar."

"Thanks." Parker stood and Elisa took that as a sign she was done talking. She started to leave when Parker said, "One more thing."

Since Elisa was now facing away from her, she indulged in a brief eye roll before turning around. "Yes?"

"If I ask you to do things, I hope you know it's to be efficient. You know the logistics of things around here better than I do."

Elisa tipped her head slightly. "You're the boss."

Parker frowned. "I don't think of myself that way. I hope you don't either."

Elisa had no idea what to make of Parker's assertion. Was it an attempt to be friendly? To cover her ass? Was Elisa supposed to take it as a compliment or an insult? It annoyed her, but she refused to ask for elaboration. She straightened her shoulders and nodded. "Sure."

And then she fled to the relative safety of her own office.

## Chapter Three

At 5:00 on the dot, Elisa shut down her computer. She didn't usually enforce regular business hours with such exacting precision, but today it was a matter of principle. Well, that and the fact she had plans. She grabbed her purse and contemplated going down the back stairs to avoid walking by Parker's office. Hating herself for such a cowardly thought, she walked purposefully toward the elevators.

"Heading out?" She was a step past Parker's office when she heard her voice.

Elisa backtracked so she could make eye contact. "I am. Hope you have a good night."

Parker had taken off her jacket and rolled up the sleeves of her shirt. The look suited her even more than the full suit. She offered Elisa an easy smile. "Thanks. You, too."

Elisa offered a wave and kept walking. As she waited for the elevator, she chided herself for noticing. She sighed. She'd done far more than noticed. Her body seemed to have an automatic switch when it came to Parker. She went from zero to aroused in two seconds flat.

It didn't seem mutual. Even knowing that was for the best, it stung. She didn't need every lesbian she encountered to find her attractive. But something about Parker—the casual confidence, the sexy butch energy that radiated from her at all times—got under Elisa's skin. Having it entirely one-sided was…demoralizing.

The elevator doors pinged open and she stepped inside. On the ride to the lobby she shook her head and rolled her eyes. Parker was her boss, for the next few months at least. Even if she asserted otherwise. And even if she'd already learned her lesson when it came to Parker.

She drove home, then walked the short distance to Maxie's. Her cousin, Sam, and friend, Mia, were already there. "Hey, lady." Mia pulled her into a hug.

"Hey, yourself."

Sam, still a relatively new addition to their group, kissed her on the cheek. By the time they'd finished exchanging greetings, Laura joined them. "No Chloe tonight?" she asked.

"Hot date. The one she met online," Mia said.

Elisa smiled. "Date number four, I believe."

Mia nodded. "Expect details in the morning."

Sam held the door and they headed into the bar. Gossip took a back seat to perusing the menu and ordering drinks. Before long, they each had some version of a martini in front of them. After a chorus of cheers and clinking glasses, Elisa took a sip. She didn't like to think of herself as ever truly needing a drink, but today, it really hit the spot. She let out a contented sigh.

"How was it?" Laura asked.

"How was what?" Mia added before Elisa could answer.

Elisa related the abbreviated version of the story she'd told Laura the previous night over margaritas. Mia and Sam listened with rapt attention, nodding and shaking their heads, and offering tuts of disapproval. "And now I'm out drinking for the second night in a row."

Her three companions laughed. "You say that like it's a bad thing," said Sam.

Laura looked at her expectantly. "So how was today?"

Elisa shrugged. "It was fine."

Mia propped her chin in her hand. Laura looked incredulous. Sam folded her hands and set them on the table.

"It was annoying and awkward and she called me into her office after the team meeting and tried to be friendly. I guess her dad died and she's been wanting to move back home to be closer to her mom. So that's a relief, right? I mean, not about her dad, but that her coming back had nothing to do with me."

Three heads nodded. Laura asked, "Is she still hot?"

Elisa sighed. "So. Fucking. Hot."

Laura looked at her with sympathy. "I'm sorry. Did she, you know, acknowledge your past?"

"I don't think what happened between us counts as a past. It was one night. Mostly we were acquaintances. Casual friends at best."

Mia shook her head. "A hookup is a hookup. Not acknowledging it is weird. You have to mutually agree to pretend it never happened or it just hangs out there."

"Which makes it a thing." Laura shook her head. "I'm sorry, but if she remembers enough to call you in and chat you up, she remembers making out with you."

"Maybe making out with me is not all that memorable." Not that she wanted to think that, but it might make her current situation more palatable.

"I think she was flirting with you." Sam pointed at her with a toothpicked olive. "If she's not technically your boss, it's not taboo to ask you out. She's chumming the waters."

Elisa curled her lip at the assertion, as well as the metaphor. "I don't think so."

Laura nodded. "Sam has a point. What exactly did she say?"

Elisa replayed the conversation in her mind. "She asked me to do something and I replied with 'you're the boss.' Then she said, 'I don't think of myself that way. I hope you don't either.'"

Sam ate one of the olives and dropped the toothpick back in the glass. "Definitely flirting. Why else would she say that?"

"Because she made a dig about me not being a partner yet and probably felt bad."

Sam lifted a shoulder. "I don't know. I think it could easily be read either way."

"Or both," Mia said.

"So what are you going to do?" Leave it to Laura to ask the million-dollar question.

"My job."

"Seriously." Mia drained the last of her lemon drop martini. "You need a game plan."

Elisa ran a hand through her hair. "I'm going to do my job and not let her get under my skin."

Laura tapped a finger to her lips, then pointed at Elisa. "But what about under your skirt?"

Elisa swatted Laura, but not hard. "You're terrible."

"I just think you need to be prepared for all eventualities."

Both Sam and Mia nodded in agreement. "Yeah."

"She's not going to get under or on top of me in any way, shape, or form. I'm really good at keeping boundaries around my work. This won't be any different." Elisa spoke with more conviction than she felt, but she embraced the idea like a mantra. "It's going to be fine."

"Famous last words." Laura raised her glass. "I'll drink to your resolve."

"Great. Can we talk about something else now?"

"Don't look at me." Laura set down her glass. "The most exciting thing at my house is the school supply list."

"Already?" Sam looked horrified. "It's only July."

"They go back mid-August."

"Right."

Elisa smiled. "And they've been on vacation since the second week of May."

Sam nodded. "Okay, that's better, then."

"How's the house?" Elisa asked Sam. Sam and her girlfriend had recently bought a house, but it needed a lot of work.

"Good. I think we'll be able to move in by September. We put Tess's place on the market this week."

"How did that go?" Laura, whose husband was in Tess's band, looked worried.

"Really well. I'm sure she'll have moments of feeling sentimental, but she's excited enough about the new place that I think it will all work out."

Elisa had been to the new house before they bought it and once since the renovations had started. "If I was moving into a place as gorgeous as the one y'all found, I'd be excited, too."

"I still need to come and see it. Let me know next time you're there for a stretch," Mia said.

"Will do." Sam slid a credit card to the waiter before he could set the check on the table, then lifted her hand before anyone could protest. "Sid Packett's prerogative."

Elisa smiled. She still forgot that her cousin was a best-selling mystery writer. Other than slyly picking up checks whenever she could get away with it, Sam didn't give much indication of her fame, or her wealth. "Thank you."

Mia and Laura echoed the thanks. While they waited for the bill to be brought back, Elisa turned to Mia. "What about you? You've been sort of quiet tonight."

Mia offered a playful shrug. "I'm good. I've got a date after this."

Exclamations and a push for details revealed nothing. Mia promised to elaborate if it went anywhere. They left the bar and Laura headed home to her family. Sam said her goodbyes quickly as well. She was off for a cooking lesson with a woman who owned a Cuban restaurant. "I'm hoping to surprise Tess before we move."

It was sweet, especially given Sam's complete lack of skill in the kitchen. Elisa sent her on her way and walked slowly in the direction of her house. She wondered if Parker would still be in the office. Then she couldn't decide what annoyed her more—that Parker might still be working or that she was thinking about Parker in the first place.

By quarter after six, Parker felt like the last person working on the entire floor. It was a far cry from Manhattan, when her workday often extended to seven or later. Although she appreciated the quiet—and might be tempted to use the time to get ahead on things—tonight she had plans. She shut down her computer and tucked her laptop into her briefcase. Her walk to the elevator confirmed that she was, in fact, the last one there.

She passed an older woman emptying trash cans into a large custodial cart. Parker smiled at her and extended a hand. "Hi, I'm Parker. I'm new."

The woman seemed alarmed at first, but when she met Parker's eyes, she smiled. "Good evening, Miss Parker."

The woman didn't give her name, but Parker noticed a name tag pinned to her shirt. "Good evening to you, Miss Ava."

Parker took the elevator down to the garage, located the spot she'd been assigned. The navy sedan screamed company car, but she didn't mind. She didn't plan to spend much time in it. She pressed the key fob that had been dropped off that afternoon and, sure enough, the lights flashed and the locks clicked.

On the drive to her mother's house, Parker thought about how different her life would be had her father not fallen for her mother, who'd been working as a waitress when they met. Well, maybe not her life, since she'd never have been born. But her mother, who'd barely graduated from high school when golden boy Edwin Jones had set his sights on her. She shook her head. New Orleans loved a rags-to-riches story, just as long as enough people stayed in rags to get things done.

Even with traffic, the drive only took fifteen minutes. Parker pulled into the driveway and took a deep breath. Her brother's car in front of hers told her he'd accepted the invitation after all. Parker said a silent prayer that his wife and kids were with him. That would at least diffuse the situation.

Before she'd even climbed out of the car, the front door swung open and Molly and Macy came running toward her. "Aunt Parker!"

Parker bent to give them hugs. They wore matching sundresses and white sandals, along with big white bows in their hair. Unlike Parker at that age, they didn't seem to mind the bows. She stood to find Eddie and Kim standing on the porch. Kim held a squirming toddler on her hip and Parker realized she'd not seen them since Chase was baptized. "He sure got big fast."

Kim grinned. "And Chase has grown a lot, too."

Eddie gave his wife an exasperated look and Parker laughed. She'd always liked Kim. At first, she worried that Eddie might try to tame her, but she gave as good as she got and held her own. At this rate, Parker might actually start to like her brother.

Kim and Eddie stepped to the side. Behind them, Stella stepped onto the porch, wiping her hands on a dish towel. Parker smiled but found her eyes stinging with the threat of tears. She blinked quickly. Now was not the time to be emotional. "Hey, Mama."

"Parker." She opened her arms.

Parker climbed the porch steps and let herself be enveloped. As always, the softness of her mother's body belied the strength of her hugs. Parker took in the scent of her, a mixture of baby powder and magnolias. She stayed there for a good minute, letting herself be glad to be home. "I missed you."

"I missed you too, baby girl." For most of her life, Parker had bristled at the term of endearment. She no longer minded it. "Come on in out of the heat and stay a while."

Stella led the way back into the house. Parker took in the smell of lemon oil and gardenias. She'd been home once since her father's funeral, but that had been close to six months ago. Little had changed in the house and she had her usual reaction—a mixture of familiarity and nostalgia, laced with unease. She'd hoped the unease would subside after her father's death. Maybe it still would, in time.

"Supper's just about ready if y'all want to head into the dining room," Stella said.

"What can I do to help?" Parker hated her mother's tendency to treat her like a guest to be served.

"Not a thing. You worked all day and I lazed around. The least I can do is put supper on the table."

Parker knew better than to argue. Like the foyer, the dining room remained unchanged. Floral wallpaper and white wainscoting, a huge mahogany table and chairs. Although she'd had many of her childhood meals in the less formal kitchen, Stella had decided about ten years prior that saving the dining room for guests and special occasions was nonsense. They'd used it, at least for supper, ever since.

The table was already set, including a big pitcher of iced tea. Stella bustled in and out of the kitchen, and the next thing Parker knew, the table was filled with food—shrimp creole, rice, stewed okra, squash casserole, and a big basket of French bread. Parker sighed, a mixture of contentment and worry. She'd missed her Mama's cooking, but it was going to be hard not to gain twenty pounds making up for lost time.

"Sit, sit." Stella waved a hand over the table. "Y'all dig in."

Parker talked a little about her job and the executive apartment the firm had arranged. She'd yet to see it, but she'd been sent pictures, and the location was ideal. Mostly, she asked questions. It was a relief to know that her mother had kept up volunteering and seemed to be going out with friends. As imperfect as her parents' relationship had been, so much of Stella's identity had been wrapped up in her husband. Parker took solace in knowing she was getting on with life.

She noticed a change in Eddie, too. His tone was easier; he was attentive to his kids. Whether that had more to do with Edwin's death or Kim's influence, she didn't know. But it made her happy to watch.

After the meal, Stella brought out a pan of bread pudding. Parker indulged in a huge piece, promising herself she'd make up for it at the gym in the morning. By the time she hugged everyone goodbye and made promises to return for Sunday dinner, it was after nine. She drove to her apartment, which was exactly as promised. After unpacking her clothes, she took a long cool shower and crawled into bed naked. It felt strange to think she'd been in her bed, in Brooklyn, not twenty-four hours prior. She smiled into the darkness. Not bad for her first day home.

# Chapter Four

Elisa eyed Parker across the table. In just over a week, they'd done initial discovery, filed motions, and generated a list of names for depositions. Without coming across as a taskmaster, Parker kept them focused and moving forward. Although she remained adamant she didn't want the role of lead counsel, Elisa admired her methods. If she ever did have to run things, she hoped she could do it with the same level of focus and style.

Today was the final prep day before taking depositions. The hope was that this would generate a strong enough case to warrant a motion for summary judgment. Or, perhaps more likely, strong enough to convince the team from Blackman they had no chance of winning. Parker ran through the list and assigned depositions across the team.

Parker, of course, planned to attend all of them. Elisa listened as Parker booked herself for no less than thirty hours of depositions. Part of her wanted to be exasperated by the control freak tendency, the other part knew she'd do the exact same thing. Not that she needed to control everything, but being in charge meant being responsible, including knowing every intricacy of the case.

Not wanting to get caught staring, Elisa shifted her focus to the other members of their team. Kyle looked bored out of his mind—not a good look for someone who'd already been caught with his head up his ass more than once. Drake looked attentive and perfectly polished, as always. And Alie was typing furiously, trying to capture everything being said. She was technically a paralegal but was one of the smartest people in the firm, and Elisa held out hope she'd take the leap and go back to school.

Parker talked with a brisk efficiency that still took Elisa by surprise. One of the things Parker had clearly lost in her ten years out of Louisiana was the lazy drawl Elisa had once found charming. The fact that she missed it irritated Elisa no end. As did the many and various fantasies her mind seemed to spin every time she let her guard down. There was the one where she went into Parker's office after hours, when no one else was around to see or hear them. There was the one where the two of them got stuck in the elevator. And her personal favorite, the one where Parker shoved all the files to the floor and took her on the conference room table.

"Elisa?"

Shit. She'd just been judging Kyle for not paying attention and now she'd been caught doing the same. "Sorry. I was strategizing. Got a little ahead of myself."

Parker nodded and Elisa couldn't figure out if she got away with the lie or not. "Okay. It looks like we're going to have to double up a couple of days this week. Since I can't be two places at once, I'm going to have Elisa and Kyle take," she glanced down at the file, "Bishop while Drake and I do Covington. Does that work for everyone?"

Elisa glanced at Kyle. He didn't seem too perturbed. Perhaps he considered her a preferable partner to Parker. "Who takes lead?" he asked.

Elisa resisted rolling her eyes. Parker didn't even look up. "Elisa."

"But—" Kyle was her senior at the firm by just over a year, a point he was, no doubt, about to point out.

Parker lifted a hand. "She handled the original discovery on him. Let's not make this a game of whose is bigger, shall we?"

She looked from Kyle to Elisa, then back to Kyle. He nodded. Elisa did, too. Elisa appreciated the call, even if it would make Kyle unbearable in the meantime. To avoid any pretense of gloating, she looked at Kyle. "I've got an hour this afternoon if you want to prep. I can come to your office."

He glowered, but didn't protest. "Sure."

"Great. I've got a meeting with Don. Let's regroup at four," Parker said.

There were mumbles of assent as everyone filed out of the conference room. Elisa started back toward her office. Kyle followed.

He hovered in her doorway as she walked to her desk. “Are you sleeping with her?”

“What?” Elisa looked past him, certain for a moment he wasn’t speaking to her. There was no one behind him.

“Jones. Are you sleeping with her?”

Elisa resisted the urge to hurl a stapler at his head. “Are you out of your mind?”

“I didn’t know if it was a chicks helping chicks thing or if it was more personal.”

How this man functioned in society was a mystery. “It’s neither. I did all the research on Bishop. I practically know what he’s going to say before we even sit down.”

Kyle shrugged dismissively. “Whatever. Senior counsel takes the lead. That’s how it’s always worked around here.”

She would not get sucked into an argument with him. “If you’ve got a problem, I suggest you take it up with Don.”

He sulked away without a reply. Elisa sat down and blew out a breath. Was he being his usual asinine self or had she allowed herself, her attraction, to become transparent? It had to be the former. She’d not done or said anything even remotely improper. And no reasonable person could argue that Parker had given her anything close to preferential treatment. No, Kyle was being petulant about playing second fiddle, to a woman no less. The insinuation was nothing more than his attempt to get under her skin. She wasn’t about to give him the satisfaction.

Parker sat at her desk and closed her eyes. Only a masochist would spend seven hours listening to financial professionals talk about their management structure and internal controls. Well, a masochist or a perfectionist. As miserable as she was at the moment, her team had accomplished more in the last two days than some tackled in a week, or more.

That was part of her strategy. By keeping an aggressive pace, she made sure the defendants remained on their toes. Without a protracted discovery phase, she could hold a certain advantage in the filing of motions and other procedural matters. It wouldn’t determine the outcome of the case, but it might improve her chances of getting a settlement before the trial even began.

Parker leaned back to stretch out her neck and shoulders. She chuckled to herself. If anyone had told her in law school that one of her top professional goals would be staying out of court, she'd have laughed. But in the world of civil litigation, efficiency mattered. Settling a case in less time and with a lower cost was the single most effective way to drum up new business. It was why she'd been chosen for the partnership with Blanchard & Breaux, and she planned to deliver.

She glanced at the clock on her desk. Although technically still business hours, only a tool asked the support staff for anything at 4:45. She did her best not to be a tool. Which meant she wasn't above making copies or getting her own coffee. She grabbed the stack of files and decided to hit the break room first. She walked out of her office and right into Elisa, nearly dropping the folders and everything in them. "Sorry."

Elisa smiled at her. "Don't be. I was in a hurry and not looking where I was going."

Parker raised a brow. "Hot date?"

Elisa smirked. "If you count my yoga mat as a hot date, sure."

Parker laughed. "Right, you're the yoga queen."

"Let's just say I need an hour of Zen after a day of depositions."

"You're telling me." Parker planned on spending some quality time with the treadmill in the gym of her apartment building later. That was her version of Zen.

"You don't have to put in crazy hours here, you know?"

Parker, whose mind had drifted to the soothing repetition of putting one foot in front of the other over and over again, looked at Elisa. "I'm sorry, what did you say?"

"I said you don't have to work crazy hours. Your reputation as the big shot is secure and Don's falling all over himself to talk about what a great job you're doing to anyone who'll listen."

"I like the work."

"You can like the work and still have a life."

The insinuation bristled. "I have a life."

Elisa lifted both hands. "I'm not saying you don't. And I'm certainly not telling you what to do."

Great, now she was acting defensive. "I appreciate the sentiment, and the compliment. Don't let me keep you."

Something flashed in Elisa's eyes. It looked like it might be regret. "Yeah, I should go."

Elisa walked briskly in the direction of the elevators, leaving Parker standing in the hallway with her empty coffee cup and stack of files. Suddenly, it seemed like a depressing way to spend her evening. She thought about Elisa's comment, the one about not working crazy hours. Then she thought about her reputation as a big shot. Elisa's tone hadn't made it sound like an insult, but Parker couldn't help but sense an undercurrent of judgment. And not the competitive kind she was used to, the kind that was more about jealousy than anything else. Elisa seemed to maybe feel bad for her.

Parker shook her head. She was perfectly happy with her choices. Going the extra mile had gotten her where she was, and she had no regrets.

Still. She didn't want to stick out like a sore thumb. Working like a dog earned her respect in her previous positions. It was the price of admission to being taken seriously. But New Orleans was a far cry from New York. She didn't need to scrap her drive, but maybe she could temper it some. Lead her team without leaving them in her dust.

Feeling oddly liberated, Parker turned and headed back to her office. If she left now, she could get in a workout, order dinner, and catch up on *Godless.* She dropped the files on her desk and grabbed her things. It felt a little strange to be leaving by six. But as she looked around on her way to the elevator, she realized, once again, she was the last one out. She chuckled to herself. Far cry indeed.

# Chapter Five

Parker looked up to find Elisa hovering in her doorway. "Hey."

Elisa offered her a smile. "Hey."

"What's up?"

"A bunch of us are going out for drinks. Care to join?"

Parker considered. She'd learned she was more likely to earn a reputation as a taskmaster than a boss who was too chummy. Buying a round could go a long way in bonding with her team. Given the amount of work they'd been tackling, it could also help in keeping morale up. "Absolutely."

She gathered her things and met a group of about ten near the elevators. Most of her team was there, along with a handful of people she'd yet to meet. On the ride down to the lobby, Elisa filled her in on the plans. "We take the streetcar down. It makes it easier for anyone who's had one too many to justify a Lyft home."

"Nice."

Parker couldn't remember the last time she rode the streetcar. It was one of those things so easy to think of as part of the charm of New Orleans and not a practical part of public transportation. But as she and ten of her colleagues piled onto one heading to the Garden District, she couldn't help but liken it to the New York subway.

The car rattled down St. Charles, making Parker realize she actually could use it to get to work every day. She made a mental note of that, not because parking and driving were that much of a pain, but because she valued anything that kept her from a potential rut.

At the corner of Loyola, she disembarked with the group and crossed the street to Superior Seafood. She hadn't been there since law school, but it seemed that raw oyster happy hour remained a thing. Inside, they took over three high-top tables in the bar. She wanted to snag a seat next to Elisa, but she'd broken off from the group and was hugging the oyster shucker.

Parker held back, waiting until Elisa returned to the group to sit. When she did, Parker was at least able to plant herself at the same table. "Who's that you were hugging?"

Elisa glanced quickly at the woman and smiled. "My cousin's girlfriend."

"I didn't realize you had family in town."

"I didn't until recently. My cousin, Sam, came last year with a plan to stay six months and then decided to stick around."

Parker nodded. She tried to avoid most of her cousins but could still appreciate the sentiment. "So, I'm guessing you're a regular. Are the oysters good? I've always avoided them in the summer." Much like no white after Labor Day or before Easter, she'd been trained to only eat raw oysters in months with "R."

Elisa shrugged. "I've never had a bad one here. And I was here just last week."

"Okay, then."

Before long, the tables were filled with trays of oysters, cocktails, and wine. Parker let herself get talked into a frozen French 75. Despite shunning most frozen daiquiris as sugary vehicles for cheap booze, this one wasn't half bad. And, like the oysters, it was half price.

After about an hour, people began to head out for the evening or home to families. Elisa lingered, and Parker wondered if she might talk her into joining her for dinner. "Where are you headed from here?"

"Nowhere for a while. Tess gets off at six." She angled her head toward the woman she'd hugged earlier. "Sam is coming and we're having dinner here."

"Ah." She might want to spend time with Elisa, but crashing a family meal wasn't what she had in mind. Before she could make a graceful exit, Elisa's attention shifted to something behind her. Parker's gaze followed and she found herself looking at a tall, butch woman who looked oddly familiar.

"Sam." Elisa waved a hand.

The woman, Sam, looked their way and smiled. "Hey."

She came over and gave Elisa a hug. Parker couldn't stop staring at her. Had they met? She knew her from somewhere, but couldn't put a finger on it.

"Parker, this is my cousin, Sam. Sam Torres, Parker Jones."

Parker shook Sam's hand. "Pleasure to meet—holy shit."

"No, no. I'm Sam." She laughed.

Parker couldn't believe it. "You're the Sam who is really Sid Packett."

"That would be me." Sam offered a casual smile.

They'd never met, but Parker had seen her in TV interviews. Just about a year ago, she went public as the woman behind the popular crime novels. It had caused a bit of a stir, considering everyone believed the reclusive best-selling author to be a man. She'd read his—her—books for years and considered it a pleasant surprise that she'd been reading a female author all along. And now she was meeting her in the flesh. "Wow. That's so cool. I love your books."

Sam glanced at the floor in a way that made her seem mildly uncomfortable with the attention. "Thanks."

"I promise I won't fangirl all over you, but it's great to meet you." She turned to Elisa. "You could have warned me your cousin was a famous author."

Elisa looked at her blandly. "Oh, no. This is much more fun."

Sam chuckled. "I don't want to interrupt if you two are still talking about work. I can go occupy myself with Tess until you're done."

Elisa shook her head quickly. "It's all good. We were just wrapping up."

"Do you have plans for dinner, Parker? We're just staying here, but you are more than welcome to join us."

Parker glanced at Elisa, who appeared to be giving Sam a death glare. A tiny part of her thought maybe she shouldn't insert herself, but it was a tiny part. She wanted to have dinner with Elisa, after all. And she wasn't about to pass up the opportunity to share a meal with Sid Packett. "If you're sure I'm not intruding, I'd love to."

Elisa took a deep breath and unclenched her jaw. She couldn't tell if Sam was being gracious to a fan or intentionally trying to make her squirm. Probably a little of both. Sam had been teasing her about Parker for the better part of two weeks. At least she'd be able to count on Tess for moral support. Before she could say anything, Tess came over to join them. She must have gotten off and ducked in the back to change; she'd traded her chef's coat and apron for a paisley sundress and sandals.

Tess and Sam exchanged a kiss and Elisa introduced Parker. Then she said, "Let me go pay my tab and we can get a table."

Parker lifted a hand. "Let me. It's the least I can do."

She didn't like the idea of Parker buying her a drink but didn't want to haggle about it. And it was the least she could do. "Okay. Thanks."

Parker went to the bar and Elisa turned to Sam. "You had to invite her to dinner."

Sam offered a playful shrug. "I was trying to be nice. I'm a little surprised she said yes."

Before she could retort, Parker rejoined them. Tess went to the hostess station, and in under a minute, they were seated at a table near the window. Parker asked Tess about her work at the restaurant and Sam about her writing. She seemed genuinely interested in the house they'd bought and were renovating. She was charming and funny, and if she weren't Parker, Elisa would say it felt like a double date. Hell, it still felt like a double date, even if Elisa didn't want to admit it.

As if on cue, Parker turned her attention to Elisa. "Do you really teach yoga?"

Clearly, she'd zoned out for a minute. "I do. Just a beginner class once a week. It's my exercise and my meditation."

Parker smiled her ridiculously charming smile. "I've never done yoga. I'd love to give it a try."

Sam pointed at her. "I warn you, it's harder than it looks. Elisa talked me into a class when I first moved here, and I honestly thought I was going to die."

Elisa shook her head and laughed. "You weren't that bad."

"Maybe not, but I could barely move the next day."

Parker leaned back in her chair. "I'm pretty fit. I think I could handle it."

Parker's voice held just a hint of arrogance. Elisa couldn't resist taking the bait. "Okay. My class is Wednesday at six. I'll give you the address."

"Excellent."

Sam looked at Parker with concern. "Take one piece of advice from someone who's been there. Don't try to show off. You'll seriously regret it."

Parker laughed. "Point taken."

Elisa glanced at her watch and realized it was after eight. Had they really just had a two-hour dinner? A waiter brought the check and Parker insisted on paying. "I did crash your dinner, after all."

Outside the restaurant, Sam asked where Elisa was parked. "We took the streetcar, actually."

"I'll drive you," Sam said. "We're heading that way anyway."

"That would be great."

"Parker, can I offer you a ride, too?"

"If it's really not an imposition. I live not too far from here."

Sam smiled. "Not at all."

"Thanks." Parker gave her the address. They got into Sam's car and Elisa wondered exactly how she'd gotten herself into not only dinner, but a chummy ride home.

Sam pulled onto St. Charles from the side street. "I rented a place not far from here when I first moved."

"Nice. Where are you guys now?"

Tess turned around from the passenger seat. "We bought a place in Algiers. That's where I grew up, and I really wanted to stay in the neighborhood."

Parker nodded. "I love it over there."

They pulled up to a modern-looking apartment building. Parker explained that it was a short-term rental arranged by the firm. Elisa wondered if Blanchard paid for it, or Parker's firm in New York. Either way, it made her realize just how big a deal Parker's presence at the firm was. She couldn't decide if that made her feel better about things, or worse. She offered a casual good night and breathed a sigh of relief when Parker was no longer sitting next to her.

Once Parker was in her building, Sam backed her car out of the drive and headed toward Elisa's house. "She seems nice."

Elisa huffed out a breath. "She's charming. That's not the same thing."

Tess turned around to face her. "You're saying she's faking it?"

"Not faking. Just…" What? "I think she turns it on and off when it suits her."

"Like at the office, you mean? At work she's all business?" Tess asked.

"Um." In truth, Parker didn't turn it off at the office. She was funny without being flirtatious. She seemed genuinely interested in the members of her team and was considerate of everyone in the office—from partners to paralegals. Elisa had even seen her chatting up the custodial staff one evening on her way out. "It's not that. She's—"

"Charming all the time and you don't like it?" Sam offered.

Elisa cringed. "That makes me sound awfully petulant."

"Not at all." Once again, Tess turned in her seat. "I hope you don't mind. Sam brought me up to speed."

"I don't." She didn't. She already thought of Tess as family.

"If she's all charm now, it leaves you to wonder if she's changed or if it's just you." Tess hit the nail on the head.

"That feels petty."

"It's not." Tess shook her head. "It's self-preservation."

"What happened between us was years ago. I probably shouldn't still be holding on to it anyway."

Sam made brief eye contact with her in the rearview mirror. "I don't get the sense you've been pining."

"I haven't." That, at least, was true. The whole thing had been a bruise to the ego, but once Parker left, she didn't dwell on it.

"But?"

"But it's one thing to be over it in some theoretical sense. Now that she's popped back into my life, I don't know how to navigate it. I'm not holding a grudge, but it feels weird to let my guard down, or to act like nothing ever happened."

"Have you told her as much?" Tess asked.

The very idea of baring her soul to Parker mortified her. "God, no."

"Are you still attracted to her?" Sam glanced at her in the mirror. "Or maybe attracted to her again?"

Elisa groaned and rolled her eyes, letting her head fall against the headrest.

Tess gave her a sympathetic look. "I'm going to take that as a yes."

"And I hate myself for it."

"But she's super attractive," Tess said.

Sam lifted a hand. "Hey. I'm right here."

Tess shrugged. "Being in love with you doesn't turn off the part of my brain that recognizes women as attractive."

Sam scowled, but without real anger. "Fine."

"The problem isn't that I find Parker attractive. That's something you acknowledge in passing. The problem is that I'm attracted to her." There. She'd said it out loud. At least she could say she'd moved past the denial phase.

Tess nodded. "I get it."

"It's kind of humiliating to want someone who hooked up with you when they were drunk, but the next morning was, 'eh, no thanks.' And now she's my boss. I'd be an absolute idiot to give her even a passing thought."

"I sort of felt that way about Sam."

Elisa had never gotten Tess's side of the story. "You did?"

"Well, the passing thought part. Not a local, a little too smooth."

"Again. Right here."

This time Tess leaned over and kissed Sam's cheek. "And I gave you a chance and now we live happily ever after."

Elisa did not like where this conversation was going. "What are you saying?"

Tess returned her gaze to Elisa. "Only that you shouldn't be so hard on yourself."

"Oh, because it sort of felt like you were telling me to give her a chance."

"That, too. Professionally, at least, and maybe as a person. I'm offering no romantic advice whatsoever. I know better than that."

And with that, they pulled into Elisa's driveway. She gave Sam and Tess half hugs from the back seat. "Thanks for dinner."

"We didn't get to buy dinner, if you recall."

Right. "Thank you for the company. Even if I'm now more conflicted instead of less."

She climbed out of the car and went to the front door. She unlocked it and offered a final wave before stepping inside. She closed the door behind her and leaned against it. How had she gone from happy hour to dinner to maybe giving Parker another chance?

Was that what she was doing? No. At least not in that way—the romantic way. But maybe she didn't need to keep her guard up quite so high either. Parker had been friendly and funny and professional. What happened between them had been a long time ago. And, like Sam said, it wasn't like she'd been pining.

# Chapter Six

Despite another grueling day of depositions, Parker had promised herself she'd check out Elisa's yoga class. Even if what she really wanted was a mindless three-mile run and a martini. She sighed. It probably wouldn't feel like a real workout, but she'd get to see Elisa, out of the office no less. Not that she'd seen much of her in the office this week. So, even if it was a total bust, it would be worth it.

Parker had no idea what to expect. Or what to wear. She regretted not asking Sam when they'd talked about it over dinner. In the end, she settled on athletic shorts and a T-shirt. Because there was no way in hell she was putting on yoga pants.

At 5:15, she changed in the office bathroom and sneaked down the back stairs so no one would see her. She drove to the address Elisa had given her and found herself in front of a tiny standalone building that looked like it used to be a shotgun-style house. The small yard out front had been set up like a Zen garden, complete with a bubbling water feature and meditating Buddha statue. Parker gave it points for charm.

Inside, most of the interior walls had been knocked down. Dark wood floors gleamed against neutral walls, making the space seem open yet intimate at the same time. A small desk sat near the door. Behind it, a woman who appeared dressed for yoga smiled at her. "Are you here for the class?" she asked.

Parker returned the smile. "I am."

"You don't look familiar. Is it your first time here?"

"First time doing yoga, actually. I'm a—" Parker hesitated for moment, unsure whether she qualified as a friend at this point. "I know Elisa and she invited me."

The woman beamed. "Great. This is a great class to start with. It's gentle, but not so gentle you'll think you didn't do anything."

A man and a woman walked in behind her, carrying water bottles and yoga mats. Shit. "So, I need to pay for the class, obviously, but do you happen to sell mats, too?"

"We've got plenty you can borrow." She pointed to a basket near the wall.

"Oh. Right. Thank you."

Although she could have paid for a single class, Parker bought a pass for four sessions. It would be good to mix up her routine. It also gave her an excuse to see Elisa outside the office. If she had any chance of making progress on that front, Parker had a feeling it would need to be outside the office.

Parker grabbed a mat and positioned herself along one wall near the middle of the room. She was contemplating introducing herself to some of the people in the class when she saw Elisa walk in. She wore black capri-length yoga pants and a snug cranberry-colored tank top. As much as Parker enjoyed Elisa's office style, this suited her, too. And showed off every glorious line and curve of her body. Parker swallowed, not ready for the stab of desire right in her gut.

Elisa glanced over and Parker realized she was staring. She offered a wave. Elisa smiled but looked incredulous. She walked over to where Parker stood. "I didn't think you were serious."

Parker feigned offense, if for no other reason than to cover the fact she'd been caught ogling. "Of course I was serious."

"And you've really never done yoga before?"

"No, but I stretch after I run and stuff."

Elisa nodded. "Okay. Just don't overdo."

Parker knew what it was like to be out of shape. She spent the first eighteen years of her life chubby and uncomfortable in her body. Yes, much of that had to do with having all things feminine forced down her throat, but she'd been lazy, too. At this moment, she was probably in the best shape of her life. "I'm good. Promise."

"All right. I'll stop harassing you." Elisa's tone was conciliatory, but her smile felt more like a smirk.

She went off to greet other students—was that what people in a yoga class were called?—and Parker focused her attention on her surroundings. Or at least she tried to. Over and over, her gaze kept going back to Elisa. Parker told herself it was because Elisa's body was on such beautiful display. It was more than that, though. She liked watching Elisa interact with other people. Just like at the office, people gravitated to her. And while Parker couldn't make out what Elisa was saying, the nods and smiles made it clear everyone liked her.

It didn't take long for Elisa to call the class together. Parker watched those around her settle on their mats and she followed suit. She sat on the floor with her legs folded and, as instructed, closed her eyes. The first few minutes seemed to be all about breathing, so Parker cracked an eye to peek around the room. Everyone's eyes were closed, including Elisa's. Parker shrugged, then tried to focus her breath in the ways Elisa described.

Parker followed the class through what Elisa called a vinyasa, going through a series of poses with names like warrior and tree and sun salute. None of it seemed all that hard, but as she went into what felt like her millionth downward-facing dog, Parker found herself glancing around for a clock. Why was she sweating so much? And how much longer would this last?

After what felt like an eternity, Parker found herself sprawled on her back with her eyes once again closed. Elisa's voice had become even more soothing as she talked the class through a centering cooldown. Parker breathed. She could get behind corpse pose. She hauled herself back to a seated position and joined the chorus of "Namaste."

As the room emptied, Parker lingered. Several people were talking with Elisa. Parker didn't want to crash the conversation; she also didn't want to leave without saying goodbye. Eventually, they left and Elisa looked over at her. "Well? What did you think?"

Parker smiled. "I think Sam was right."

That earned her a bland look. "Really?"

"But in a good way. I didn't expect it to be so much of a workout."

"I'll take that as a compliment."

"It is. I go to the gym at least five days a week and I feel like I used muscles today I didn't know I had."

Elisa smiled. "Definitely a compliment."

In that moment, the last thing Parker wanted was for them to go their separate ways. "So, are you done now? I'd love to buy you dinner as a thank-you for introducing me to yoga."

Elisa's smile didn't falter, but a shadow passed through her eyes. "I'm sorry, but I have other plans."

So, clearly that was an overstep. Not wanting to stick her foot in her mouth any farther, Parker offered a casual shrug and smiled. "No big deal. I am grateful, though."

Elisa nodded. "No thanks necessary. I'm glad you liked it."

"I should warn you, I bought a four-session pass."

The warmth returned to Elisa's eyes. "There are other classes with far better instructors. But you're welcome to become one of my regulars if you'd like."

Parker wanted there to be something flirtatious in the comment, but she was pretty sure Elisa was being, at best, friendly. Hell, she might only be offering out of some sort of yoga enthusiast sense of obligation. Still, Parker wasn't about to turn her down. "I'd like that."

"Okay. Great." Elisa glanced toward the door. "I should go."

"Of course. I'm sorry I kept you."

Elisa smiled. "Have a good night."

"You, too." Elisa walked away, leaving the studio with a group of three other women.

Rather than being sorry she didn't score an invitation, she was relieved Elisa seemed to have real plans. Parker rolled up her mat and returned it to the basket. She'd have to get one of her own before the next class.

"Did you like it?" The woman who'd greeted her initially remained at the desk near the door.

Parker smiled. "I did. More than I thought. I might have to become a regular."

"Elisa's great. She's only been an instructor for about six months, but you'd never know it."

The comment made Parker wonder about the other aspects of Elisa's life outside the office. "She's a natural."

A trio of women came in and Parker realized that another class must be starting soon. She took that as her cue to exit. She left the studio and got in her car. It was hotter than a sauna, and her steering wheel nearly burned her fingers. New Orleans would be so much more palatable without the months of July and August. She cranked the AC and started toward home.

After a mental rundown of the contents of her fridge, she made a detour to the grocery store to pick up salad stuff so she wouldn't have to cook. After only a moment of hesitation, she grabbed a pint of Blue Bell pralines and cream. She'd definitely earned it.

## Chapter Seven

Elisa saved and closed the motion she'd just finished proofing. She did a quick check of her email, then looked around her office. She drummed her fingers on her desk. Tess's words echoed in her mind. "You should invite Parker."

She'd said it casually, but the result was anything but. Elisa scoffed at first, but then she thought maybe her refusal said more than inviting Parker along. She'd hemmed and hawed for the better part of a week, a fact that left her feeling ridiculous. She stood up and marched down the hall to Parker's office.

As usual, Parker sat at her desk, completely absorbed in whatever was in front of her. Today, she was typing furiously with a look of intense concentration on her face. Her sleeves were rolled up and her suit jacket hung on the back of her chair. Just like the first time she saw Parker that way, Elisa's reaction was instant and visceral. She fought the urge to leave before Parker noticed her and knocked lightly on the open door.

Parker looked up, blinked a few times, and smiled. "Hi."

"Hey. I finished reviewing the motion. The updated version is on the server." She could have said as much in an email, but this made it seem like she had actual business and wasn't only there to extend an invitation.

"Excellent." Parker leaned back in her chair. "I really appreciate the second pair of eyes."

Elisa smiled. "It was really good. I only made a couple of changes."

Parker nodded. "Fingers crossed the judge agrees."

"Do you remember Tess, my cousin's girlfriend, who works at the restaurant?" Okay, so no points for a smooth transition.

"I do." Parker's face registered the abrupt shift, but she didn't comment on it.

"She's in a band—a really good band, actually—and they have a show tonight. You seemed to like them when we all had dinner, so I thought I'd see if you wanted to come." God. Could she sound any more awkward? Parker didn't answer right away, making Elisa even more uncomfortable. Maybe she had plans already. Or maybe she was deciding how to tell Elisa such an invitation was professionally inappropriate. Or maybe she was wondering whether Elisa was asking her on a date. "It's super laid back. It's at a townie bar in Algiers."

"I'd love to."

"Great." At this point, she almost wished Parker had declined. "I, um, I'm going to go home and change. They go on at eight."

"Since it's across the river, do you want to ride together? We could grab dinner first."

"Okay." Elisa's mind raced. She needed to keep this as far from date territory as possible. "There's a food truck that sets up at the bar. Do you want to just do that?"

"Sure. How about I pick you up at 6:30?"

"Yeah. Sounds good." Elisa hovered for a moment, trying to find a graceful exit. "I'll see you later." Not remotely graceful, but whatever. She turned to leave, but Parker called her name. She turned back.

"I'm sure I could find your address in the system, but that seems sort of creepy."

Elisa laughed. "Right." She walked to Parker's desk and picked up a pad of sticky notes. She wrote her address and handed it to Parker. "It's off Magazine Street. Only about ten minutes from here. Close to the yoga studio."

"Got it." Parker looked at the address, then Elisa. "Thanks for thinking of me."

Elisa nodded. She tried not to notice how long Parker's eyelashes were, or how the patch of skin exposed by her open collar had freckles on it. She definitely didn't think about what it would be like to kiss Parker from that vantage point, placing her hands on the arms of the chair and—

"Jones, I thought we had a meeting."

Elisa jumped as though she'd been caught doing what her brain was imagining. She whipped her head around to find Don standing in the doorway. He looked at her with disinterest.

Parker stood. "On my way. I wanted to have the finalized motion to go over with you, and Elisa was helping me with a read-through."

"Ahead of schedule. I like it, Jones. I'll be in my office."

Elisa looked at Parker, trying to figure out if she made a quick recovery or if her mind was nowhere close to where Elisa's had been. Parker offered her a playful shrug, followed by a wink. "I'll look forward to seeing you later."

They walked out of Parker's office and headed in opposite directions. Back in her own office, Elisa flopped in her chair and let her head fall back. She could tell herself a hundred times over she never would have acted on that flash of attraction, but doing so couldn't erase the attraction itself, or how badly she'd wanted to know if Parker's mouth would taste and feel the way she remembered. She shook her head. What on God's green earth was she thinking?

Despite running ahead of schedule on several fronts, Don managed to dump a ton of new work in Parker's lap. Not that she minded the work, but Don had a way of making her feel less like a colleague and more like a hired gun. She'd hoped to leave that kind of boss behind when she left New York, but it seemed they were inescapable. Not for the first time, Parker thought about what it would be like to work for herself.

It didn't help that Kyle came in to whine about Drake getting the better research assignments. By the time she talked him down in a way that wouldn't make him insufferable, she was late to her mom's doctor appointment. And an accident on St. Charles didn't put her back in the office until four. Not that those things were Don's fault, but the combination wore her patience dangerously thin.

Had the invitation to go out come from anyone but Elisa, she would have bailed so she could stay late at the office and get some work done. But it was Elisa, so at 5:30, she closed up shop and headed home to change. Giving herself only ten minutes to get ready kept her from spending too much time contemplating her look for the evening. She changed out of her suit into a pair of washed-out red shorts, a light blue chambray shirt, and her deck shoes.

When she pulled into Elisa's driveway, she had a moment of panic that she'd underdressed. Elisa stepped out her front door in a dress with a geometric print, too short for work, but incredibly sexy. Parker jumped out of the driver's seat and walked around the front of the car. "Did I go too casual?" she asked.

Elisa looked her up and down and offered a playful smile. "You'll do."

Hating that she needed the reassurance, Parker opened the passenger door. "I'm serious."

"It's casual." Elisa gestured to herself. "I'm casual. We're all good."

Parker laughed at herself then. "I think New York messed with my fashion sense, at least when it comes to summer."

"This place isn't much more than a dive. Relax."

Parker returned to the driver's seat, realizing it was Elisa's opinion she worried about, not her fellow bar patrons. "Relaxed. Promise."

Once they were over the river, she followed Elisa's directions to the Old Point. They parked on a side street and walked toward the bar. Although the sun was beginning to set, the air remained thick and hot. The heady fragrance of morning glories and bougainvillea wafted from the yards they passed. "Yeah, I'm glad I went with shorts."

Elisa laughed. "Good. Let's pop inside to say hi to Tess and grab a drink. Then we can think about food."

"Sounds like a plan."

Inside, the air was cooler, if not fully cool. Low lighting helped, and the crowd wasn't too dense. Fans kept the air moving. Parker was taking in her surroundings when she heard Elisa's name called. She turned in the direction of the voice and saw Tess waving enthusiastically. Elisa returned the greeting and Parker followed suit. Tess hurried over to join them.

"No Sam tonight?" Elisa asked.

"Looming deadline. She's decided to rewrite the last third of the book a week before it's due."

"Why does that not even surprise me?" Elisa shook her head but smiled.

Parker chuckled in spite of her disappointment. She really liked Sam. Although, without her, hanging out with Elisa would be much more like a date.

"Hey, Tess?" One of the guys onstage was looking their way.

"Don't let us keep you." Elisa gave her a hug. "We're going to grab food and drinks, but we'll be in for the show."

"Thanks so much for coming." Tess looked at Parker and, without hesitating, gave her a hug, too. "Both of you."

Tess returned to the stage and Elisa pointed to the bar. "Shall we?"

"Yes, please."

Beers in hand, they stepped outside. People stood in groups and sat at picnic tables along the wall. Many were already eating. They joined the line and, a few minutes later, Parker found herself staring down a mammoth pulled pork sandwich mounded with coleslaw. Elisa had the same thing, only with chicken. They found an empty table and sat.

Parker took a bite of her sandwich and groaned. "God, this is good."

Elisa raised a brow.

"Sorry."

"Don't apologize. I just wasn't expecting that level of conviction."

Parker laughed. "I love to eat. I practice restraint only so my clothes will fit."

Elisa snickered. "I know that feeling."

They finished their sandwiches and returned to the bar. A crowd had formed around the stage. "Another beer?" Parker asked.

"Sure."

"You get us a spot and I'll come find you."

While she waited for the bartender, Parker studied the crowd. While older patrons sat at the bar or the small tables in the back, the people waiting to hear Tess's band skewed younger, more hip. Elisa fit right in, aside from being the most gorgeous person in the room. Since her attention was focused elsewhere, Parker allowed herself to stare. In spite of their history, she'd not anticipated being this attracted to Elisa.

Parker didn't mind the attraction. She just didn't know what to do with it. She'd started to convince herself that Elisa didn't feel the same, but it was now the second time they were spending time together outside of work. Even if yoga didn't count as a personal invitation, this certainly did. Maybe things weren't so one-sided after all.

She carried two bottles of beer to where Elisa stood, joining her just as the first set began. She'd come to spend time with Elisa, and because Tess seemed nice. But once she heard the first song, Parker realized the music would have been enough of a draw on its own. Tess's voice was incredible and her band, Sweet Evangeline, had a sound that seemed to meld jazz and pop and blues in a way that sounded both original and familiar.

After the first set, the crowd thinned. Elisa offered to buy another round and they snagged a pair of stools at the bar that kept them in close proximity to the stage. Parker almost declined the drink but didn't want to come across as stuffy or uninterested. When the second set started, they turned to face the stage. Elisa's thigh brushed against Parker's and remained there, just touching. Parker spent the next hour listening to music and doing her best to stay still so as to not break the contact.

When the music ended, Elisa hopped down from the stool to clap and cheer. Parker followed suit. When she stood, she realized her head was completely fuzzy. "Crap."

Elisa looked at her with concern. "What's wrong?"

"Nothing. I just skipped lunch today and now I'm buzzed."

Elisa laughed. "You ate that giant sandwich."

"Oh. Right. So, how harshly will you judge me for being a lightweight?"

Elisa gave her a quizzical look. "I wouldn't judge you."

Parker chuckled. "I forget you're not a native. If you were from New Orleans, you'd definitely be judging me right now."

"Your lucky day, I guess. If you don't mind me driving your car, I'll take you home."

Parker searched Elisa's face for meaning. Was there something more than a friendly offer there? Or did she simply want there to be? "I'd be forever in your debt."

Elisa smirked. "That could come in handy."

Again, it felt like there might be a double meaning to her words. Even with her fuzzy brain, Parker was picking up all sorts of unspoken signals. She fished her keys out of her pocket and handed them to Elisa. "I place myself in your hands."

They walked to Parker's car and climbed in. Elisa spent a moment adjusting the mirrors and they were off. Parker took advantage of not having to focus on the road and studied Elisa's profile. "Thanks for tonight."

"Thanks for coming."

Parker swallowed. "And thank you for driving me home. I'm still used to New York, where I never drove anywhere. It was irresponsible of me to get tipsy."

Elisa's smile was soft. "It's okay. You didn't have that much, really."

"Yeah. Despite having my first daiquiri at fourteen, my tolerance was never all that high. And since I lost weight, it's even less."

Elisa glanced at her with what looked like surprise. "When did you lose weight?"

"Junior year of college. I was a chubby kid. Then, in high school, being heavy was a way to avoid male attention and an excuse to wear the clothes I wanted."

"I'm sorry. That sounds hard."

Parker shrugged. She hated it when people acted like losing the weight was her biggest life accomplishment. "It was my coping mechanism. I've had a lot of therapy since then."

Elisa didn't respond and Parker wondered why she'd answered so honestly. Maybe she was drunker than she realized. Or maybe Elisa had that effect on her.

As they made their way back across the river, Parker realized she was supposed to drop Elisa off. "If you want to take my car home, I can come get it tomorrow. You just have to let me into my apartment first."

Elisa nodded. "Sounds good."

At Parker's building, she directed Elisa to her assigned spot. "I can run up to let myself in and come back, if you want."

"It's okay. I'll walk you up."

They entered the building and Parker pressed the button for the elevator. She glanced over and caught Elisa staring at her. It wasn't the first time, either. Combined with the flirty comments, it made her think maybe Elisa felt the chemistry between them, too. And Elisa was coming up to her apartment, had offered to. A flutter of anticipation filled her chest.

When the elevator pinged, she led the way to her apartment. Elisa handed her the keys and she unlocked the door. “After you.”

Elisa didn’t decline. She walked ahead and Parker followed, flipping on a couple of strategic lights. “Can I get you something to drink?”

“I’m good, thanks.” Elisa turned to face her. Parker couldn’t read her expression—it fell somewhere between amused and intrigued. For Parker, it was enough encouragement for her to take the lead.

“Same.” Parker closed the short distance between them. She could just make out a hint of Elisa’s perfume. Parker breathed it in, thinking how odd it was that it felt familiar. She looked into Elisa’s eyes, then at her lips. She’d not expected the night to end this way, but she couldn’t imagine anything better.

## Chapter Eight

Elisa sensed it coming, but she was powerless to stop it. The press of Parker's mouth was gentle but confident. Even as her brain screamed no, the rest of her body responded with enthusiasm. The kiss felt at once familiar and new, throwing her back to the last time, so many years ago. It was even better than she remembered.

It took far more effort than she cared to admit to plant her palms on Parker's chest and push her back. "Stop."

Parker opened her eyes, blinked a few times. "I'm sorry. I thought you…I must have read your signals wrong."

Elisa took a deep breath and tried to slow her racing pulse. "Not entirely wrong."

Parker gave her a look that seemed more confused than angry. "What does that mean?"

"It means I may have sent you signals that I shouldn't have."

"Wait. Does that mean you are attracted to me or you aren't?"

How could she have made such a colossal mess of things? "It means I'm attracted to you, but I know better than to indulge it."

Parker offered her a smile. "I don't know. If I'm remembering correctly, we had pretty good chemistry."

The mention of their past hookup felt like a slap to the face, or perhaps a bucket of cold water. "Yes. You were drunk then, too. And the next morning, you made it clear I was nothing but a mild distraction."

"I never said that to you."

Elisa's indignation was in full force now. "No, you said it to George. George fucking Fitzhugh, of all people, and I heard you."

Parker's face fell. "That's not what I meant."

"I'm not sure how else to interpret 'She's hot, but who's got time for that? Maybe after I make partner.' "

Parker scrubbed her hands over her face. She vaguely remembered the conversation. Part of it had been playing it cool. The other part was her singular focus on passing the bar and getting the hell out of Louisiana. She'd never meant Elisa to hear it. And since Elisa had brushed her off the next time she saw her, Parker figured the feeling was mutual. "I'm sorry."

Elisa's face registered disdain. "Sorry you said it or sorry I heard it?"

"Both. I was an ass."

"Well, we can agree on one thing, it seems."

"I hope you know it didn't have anything to do with you. I had a great time that night, but I wasn't looking for any sort of relationship."

Elisa sniffed in disgust. "Eyes on the prize, right?"

"Yes."

"I hate that competitive bullshit. I hated it about law school and I hate it about lawyers. Why don't you all just whip out your dicks to see whose is biggest? It amounts to the same thing."

Parker shook her head and wished she was completely sober. "It's not like that. I'm not like that."

"Could have fooled me."

"I mean, I get how it came across, but my motivations were different."

Elisa didn't say anything. She simply folded her arms and waited.

For the first time in as long as she could remember, Parker wanted to talk about what led her down her chosen career path. She wondered if it was the result of her fuzzy brain or the woman in front of her. "My father was an asshole."

Elisa's face softened. "You mentioned that."

"He hated that I was gay and hated even more that I refused to dress like a girl."

"I'm sorry. I'm sure that made things hard."

"It was hard because my mother tried to run interference, to her own detriment. I hated her being in the middle." She hated even more not being brave enough to stand up to her father.

"Sure." Elisa's shoulders relaxed and she no longer looked angry.

Parker sighed. "I thought being successful would settle the waters."

"But it didn't?"

"It helped, but only a little. I knew I needed to leave, but running away for any reason other than an amazing job would have broken my mother's heart."

"So you got the amazing job."

Parker chuckled, realizing how juvenile it sounded now. "Yeah."

"Did it work?"

Parker thought for a moment. No one had ever asked her that, at least not point-blank. She'd done it well enough that people had taken her choices—and her aspirations—at face value. "Mostly."

Elisa offered a wry smile. "She missed you."

The familiar guilt crept through Parker's chest. Her mother never so much as hinted that she should move home. Still, Parker knew it was hard for her, even when Parker's presence created tension. "She did. I missed her, too. Sometimes I can convince myself that I was making things easier for her by not being around. Other times, I know I was a huge coward."

"It sounds like you made the best of a bad situation."

Parker shrugged. "I don't know if it was the best thing or not. It doesn't matter now, I guess."

"I'd say what matters is that you're home now." Elisa smiled. She had a way of looking at Parker that seemed sympathetic without feeling sorry for her. Parker nodded, feeling better about her choices than she had in a while.

"Hey, do you want to sit for a spell? I feel like an idiot having this conversation standing in the kitchen." She felt like an idiot no matter what. But even with Elisa's rebuff of her physical advances, Parker didn't want her to leave.

"I don't know. It's getting late."

Parker gave Elisa her most sincere smile. "Come on. I just bared my soul. I promise I won't try to kiss you again."

Elisa hesitated long enough that Parker thought she'd decline for sure. "Okay. A few minutes."

"Something to drink? I have bourbon."

"Fine. I know how you Southerners feel about your hospitality."

"Thanks for humoring me," Parker said. Elisa walked over to the sofa. Parker opened a cabinet and pulled out two highball glasses. She poured a couple fingers for Elisa, a bit more for herself. Since she didn't have to drive anywhere, and any chance of moving things to the bedroom had gone out the window, she figured it couldn't hurt. And she'd meant what she said. She had just bared her soul.

They sat on the sofa and Parker steered the conversation toward Elisa. She learned about Elisa's family, growing up in a traditional Cuban household. She asked about Elisa's ex, the one who brought her to New Orleans in the first place. Whether it was the drink or the fact that Parker opened up first, Elisa seemed less guarded. She shared personal details, a few embarrassing moments. Parker had always considered her beautiful, but she found herself drawn to Elisa on so many more levels.

After a while, Elisa turned the attention back to Parker. She asked about first kisses and college girlfriends. When she hinted at Parker's reputation in law school, it seemed to be without judgment or hard feelings. They talked and talked. It reminded her of college, where the intimacy and intensity of late night conversations made relationships, but also fueled self-discovery.

When there was an eventual lull in the conversation, Parker's mind went back to what started it in the first place. "I shouldn't have said what I said." Parker's lids felt heavy, but it seemed suddenly urgent that Elisa understand.

"I know." Elisa offered her a tender smile. "But I won't hold it against you anymore."

Parker felt a weight she didn't know she'd been carrying lift. "I wanted to talk to you, you know? I wanted to explain."

Elisa shook her head. "You don't have to say that now."

"It's true. But the next time I saw you, you were so cool and aloof. I thought you didn't care."

Elisa sighed. "I didn't want you to see that I did. After hearing what you said to George, I wasn't about to own having a crush on you."

Parker straightened. "Wait. You had a crush on me? You never said that."

She laughed. Parker loved the sound of her laugh. "I'm pretty sure that's how crushes work."

"You have a point." Parker thought back to that time. She

wondered if knowing Elisa's feelings would have made a difference. Sure, she'd have been less of an ass, but would it have been more than that? "I think, had I allowed myself crushes, you would have been one of them."

Elisa looked at her with skepticism. "Let's not get carried away."

Parker smiled. "I think you underestimate how attractive you were. Are. Were and are."

She laughed again and Parker realized how much she didn't want the night to end. "Would you stay? I promise I'll be a gentleman."

Elisa studied Parker. Her hair was askew, shirt wrinkled. Other than yoga class, she wasn't sure she'd ever seen Parker anything but put together. Seeing her like this had an unsettling effect on Elisa, and she didn't like it. "I'm not sure—"

"How about a movie, then? Just a friendly, relaxing movie."

Almost more than the disheveled look, the way Parker asked her to stay—not at all aggressive, vulnerable almost—caught Elisa off guard. Part of her brain screamed at her to run. The same part that knew it was after midnight. But she felt a draw that she hadn't experienced before. More than physical attraction, she wanted to be near Parker. And she couldn't help but think Parker wanted her close, needed her almost. "Nothing too serious, or bloody."

"Deal." Parker picked up the remote and turned on the television. She navigated to the menu. "I'll even let you pick."

She considered a few newly released comedies, but they all seemed loud and boorish. She definitely didn't want anything sentimental. Elisa scrolled through the classics section and settled on one she hadn't seen before, an art heist comedy starring Audrey Hepburn and Peter O'Toole. "How's this?"

Parker smiled. "I love old movies. And Audrey Hepburn."

Elisa pressed play and Parker leaned over to dim the lamp. Even without cuddling, it felt intimate, romantic. Elisa hoped she wouldn't regret giving in to Parker's request. She pulled her feet up and picked up one of the throw pillows to hug against her. She hadn't realized the movie was set in Paris.

She didn't remember dozing off, but when Elisa opened her eyes, the screen saver was on the television and Parker was sound asleep. In her lap.

She should freak out. Everything about this moment should make her uneasy, uncomfortable, and probably several other un- words. But it didn't. Elisa struggled to wrap her head around just how right it felt.

She'd never seen Parker's face more relaxed. Maybe that was it, combined with the deeply personal conversation. She'd like to blame the whiskey, but she'd not had enough to affect her judgment. Not that she'd used good judgment. She just couldn't blame the whiskey.

This had to be a bad idea. Although, as she studied Parker's features, thought about running fingers through Parker's hair, she had a hard time remembering why.

Unfortunately—or was it fortunately?—her left foot was asleep. As she became more awake, it did, too. It didn't take long for the tingling to become unbearable. "Hey, Parker." Parker moaned, but she didn't stir. Elisa shifted, sending a rush of blood and pain down her leg. "Parker, wake up."

"What?" Parker bolted upright, bringing the top of her head into crushing contact with Elisa's nose.

"Fuck." Elisa jerked back, pain radiating and blurring her vision. She lifted her hand to her nose, fully expecting it to be bleeding.

"Oh, God." Parker turned to her, a look of horror on her face. "I'm so sorry. Are you okay?"

Elisa pulled her fingers away. No blood. The initial shock faded and she pinched the bridge of her nose gingerly. Everything seemed in place. "I'm fine."

"Are you sure? You don't look fine."

She wiped at her watering eyes and chuckled. "I'm sure. Just caught off guard."

"I didn't mean to fall asleep like that."

Elisa wondered whether "like that" referred to sleeping in general or the fact that Parker had fallen asleep on her. "It's okay. I dozed, too."

Parker looked at the television, then picked up her phone. "It's after four."

"Is it? Wow. We must have really conked out for a bit."

Parker scrubbed her hands over her face. "Real smooth on my part, right?"

Elisa laughed and ran her fingers through her hair. "It's fine. I, um, I had fun. It was fun."

Parker shot her an incredulous look. "You don't have to say that."

She wasn't about to admit how natural it felt to wake up cuddled together. "I mean it. Getting to know you, hanging out. That part was really nice."

"Yeah. It was."

Elisa couldn't be sure, but she thought for a second that Parker looked bashful. It was a disarmingly good look for her, especially in contrast to the confidence she typically radiated. She wondered if it might be a fluke or if, like their conversation earlier, she was seeing another side of Parker. "I should get home."

Parker looked genuinely disappointed. "The sun will be up soon. Do you want to grab breakfast first? I know a great place open all night."

She really shouldn't. But she had yoga at nine, which meant going home and crawling into bed wasn't an option. In spite of herself, Elisa found herself nodding. "Okay."

The diner was a dive and the omelets were amazing. To Elisa's surprise, they hadn't run out of things to talk about. She made it home with just enough time to change and get to the studio. Despite being exhausted, both her mind and body were relaxed. She had a great class and let herself get talked into lunch with Laura, where she talked about anything and everything but Parker.

Something had definitely changed between them. But Elisa was far from deciding what that meant or what to do about it. At the very least, they seemed to have crossed the line into friendship. But Parker's kiss—however brief or abruptly ended—told Elisa the attraction that had been nagging her was mutual. The temptation to indulge it was growing by the minute. If not a good idea, maybe it was no longer a terrible one. Especially once the case ended. And especially if she was the one calling the shots.

## Chapter Nine

The flash of a notification on her phone caught Elisa's peripheral vision. She glanced from her computer monitor to the screen.

*Don calling a meeting in 10. Expect good news.*

Elisa's excitement was tempered only slightly by the fact that Parker had the news first. But since Parker was still lead counsel, it wasn't like it could have gone any other way. *How good?*

She'd know soon enough, but part of her wanted to know how much Parker would share. Not like a test or anything.

*Short of an admission of wrongdoing, everything.*

Elisa didn't really get adrenaline rushes from her work, but this came close. Whether it had to do with the case and their clients, or with Parker, she couldn't be sure. *Congratulations, Counselor.*

When Parker didn't immediately respond, she looked back to her computer screen. Sure enough, an email from Don appeared at the top of her inbox. The meeting summons was cagier than Parker's text, not even hinting that a settlement had been reached. She grabbed a pad and pen and headed to the conference room.

Parker was already there when she arrived. For some reason, it made her feel better about the fact that she hadn't responded to Elisa's words of congratulation. The rest of the team trickled in. Kyle looked peeved, like he had a million other places he'd rather be. True to form, Don came in a full five minutes after everyone else. For a guy who lived and died by the billable hour, he didn't mind making everyone wait so he could make an entrance.

He moved to the head of the table like a king holding court. A tubby, balding king, but a king nonetheless. "I appreciate that everyone is paying attention to their email."

A round of chuckles made its way around the table. "Are you here to hand out work or bonuses?" Kyle asked.

The second round of laughter had more teeth.

"Neither. Although with your slick attitude, I'm tempted to pull out the pink slips."

It was yet another round of the back and forth they had in nearly every meeting. Kyle had a mouth, but he did good work. Don would never inconvenience himself enough to fire someone like that. If anything, they seemed to enjoy antagonizing one another. Elisa rolled her eyes, then glanced around to see if everyone else looked as bored by it as she was. They did. Elisa locked eyes with Parker, who hadn't taken a seat. Parker offered her a wink, then moved to stand next to Don at the head of the table.

"Ms. Jones, would you like to do the honors?" Although Don usually had terrible posture, he stood tall, with his chest puffed out.

All eyes trained on Parker. Elisa was impressed that Don deigned to share the spotlight. Before she could start to tease out the potential meaning of that, Parker began to speak. She walked through the details of the settlement, citing how unusual it was to get the full damages—all the bogus fees, plus interest and legal costs. "That would not have happened without the diligence and attention to detail by each and every member of this team, so give yourselves a round of applause."

Attorneys didn't typically need much prompting to be self-congratulatory. Clapping and a couple of cheers filled the room. Elisa watched her colleagues celebrate, but her gaze quickly returned to Parker. She seemed glad, satisfied even. But it looked to Elisa that her mind was at work. Perhaps she was already thinking about the next case. Elisa shook her head. She hoped she never got so consumed by her ambition that she couldn't even take a moment to enjoy a job well done.

Parker looked her way. She must have caught Elisa staring, because her expression turned questioning. Elisa thought for a moment she might say something, but before she could, Don raised his hand. "While I enjoy a celebration as much as the next person, we're still in regular business hours, and there are other cases to be won."

Don's comment earned him some groans and a couple of eye rolls.

Most of them were good-natured, though. Everyone around the table knew where their bread was buttered. As people began to get up, Parker spoke again. "Which isn't to say that a proper celebration isn't in order. It would be my pleasure to buy the first round this evening. Shall we say Marcello's at five thirty?"

Parker's offer to buy drinks earned as many cheers as the news they'd reached a settlement. People filed out of the room, but Elisa held back. Don said something to Parker that Elisa couldn't hear. Parker laughed, but then looked her way. Parker thumped Don on the back and started walking toward her.

Elisa took in Parker's confident stride and perfectly tailored suit, her warm brown eyes and close-cropped hair. It couldn't have taken more than a few seconds for her to cross the room, but it was all the time Elisa needed. The case was done. She had no idea if Parker would stick around or disappear tomorrow. Not knowing fueled Elisa as much anything else.

"Congratulations," Parker said.

"Same to you."

Parker offered her a curious smile. "Is that it? I got the feeling you wanted to ask me something."

Now wasn't the time to show her cards. "I was wondering if I could get a ride with you tonight, to happy hour."

Parker's smile warmed. "Of course. I'll swing by your office around five."

"Thanks."

Parker nodded and Elisa watched her leave. She stood in the conference room for a moment, letting her decision percolate. She was going to finish what she and Parker had started twice now. And she was going to do it one hundred percent on her terms.

Parker shook Kyle's hand and watched him leave. His departure meant that only she and Elisa remained from the original group of ten. That fact filled her with uneasy anticipation. They'd not had any time alone together since their pseudo-sleepover. Parker didn't regret it, but she wasn't sure where it left them. She turned back to the high-top table and found Elisa studying her.

"It was nice of you to buy all the drinks," she said.

Parker smiled. "I figure it was the least I could do. It really wouldn't have come together without everyone pulling their weight and more."

Elisa angled her head. "You're more humble than you used to be." She smirked. "Or maybe than I gave you credit for."

"Should I take that as a compliment?"

Elisa smiled fully then. "I meant it as such."

"Ah."

"A lot of things about you are different than I remember."

Parker hoped that was a compliment, too. "I like to think I've grown up at least a little since law school."

Elisa lifted a shoulder. "That, but I realize now I didn't really know you then."

Parker wished she could decipher the underlying meaning of Elisa's words, or at least the direction she was now steering the conversation. "I'm sorry that we weren't closer."

"Don't be." Elisa shook her head. "I'm only saying I'm glad I've gotten to know you now."

Parker swallowed. Why did it feel like she was standing on the edge of something monumental? "The feeling is mutual."

"Do you want to grab some dinner?"

While the casual invitation should have relaxed her, Parker's anticipation only increased. For the first time since she was twenty, she consciously told herself to be cool. "I'd love to."

They walked a few blocks to Cochon. Despite not having a reservation, they were able to get a table on the patio without much of a wait. Parker watched Elisa peruse the menu. It felt like they were on a date. And not even a first date. Between knowing each other through work and the awkward kiss and falling asleep together, she felt closer to Elisa than most of the women she'd dated in the last few years.

For perhaps the millionth time, Parker wondered if she'd blown her chance.

"Do you want to share some things?"

The question snapped Parker out of her reverie. "That would be great. You choose."

Elisa lifted a brow, but didn't argue. "How about grilled oysters, boudin, and a mixed green salad?"

Parker nodded. She'd have agreed to just about anything, but Elisa chose things Parker would have selected herself. "Perfect."

Elisa ordered and the food seemed to appear in a matter of seconds. Parker couldn't figure out why time seemed to be moving so quickly all of a sudden. The next thing she knew, their plates were being cleared and Elisa was slipping a credit card into the folder with the check. "You don't have to—"

"I insist." Elisa smiled. "You can get the nightcap."

Parker was surprised by the suggestion. She'd been surprised by the dinner invite as well, but that at least fell in the realm of casual friendship. This felt neither casual nor like friendship. "If you're agreeing to a night cap, then I'll concede the check."

Elisa's gaze never left hers. "I thought we might go back to your place."

All of the air rushed out of Parker's lungs and time—that had been hurtling along just a moment before—seemed to stop. "Uh…"

Elisa laughed. The sound was sexy and rich and made Parker think perhaps Elisa was simply messing with her. But then she looked at Parker again and her eyes were all suggestion. "Not interested?"

"Oh, no. I'm interested." Parker grasped for a coherent sentence. Nothing.

"I mean, with the case done, it feels like cause for celebration."

Again, Parker couldn't decipher her meaning. It was infuriating, in part because reading people was one of her biggest strengths. The other part was just how desperately she wanted to understand exactly what Elisa meant. Asking might make everything unravel. She needed to relax, and to follow Elisa's lead. She angled her head. "Let's get out of here."

"I thought you'd never ask."

## Chapter Ten

Half an hour later, they sat on Parker's sofa, sipping cognac. For the life of her, Parker couldn't figure out if Elisa was waiting for her to make the first move or if she'd somehow imagined the meaning behind Elisa's suggestion. "So."

Elisa set down her glass and leaned in very close. Her smile was slow and sultry. "So, are we going to do this?"

She hadn't imagined it. Elisa was in her apartment and giving her the green light. Without taking her gaze from Elisa, Parker reached over and set her glass on the coffee table. She decided to reuse Elisa's phrase from earlier in the evening. "I thought you'd never ask."

Parker kissed her, more tentatively than she had the last time. The time Elisa pushed her away and looked at her like she was insane. This time, there was no pushing away. If anything, Elisa's response urged her on.

Parker took the kiss deeper, allowing her tongue to slide between Elisa's lips. Elisa's mouth opened, welcomed her in. She tasted sweet, with a lingering hint of spice. Parker wondered if it was the cognac or a trick of how long she'd been thinking about kissing her.

Elisa slid a hand around the back of Parker's neck, scratching her nails lightly through Parker's hair. The gesture—sexy, confident, commanding—sent Parker into overdrive. As tempting as it might be to go with it, plow forward and never look back, she needed to stop while she still could. Parker broke the kiss and leaned back. No matter how badly she wanted this, she couldn't risk it being something Elisa would regret. She searched Elisa's face, trying to read her thoughts.

"What is it? What's wrong?"

"I don't want this to be a mistake."

Elisa laughed, an incredibly sexy sound that tested Parker's restraint. "I'm not the fragile 2L you hooked up with all those years ago."

Despite the humor in Elisa's voice, Parker hesitated. "You weren't fragile then and I don't think you're fragile now."

"So what's the problem?" Elisa trailed a finger between Parker's breasts, stopping right above her belt.

Parker swallowed. "Not a thing. Just tell me—say out loud—this is what you want."

Elisa's smile was slow, sexier even than her laugh. "I want this. I want you. No strings, no promises, no expectations."

For some reason, the adamant declaration left a hollow feeling in Parker's chest. It must be the adrenaline. She nodded, as much to herself as in agreement with Elisa. "That's good. Because I want you, too. And not acting on it has just about killed me."

"We can't have that." Elisa leaned in and resumed the kiss that Parker had interrupted. She reveled in the heat of Parker's mouth and the hard muscles of Parker's arm under her hand. She meant what she'd said. She did want this. Only this. Knowing that going in, deciding it, made all the difference.

Parker shifted and Elisa found herself beneath her on the sofa. Parker braced one arm over her head. This time, when she pulled her lips away, it was to trail kisses down Elisa's neck, along her collarbone, and across the neckline of her dress. Elisa sighed with pleasure.

She kept one hand in Parker's hair, used her other to untuck Parker's shirt. She trailed her fingers up Parker's side and then across her stomach. Parker's abs tensed at the touch. Elisa wanted her naked, so she could see and touch and taste. She began fidgeting with buttons, fumbling in the limited space between them.

"Wait." Parker pulled away again, and it was all Elisa could do not to groan in frustration.

"What now?"

Parker's face was playful this time instead of concerned. "If we're going to do this, it should at least be in a bed."

Elisa laughed. When was the last time she'd been turned on enough not to care about her surroundings? "I guess you have a point."

Parker stood and took Elisa's hand. Elisa followed her to the bedroom. The space was modern, with clean lines, cool grays, and nothing personal. She remembered, then, it was a corporate apartment, a temporary rental arranged for Parker by the firm. The thought of the firm, and the case, dampened her libido. Elisa intentionally shoved aside those details, along with any doubt or hesitation. The case was done and this was happening, and she planned to enjoy it.

Parker turned to face her and Elisa resumed her efforts to rid Parker of her shirt. Parker helped by undoing the buttons of her sleeves. Elisa yanked the rest of the hem from Parker's pants, then pushed the shirt from her shoulders. Underneath, Parker wore what looked to be a combination undershirt and sports bra. Elisa ran her fingers over the snug knit fabric. "I like this."

Parker offered a small shrug. "It's my compromise."

Elisa laughed. In law school, Parker had a masculine energy, but it was more the sporty/preppy variety. The evolution to professional butch made Elisa's insides all hot and bothered. Not that she'd admit that out loud. "It suits you."

"I'd say this dress suits you," Parker reached around and slid the zipper down, "but I'm dying to know what you've got under it."

Elisa let Parker ease the dress from her shoulders. She stepped back so it could slide down her body, relished the lust that sprang into Parker's eyes. Knowing that Parker wanted her, combined with being in control of the situation, felt a lot like vindication. She enjoyed it for a moment, then set it aside. Tonight wasn't about that. It was about incredible sex, and she intended to have it.

Parker stayed an arm's length away. "You're stunning."

Elisa smirked, allowing her gaze to travel up and down Parker's incredibly toned body. "You're not so bad yourself."

Parker closed the space between them, pushing her fingers into Elisa's hair and pulling her into a kiss. Elisa took advantage of her position and worked at the clasp and zipper of Parker's pants. She pushed them down, then slid her hands around Parker's waist and over her ass, enjoying the way her boxer briefs stretched tight across it. Elisa squeezed and Parker groaned against her mouth.

Whatever playfulness had been between them vanished. In its place, a hungry determination. Parker's tongue slid seductively across Elisa's bottom lip. Elisa responded by pulling it into her mouth, sucking and biting it gently. One of Parker's hands moved down her back, unhooking her bra with a practiced flick. Craving the feel of skin against skin, Elisa yanked at the hem of Parker's undershirt, pulling it up and over her head. Underwear quickly followed.

Just a quick brush of their bodies and then Parker's hands were on her breasts. Instead of pinching or playing with her nipples, Parker held them like some sort of precious treasure. And then she dipped her head, taking one hardened peak, then the other, into her mouth. Elisa arched and let out a cry, unprepared for the intensity of the sensations Parker evoked.

They tumbled into the bed and Parker pressed her leg between Elisa's thighs. Again, the force of her reaction caught Elisa off guard. Unwilling to cede control, Elisa shifted. She hooked a leg over Parker's and rolled, reversing their positions.

She enjoyed the play of emotions across Parker's face as she straddled her. Surprise morphed into a smile of satisfaction. When Elisa moved against her, Parker's smile gave way to a look of pure desire. Parker put her hands on Elisa's hips and closed her eyes. It was Elisa's turn to smile then.

She slid over Parker, pleasuring herself and, from what she could tell, Parker as well. After a moment, Parker opened her eyes. She dug her fingers in a little deeper but didn't try to control the pace. "You are so fucking sexy."

Elisa didn't reply. Instead, she eased away. Parker let out a small moan of protest, but before she could do anything else, Elisa slid her hand between Parker's legs.

She'd expected Parker to be turned on, but Elisa didn't think she'd ever touched a woman as hot and wet as Parker was in that moment. It made her gasp. She squeezed her legs together in an effort to stem her own arousal.

"Fuck." Parker's eyes rolled back in her head.

Elisa forgot her desire and focused on the task at hand. She intended to make Parker come undone.

Elisa slid her fingers up and down, stroking on either side of Parker's clit. She watched Parker writhe—in pleasure, but also in search of more direct stimulation. She refused to hurry, to give in to the quick release. It wasn't a chore. She could stare at Parker's body all day long and never grow bored. Seeing it rise to meet her hand, covered with a light sheen of sweat, took it to another level.

When it seemed like Parker had settled into a rhythm, content to let Elisa set the pace, Elisa shifted tactics. She stroked squarely over Parker's center, then pressed two fingers into her. Parker's eyes flew open and she came part way off the bed. "Elisa."

The way Parker spoke her name sent a shudder through her. She shook it off before it could get anywhere near her heart and smiled. "I've got you."

Parker fell back. Her words became mumbles Elisa couldn't decipher. She did catch "more" at one point, so she added a third finger. The way Parker clenched around her, seemed to want her closer and deeper, made Elisa's pulse thud in her chest and between her legs. Her own pussy clenched, even though there was nothing for her to grab on to.

She curved her fingers slightly each time she pulled out. Parker writhed, pushing against her with abandon, giving Elisa a taste of the power she'd been seeking. She used her free hand to massage the hard bud of Parker's clit, stroking it in time with her thrusts. If it was possible, Parker pulled her in deeper, so much that Elisa thought she might lose feeling in her fingers. She almost laughed at the idea—such a small price to pay for having Parker completely at her mercy.

When Parker's legs began to tremble, Elisa braced herself. Even then, the intensity surprised her. It took all her strength to ride it out. The sound of Parker calling out her name almost did her in.

After what felt like an eternity, Parker's body stilled. Elisa let out a shuddery breath and eased her hand away. She wasn't supposed to be this affected.

Parker's eyes opened. "Damn."

Elisa smiled. "Agreed."

She expected Parker to take a few minutes to recover, but she sat up. "If we'd done that the night we almost hooked up in school, I might have never moved to New York."

The playfulness of the comment helped defuse Elisa's jumbled emotions. It was relief she felt, not regret. "I guess it's a good thing we didn't."

Parker's eyes gleamed with mischief. "I don't know. It might not have been so bad after all."

Before Elisa could protest, Parker's mouth was on hers. With one searing kiss, all illusions Elisa had of running the show vanished.

Parker's hands guided her expertly until she was flat on her back.

Parker braced herself on one elbow, but much of her weight pressed into Elisa. Between that and the slow, sensuous assault on her mouth, Elisa was done.

Despite the speed with which Parker turned the tables, she took her time driving Elisa crazy. The kiss became a lazy exploration of Elisa's neck and shoulders. By the time Parker took one of Elisa's rock-hard nipples into her mouth, Elisa was ready to be fucked senseless. But Parker continued, spending a ridiculous amount of time sucking and biting and swirling her tongue over the sensitive peaks.

Elisa felt her control slipping. Because she'd expected Parker to be urgent and this unhurried pace was the exact opposite. Parker was keeping her on her toes, not getting under her skin. She was attempting to win this argument with herself when Parker eased inside her.

Arguments vanished. Her mind went blank. All that remained were the sensations Parker evoked. She managed to be at once gentle and demanding. She coaxed Elisa to open for her. But as Parker filled her, she seemed to be giving herself to Elisa. It gave Elisa a feeling she couldn't quite wrap her head around.

As she stroked, Parker bent over her. She resumed lavishing attention on Elisa's breasts, layering pleasure in a way that threatened to consume her. Elisa closed her eyes and shook her head. She craved release but couldn't bring herself to end the onslaught.

Parker's mouth moved up Elisa's breastbone to her neck. It was enough of a reprieve that Elisa could focus on the way Parker was fucking her. She moved with Parker's hand, against it. The thrusts carried just the right force, paired with the upward strokes of Parker's thumb. She hit every nerve ending, like she knew every button to push, every one of Elisa's secret spots.

"Harder." The command came out more like a plea. Elisa didn't want to own how desperate she felt—for release, but also for something that would break the spell threatening the thin thread that kept her grounded in reality.

Parker obliged. The increased force lit the fuse of her orgasm. She let it take her, crash over her, pound through her. Lightning flashed behind her closed eyes and her whole body shook. It left her feeling spent, but sated.

"Yeah, I definitely would have stayed." Parker's mouth was at her ear. "You're incredible."

The meaning of Parker's words sank in and made her panicky. Elisa opened her eyes. "Stop."

"Just saying." The gleam in Parker's eyes remained playful. Thank God. Elisa didn't think she could handle any kind of emotional declaration at this point. "Will you stay the night?"

Part of her mind screamed that she needed to get as far away as she could as fast as she could. But that would be admitting the effect Parker had on her, and Elisa was not willing to do that. "Of course."

❖

Parker woke to find herself alone. She looked around the room. Not only was Elisa gone, all traces of her—dress, shoes, that sexy bra—had vanished. She climbed out of bed and headed to the kitchen, knowing Elisa wouldn't be there but hoping for it just the same. She picked up her phone from where she'd abandoned it the night before. Elisa hadn't sent a message, so Parker did. *Are you okay?*

While she waited for a reply, Parker started a pot of coffee. She still had an hour before she needed to be in the office. She was on her way to the shower when her phone chirped.

*I'm great. Didn't want to wake you, so let myself out.*

The explanation made sense, especially for a workday. Still. Parker didn't like the one-night stand feel of it. *I would have happily driven you home at least. We're going the same way, after all.*

She added a winky face, wanting to make sure she didn't seem needy. Despite wanting to wait for an answer, Parker needed to start getting ready or run the risk of being late. She brought her phone into the bathroom and picked it up the second she stepped out of the shower.

*I'd just as soon not saunter into the office together.*

The lack of emojis left Parker hanging. Was Elisa being playful or shutting her down? A feeling akin to despondence settled in the pit of her stomach. *Are you sure you're okay? Not regretting last night, I hope?*

Parker hesitated before hitting send. She needed to know the answer to that question, but she dreaded it all the same.

*I had a great time. But let's not pretend like it was more than it was.*

Elisa's reply left Parker feeling even less certain about where they stood. She scrubbed her hands over her face and studied herself in the mirror. Angsting about it wouldn't solve anything. She went to her room to get dressed.

Parker stood in front of her closet, resolutely refusing to look at the bed. The tousled sheets, the pillow she knew smelled like Elisa. It didn't stop her mind from revisiting what she'd been doing in that bed only a few hours before. The feeling of Elisa straddling her, the smell of her perfume mixed with arousal. She could still see the look on Elisa's face when she came.

Parker shook her head. She didn't have a problem with one-night stands. If anything, she loathed the awkward attempts at turning a physical connection into something more. But the idea of putting Elisa in that category made her queasy.

She told herself it was their shared history, the lingering guilt that she'd led Elisa on all those years ago. It was her conscience, wanting to be sure she didn't repeat the juvenile mistakes of her past. But even as Parker reassured herself, she knew it was more. She had feelings for Elisa. Worse, Elisa didn't seem to have any in return.

## Chapter Eleven

"Could you sign these?"

Elisa looked up to find Alie standing in the doorway. It was the third time in as many hours she'd been caught staring out the window. Fortunately, it had been someone different each time, so she wasn't in danger of looking like a complete slacker. "Of course."

Alie brought the files over. "Did you see Parker this morning?"

"No." She answered a little too quickly, but that was okay. "Why?"

"Drake said she went into Don's office almost an hour ago."

Elisa tapped her pen on the desk. That could mean a hundred different things. Most likely, though, was Don offering her a full-time position with the firm. The fact that the meeting was still going on told her Parker was probably negotiating. To her knowledge, Blanchard & Breaux never brought in new associates as partners, but Parker wasn't technically new. She'd certainly proved herself in the short time she'd been around. And she'd already made partner at Kenner. "I don't know what it's about. Sorry."

Alie shrugged. "I wasn't looking for scoop, really. I kind of just wanted you to know."

Elisa studied the woman whom she'd come to think of as a mentee. She realized there was more to their relationship than shared lunches and words of encouragement. She trusted Alie and considered her a friend. "Thanks."

"Are you okay?"

"I slept with Parker."

Alie's eyes got huge. "Seriously?"

"Yeah." There wasn't a policy against it. Elisa had checked. It wasn't encouraged, though, and if Parker took a permanent position at the firm, they'd have to disclose it. If Parker became partner? Elisa shook her head.

Alie took the file back but, instead of leaving, sat in one of the chairs opposite Elisa's desk. "Do you want to talk about it?"

"Maybe, but not right now. And certainly not here."

"I hear you." Alie bit her lip. "We're friends, right? Not just coworkers?"

As much as that was true, Elisa had a feeling she wouldn't like whatever Alie had to say next. "Absolutely."

"I've seen the way Parker looks at you."

So much for being subtle. "How's that?"

"Like she's the hero in a Nicholas Sparks movie and you're the heroine."

Elisa narrowed her eyes. "Is that a compliment? I can't tell."

"Come on." Alie leaned forward and smacked the file against Elisa's desk. "Like attraction and admiration rolled into one. Sex, but with respect. A little adoration thrown in for good measure."

Elisa laughed at the over-the-top description. "I think you've watched *The Notebook* one too many times."

"Maybe, but I know it when I see it. No one has ever looked at me that way. Not yet, at least."

Elisa sighed. What was she supposed to do with that? "There's definitely something there, but I think you're romanticizing."

Alie shrugged again. "Whether that's true or not, you should also know I'm not the only one."

"What does that mean?"

"A few of the guys in compliance have a pool going."

Mild curiosity became a gnawing feeling in her stomach. "A pool?"

"If and when you and Parker are going to hook up."

In that instant, the vague concerns of an office romance became a tangible, glaringly real problem. "Fuck."

"I think it's up to a couple hundred bucks." Alie cringed as she spoke.

Elisa's mind swirled with a mixture of outrage and indignation. A little panic joined in the fray. If it got around that she and Parker actually had slept together, she'd never live it down. And a good half the men she worked with would never take her seriously again. "You can't say anything."

"Of course not."

Elisa took a small consolation from how offended Alie seemed by the suggestion. "How do they think they'll even find out?" A horrible thought occurred to her. "Do they think Parker would spill?" Would Parker spill?

"I think it's more an exercise in asinine male bonding than someone actually winning."

That did not make her feel better. She needed to talk to Parker. To give her a warning. Not to mention make sure they were on the same page when it came to discretion. But at this point, she didn't even want to be seen in the same room as Parker. What a colossal mess. Alie coughed and Elisa remembered she was still sitting across from her. "Thank you for telling me."

"Is there anything I can do?"

Elisa shook her head. "No. Thank you, though."

"Okay. You know where to find me if you need anything."

Elisa nodded and Alie left. Elisa picked up her phone. She started a text to Parker, but didn't want to chance her phone going off in the middle of Don's office. She started a different message to Laura but couldn't decide what to lead with—sleeping with Parker, Parker perhaps becoming her boss permanently, or being the laughingstock of Blanchard & Breaux. She set down her phone and pressed her fingers to her temples.

The sound of an incoming text made her jump. She picked up her phone. The message was from Parker.

*Can we talk?*

Elisa rolled her eyes. Of course Parker would give nothing away. *Yes, but not here.*

She waited impatiently for a reply.

*Agreed. Want to take lunch and meet at Lemongrass?*

It annoyed her to still have no sense of whether Parker had good or bad news to deliver. Not that they would even agree on what constituted good news. *Sure. See you there.*

Elisa grabbed her purse and headed to the elevators. There was no sign of Parker, and Elisa wondered if she was giving her a head start so they wouldn't be seen together. It didn't make sense, given that Parker didn't know about them being the talk of the office, but maybe she was being cautious. Or maybe she did know. Maybe she was part of it.

Parker being part of the boys' club in that way didn't seem completely implausible. She had that competitive streak, after all, and what better way to earn points with the bros. The idea of it turned Elisa's stomach.

By the time she got to the restaurant, Elisa had worked herself into a state. Seeing Parker out front, looking cool and polished despite the oppressive heat, only added fuel to the fire. For the first time in her life, Elisa was tempted to make a scene right there on the sidewalk.

Parker turned and smiled. Although Elisa couldn't see her eyes behind the dark sunglasses, there seemed to be genuine joy on her face. In spite of herself, Elisa softened a little. She took a deep breath and reminded herself that her anger was based on conjecture, at least for now.

"Hi." Elisa didn't smile, but she didn't scowl, either.

"Hey." Parker continued to smile, leaning in to give Elisa a light kiss on the cheek. "Thanks for accepting my last-minute lunch invitation."

"Since you asked to talk in the middle of the day, I figured it had to be important."

Parker opened the door to the restaurant, holding it for Elisa to go ahead of her. "Something like that."

They were early for the lunch crowd and were seated immediately. A waiter appeared in under a minute. Elisa ordered Pad See Ew and an iced tea, although she had absolutely no appetite. Parker ordered as well and the waiter disappeared. Elisa folded her hands on the table, then unfolded them and stuck them in her lap. Parker may have been the one who asked to talk, but Elisa didn't think she could just sit there, waiting. "I don't think we can keep seeing each other."

For the first time since they arrived, Parker's smile faltered. "Why do you say that?"

Elisa swallowed. She needed to stay calm and keep the upper hand. "I don't regret that we slept together. It was good, better than I imagined, even."

Parker's face gave nothing away. "But?"

"But I'm pretty sure Don offered you a permanent position at the firm this morning and I can't be romantically involved with a colleague, much less a boss." There. She'd said it. That was reason enough. She didn't even need to find out if Parker had been part of the rumors or the pool or anything else. Not knowing would help her keep her distance, maintain boundaries.

"What makes you so sure Don offered me a job?"

Elisa gave her a bland look.

"Okay, what makes you so sure I would accept the offer?"

"You want to move back to New Orleans. The firm is a good match for your specializations. Everyone seems to like you. So unless he didn't offer you enough money—"

"It wasn't about the money."

Parker's comment came just as their food arrived. They thanked the waiter, assured him everything looked delicious, and promised there was nothing else they needed. Elisa ignored the food in front of her and looked at Parker. "What did you say?"

"I said it wasn't about the money. I didn't take the offer, but it wasn't because of the salary."

Elisa's mind raced. Surely it didn't have anything to do with her. The idea it might both thrilled and terrified her. "Why didn't you?"

Parker's smile returned. "I've decided to start my own firm."

Relief filled her chest. Surely that decision was larger than any feelings Parker had for her. If the relief was tinged with disappointment, she readily ignored it. "Wow."

Parker nodded. "I've always wanted to. This seems like the perfect time."

"That's really cool."

"So will you reconsider?"

"Reconsider what?"

"Your assertion that we can't keep seeing each other."

For a second, Elisa forgot she'd opened the conversation with that. And she'd been so focused on the reasons they shouldn't, she'd not given much thought to what would happen if those reasons went away. "I don't know."

"I'd be lying if I said you weren't part of my decision."

Elisa's heart thudded in her chest. "Really?"

"Not the only reason, mind you. That would be professionally foolish and romantically presumptuous of me."

Elisa laughed. With that one comment, she remembered all the reasons she fell for Parker, beyond the physical. "Oh, well. That's a relief."

Parker shrugged. "But you were part of it. I figured you'd nix a long-term office romance. And I heard from Niecy that people had started to pick up on our chemistry. It wouldn't be good for either of us to be the subject of gossip."

The matter-of-fact tone told Elisa that was the extent of Parker's knowledge about the chatter. A weight lifted from her chest. "I just found out about it this morning."

"So, yeah. Not a reason to take my career in a new direction, but a nice perk for sure. Assuming, of course, you'll reconsider."

Elisa nodded.

"I mean, you should tell me if it's something besides the whole work thing. If you hate the way I laugh or think my breath is terrible, we should get that out in the open."

"I love your laugh. And your breath is fine." For the first time since they'd slept together, Elisa allowed herself to imagine the possibilities. Really imagine them, not just catch herself in an errant daydream.

"Whew." Parker grinned. "I think you are the smartest and sexiest woman I know. I love that you're amazing at your job but don't let it consume you. I love that you kick my ass in yoga and will stay up all night talking about whatever. And I'd really like to see where this goes."

Elisa smiled. "I'd like that, too."

## Chapter Twelve

Parker set down the box and groaned. Why did law books have to be so heavy? She looked around the space, surprised at how quickly it was transforming from a set of empty rooms to a law office.

It helped that she had movers. And furniture delivery guys. And the financial leverage to sign a lease the second she found a place she liked. Parker didn't take any of that for granted. But still, she'd worked harder in the last two weeks than in the months leading up to being named partner the first time.

"Honey, are you sure you won't let me help with those?" Stella put her hands on her hips and looked at Parker expectantly.

"No, Mama. I've worked you hard enough." Not only had Stella shown up with lunch, she'd helped Parker hang her diplomas and several paintings. She'd also helped to arrange the furniture in the reception area in a way that was far more inviting than anything Parker could have conjured.

"I am an able-bodied woman, not too far past her prime. I can move a few boxes."

Parker crossed the room to give her mother a kiss on the cheek. "As far as I'm concerned, you're one hundred percent still in your prime."

Stella smiled at the compliment, but she had an extra gleam in her eye. "I'm glad you think so."

"Why? What's going on?"

She shrugged. "Nothing much. I'm just going on a date this evening."

"A date?" The words came out pitched higher than Parker wanted. She cleared her throat. "With whom?"

"The instructor of a gardening class I took at the Botanical Society. He's a widower." She said the last part with something that sounded like satisfaction.

"Well, I'm happy for you." She was. Her mother hadn't shown much interest in men after her father passed away, which was fine, but Parker liked the idea of her getting to have some fun. "Just don't do anything too crazy."

Stella gave her a playfully disapproving look. "Don't do anything you wouldn't do?"

Parker laughed. "Something like that."

"Speaking of things you would or wouldn't do, how're things with Elisa?"

"Subtle, Mama." She'd confided most of the details of her budding relationship. And unlike when her father was alive, Stella's happiness for her wasn't tinged with worry.

"When have I ever been subtle?"

"One of my favorite things about you." Although it had created some tensions through the years, Parker meant it. She liked to think she got her grit from her no-nonsense mother. "Things are good."

"She wasn't disappointed you left the firm?"

"Quite the opposite. She had major issues with the idea of dating her boss."

"Even though you weren't technically her boss."

"I was close enough." She hadn't wanted to admit it, but Elisa's reasoning on that had been sound. It would have complicated things—maybe not for them, but in the office as a whole. "I think this arrangement will be much better."

"I'm glad." Stella smiled. "Seems to me it's about the time you should be bringing her around for supper."

Again, not subtle. "I will. Promise."

"Okay. I'll get out of your hair, then."

"Thanks for all the help. I hope you have fun on your date."

Stella's eyes sparkled. "I think I will."

Parker walked her to the door. When she'd gone, Parker glanced at her watch. She had just about an hour before Elisa would be stopping by. Parker was excited for her to see the space, but a little nervous. Fortunately, she had plenty to keep her busy in the meantime. She eyed the stack of boxes. Plenty.

❖

Elisa pulled up at the address Parker had given her. It wasn't, as she'd expected, an office building. Rather, Parker's new office occupied the left side of an old shotgun-style duplex. It exuded the kind of character and charm she often wished her office had. Once again, Parker had managed to surprise her.

She grabbed her purse and the box from the front seat, along with the bottle of champagne she'd hidden in the break room refrigerator after lunch. She made her way down the gravel path and up the steps of the front porch. She peered in the front door and saw Parker, in jeans and a black T-shirt, bent over a box. Elisa tapped lightly on the glass before going in.

Parker looked up and smiled. "I didn't expect you here this early."

Elisa offered a playful shrug. "You know me. I never let work get in the way of what really matters."

Parker crossed the room and slid her hands around Elisa's waist. "I've heard that about you."

"Just don't tell my boss."

Parker smirked. "Your reputation as a powerhouse remains intact."

Elisa laughed. "Don't be spreading rumors, now."

"I speak only the truth."

Despite Elisa's full hands and their somewhat lopsided embrace, Parker leaned in and kissed her. Not too long or passionate, but enough to send ripples of warmth up and down Elisa's body. She had an image of Parker taking her right there in the reception area, bent over the antique desk they'd found at a flea market the previous weekend. At least the intensity of her desire for Parker no longer freaked her out. She filed the image away—they'd get around to it, she was sure. "I brought you a present."

She slid out of Parker's arms and lifted her hands. Parker glanced at the bottle and the box. Her eyes lit up. "I love presents."

"This first." Elisa handed her the box. Parker tore into it like a kid on Christmas morning. Elisa watched as her eyes registered what it was. Parker looked at her, then back at the box, a wide grin spreading across her face. She lifted the slate sign from the tissue and held it up. The white block letters—The Law Offices of Parker M. Jones—stood out even better than Elisa imagined when she commissioned Tess's friend Jenny to paint it.

"I love it."

"They're reclaimed roof tiles. Since you're literally hanging out your shingle—"

Her moderately amusing pun was cut off with a kiss. Unlike Parker's greeting a moment before, this one packed a healthy wallop of passion. Elisa felt it straight down to her toes. "It's perfect. You are perfect."

Elisa was about to rebuff her when realization hit. "Crap, I forgot glasses."

"Okay, almost perfect."

Elisa cringed. "I guess we could swig it right from the bottle."

Parker raised a finger. "The water cooler was delivered this morning."

Elisa glanced in the direction Parker pointed. A five-gallon Kentwood Springs jug sat perched in a stand. "Beggars can't be choosers, right?"

She handed Parker the champagne and got two paper cones from the dispenser. Parker popped the cork. Elisa smiled at the decidedly festive sound. Parker filled the cups and Elisa handed her one. "Thanks for helping me celebrate."

"It's a gorgeous space." Elisa lifted her makeshift glass. "To fresh starts and new beginnings."

Parker did the same, and they each sipped from their tiny paper cups. Parker looked at her, eyebrow raised. "You know, there's an extra office on the second floor."

Elisa offered a bland look. "I just got rid of you as my boss." Not that the prospect of a more personal firm, with clients of her own, didn't appeal.

"Which is why we'd be partners—equals, in it together for the long haul."

Something in Parker's eyes said she was talking about far more than the practice of law. The prospect both thrilled and terrified her.

Parker must have sensed her reaction because she smiled. "Not tomorrow. Eventually, once we know for sure we're compatible."

Okay, she was definitely talking about more than work. "I like the sound of that."

"Good. For what it's worth," Parker drained the champagne from her cup and smiled, "I have the feeling we're going to be phenomenally compatible."

Elisa allowed the possibility to sink in. It wasn't so long ago that the prospect of working with Parker was as off-putting as the prospect of dating her. Now she could easily imagine a future with her—professionally, romantically, everything. She looked around the office, thinking about what it would be like to come in each morning, together. And then, at the end of the day, go home together. Yeah, she could definitely imagine it. She returned Parker's smile. "Counselor, I think we might be in agreement."

Parker's eyes gleamed. "Then I rest my case."

# For Your Eyes Only

*Julie Cannon*

# Part I: Riley

## Chapter One

"I so do not want to be here," I said to my reflection in the bathroom mirror. I'd snuck away from the raucous crowd down the hall for a few minutes of peace and quiet. The party was in full swing, but then again it wasn't every day someone crossed the threshold of the big five-O.

I'm an introvert and I don't do parties. But Ann was my BFF and when she decided to throw herself a "Hawaii Five-O" themed birthday party, I couldn't not come. She assured me there was nothing I needed to do, but as her BFF, I took my role seriously, which, tonight, meant making sure she had a good time.

I'd kept an eye on her for most of the evening, but it was eleven thirty and there was no sign the festivities were anywhere near winding down. It was Saturday, so I couldn't blame the dozen ladies in the living room for having their fun, but I had a half-marathon to run in the morning and my start time was seven thirty. It was going to be a short night and a very long run.

I splashed cold water on my face and patted it dry with a thick hand towel folded neatly on the counter. Ann had good taste in home décor and had not scrimped on towels for the guest bathroom. I would know; she dragged me along one day to every store in a ten-mile radius to buy them as well as several sets of sheets. I'd had a boatload of work to do, my normal weekend activity, but Ann had hauled me out of my house nonetheless. She rarely took no for an answer.

I double-checked that my shirt was still tucked in. One side had come untucked from the monster hug Ann gave me when I walked in her front door, and I'd immediately felt completely disheveled. I'm a stickler, if not a little compulsive about my clothes. Being a female chief financial officer was hard enough, but having shoulder-length blond hair abd blue eyes and being an out lesbian added to the challenges of being taken seriously. I needed every advantage I could get. Whoever said we've come a long way, baby, didn't have my seat in my boardroom.

No one has confidence in their CFO if she is frazzled and doesn't have complete control over everything, including her life. I had complete control of my appearance, which was always flawless. It was also my shield of armor. I'd taken advice from an instructor in grad school to heart. As a result, my car was washed every Sunday, my hair trimmed every eight weeks, and my clothes perfectly tailored to fit my five-foot-five-inch frame. Tonight wasn't a work event, but I still maintained my standards. Several weeks ago, Ann informed me, in her absolute candor, that I'd turned into a stick in the mud. Maybe she was right.

I've always been reserved and cautious, but I'd worked hard to come out of my shell. I had a few friends and went out when invited. Some nights, I didn't stay long. Tonight was one of those where I'd leave much later than I wanted to.

"Riley, what are you doing? You got a girl in there?" It was Ann.

I took a deep breath and opened the door. She peered around me, looking for any sign of the girl she accused me of having inside. Hoped was probably a better word. She'd been after me forever to get a girlfriend.

"Riley?" she repeated. "You've been in here a long time."

"I didn't know you were bathroom monitor along with the birthday girl," I said, maybe a bit too sarcastically judging by the look on Ann's face when I stepped out.

"I know this isn't your thing, but I love you for coming." She kissed me on the cheek and hugged me, which also was not my thing. I tried not to stiffen in response.

To say I'm cold is a bit much, but I'm not big on PDA or even Private DA. My family didn't show much affection, so I'm not used to it or comfortable with it. Makes it kind of tough with a girlfriend, but I haven't had many of those either. I used to think there was something wrong with me, a comment echoed by several women I dated. I feel things—inside—I just have a hard time showing them. I want to touch someone, hold their hand, but I just can't. Freud could have a field day with that if he were still alive.

I saw a shrink for a while, but when he said I was frigid, I never went back. I thought that was the most condescending statement I'd ever heard. I went so far as to report him to the State Board of Mental Health. I guess that's the chance you take when you pick someone off a list. I really didn't have any choice; I wasn't going to ask someone for a referral.

"You know I'd do anything for you, Ann. This is just another on the long BFF list and I certainly wouldn't miss your birthday party." However uncomfortable it makes me, I thought but didn't say. Ann gave me another quick peck on the cheek.

"Stop," I said, stepping back. "People will think we're together." I pretended to be appalled at the idea. At one time, I'd thought about something more with Ann, but then realized I needed a friend more than I needed a lover. Making friends was hard for me, so I didn't dare squander the opportunity. I could always be my own lover, and often was.

"Come on," Ann said, taking my arm and pulling me back into the festivities. "The real fun is about to start."

Her statement worried me, as there was already enough fun for me, but I dutifully followed. Like I had any choice with the death grip she had on my left wrist.

When she finally let go I made a beeline for the stool at the end of the massive island that separated the kitchen from the great room. If I couldn't leave, then ten feet of two-inch granite between me and the partygoers would have to do.

The doorbell rang just as I sat down, and Clarice, a robust woman in a red top and way too tight pants, shrieked in excitement. "Let's get this party started," she shouted to the delight of the other dozen women in the room. A tingle of apprehension went down my spine. What did they know that I didn't? Ann opened the front door and motioned someone inside.

I stopped breathing as the most stunning woman I'd ever seen stepped in. The woman was tall—at least five feet ten inches—and moved with the confidence and grace that I'd only read about in the sappy romances on my bookshelf. Another one of my idiosyncrasies

I keep to myself. The woman had very short hair that didn't quite control errant waves and, if the way she looked in her clothes was any indication, a perfect body.

She was wearing Levi's that were long enough to be crumpled over the tops of her boots—well-worn, scuffed cowboy boots. Her shirt fit like a glove, a trite cliché I admit, but completely appropriate for a butch who probably wasn't yet out of college.

I didn't know her, but I immediately wanted to. The way my heart was racing and my girl-parts were reacting, I wanted to know her in the biblical sense. What the hell? I'd never reacted like this just seeing someone for the first time. I don't believe in love at first sight, but I certainly was experiencing lust at first sight.

She fiddled around in a large bag and pulled out a pair of small speakers and set them on the floor. Ann was introducing her to the other women and I froze when I realized I'd have my turn. What would I say? What should I say? Certainly not "How about we slip upstairs for a few minutes or hours or days?" No, that would be totally out of character for me and definitely so far out of my comfort zone I might as well be in *The Twilight Zone*. Oh my God, she was walking my way. I wanted to disappear, but there was no place to go that I wouldn't be missed.

"And this is my BFF, Riley. She's a little shy."

A little shy? Thanks, Ann, for making me seem like a fourteen-year-old virgin. I reminded myself to fuss at her later.

"I'm not shy," I said stupidly. But then again my brain had shut down all sensible connection to my mouth.

"I'm Jess," she said, extending her hand. Her nails were short enough to not be dangerous but long enough to make her hands look very, very sexy. I stared at her hand like it would bite, but what I wanted was to feel it and its companion all over me. I shook myself out of my stupor and took it.

"Riley Stephen—" I stopped myself before disclosing my full name. I met so many people it was just habit.

"Hello, Riley Stephen," the woman said, her voice bedroom husky.

The instant our hands touched, a jolt of electricity shot up my arm and ignited what had been a dull throb between my legs. My eyes shot to hers. She looked just as surprised as I was. My heart didn't know whether to stop or race, and the tingling in my stomach dropped several inches south.

Who was this woman and why did she affect me so much? Before I had a chance to say anything else—and that was doubtful based on my previous attempt—music started blasting out of the Bose speakers.

Jess's eyes twinkled and she started to move to the heavy beat. She was still holding my hand and I could feel her body move all the way to my toes. My throat was suddenly very dry and I was barely able to keep my jaw from dropping open.

Jess kept her eyes on me as she started to dance, her movements fluid and confident. Hoots and hollers from the other women drew her attention and she released my hand to turn to face them. I immediately felt the loss of connection, like electricity being switched off.

In my jacked-up stupor, it took me several minutes to realize what was happening, what exactly was happening. Jess was the party. She was a stripper. A dozen conflicting thoughts raced through my head. I wanted to run, but I wanted even more to stay. I didn't want to look, yet I couldn't help but stare unabashedly like everyone else in the room. My right brain screamed don't look, my left turned on its video recorder.

As the music pounded, Jess moved around the room. She stopped in front of each of Ann's guests, giving them their own personal lap dance. Her body moved more seductively with each dance as if the woman before was a warm-up for the woman after.

She pulled her shirt out of her pants, a glimpse of tan flesh flashing the woman in front of her. She unbuttoned the bottom button, then the next before giving her undivided attention to Ann. She moved in close and undid the next button, inches from Ann's face. Ann reached around and stuffed a bill into Jess's back pocket, the move putting her face even closer to Jess's not-quite-bare midsection. Jess stepped away from a protesting Ann and into the center of the room, turning and spinning.

Clarice pulled off Jess's boot and Jess rubbed her socked foot into Clarice's crotch. A collective moan could probably be heard down the block. I, however, clenched my jaw together so tight I should have broken several teeth.

Jess teasingly opened another button on her shirt, showing just enough flesh to encourage the women to ask for more. And they did, stuffing dollar bills into Jess's pockets, their hands lingering over the denim. No wonder Ann didn't tell me this part of the party. She knew there was no way in hell I would come.

Jess was a master at teasing without being a tease. When one of the women reached for more than a place to put her cash, Jess smoothly sidestepped the move. When she came back, the woman kept her hands to herself.

As Jess made her way around the circle, I realized she was going to include me in her performance. My hands started to sweat. She looked at me, her eyes riveting. I couldn't tear mine away. Hers sparkled with mischief and pleasure and something else I couldn't quite describe. Her gaze held mine.

The closer she came, the narrower my field of focus became; the awareness of my surroundings disappeared until there was nothing but ocean blue eyes in front of me. There is something just plain sexy about direct eye contact. But Jess doing it made me uncomfortable. Maybe it was because of my initial reaction to her, but there was no way I was going to break eye contact first. Not after I stupidly proclaimed that I wasn't shy. She stepped closer. The look in her eyes told me she knew exactly what I was thinking, daring me to keep it up.

I didn't have any money, but that didn't deter Jess from unbuttoning the last button between fabric and flesh. My fingers burned to pull apart the edges of her shirt, but she stepped back before I had a chance. I felt ridiculous that I didn't have any cash to reward her for her hard work. I debated telling Jess as much when Ann ran over and pressed something into my hand.

"My apologies, Jess. I didn't tell Riley that you'd be here, and she never carries cash." Ann stepped away, but not before whispering loud enough for Jess to hear, "Have some fun, Riley. You need it."

Not caring what Jess thought, I looked down and saw more than a few five dollar bills in my hand. Five dollars? What happened to ones? I guess inflation has hit everywhere.

"Do I make you uncomfortable?" Jess asked, her breath smelling like cinnamon.

"No," I answered too quickly. That happens when I lie.

"Why didn't Ann tell you I'd be here?"

"Now that she's fifty, she forgets things," I managed to say.

She laughed and I almost slid off my stool. She was stunning when she smiled.

"Stop hogging the entertainment," someone yelled. "You might not want to see more, but the rest of us do." Clapping and a few whistles followed the statement.

"Is that true?" Jess asked, her body moving seductively in front of me.

I felt heat rise from my crotch to my face. I hoped it didn't show. "No." My voice held more conviction than I felt.

Jess pulled her shirt off her shoulders, giving me a glimpse of perfect breasts before turning her back to me. Holy perfect tits! If what I saw in a glance was any indication, I'd probably have a heart attack. Instead, as every other pair of eyes in the room was ogling her front, I openly admired her smooth muscular back and the way her ass filled out the back pockets of her jeans.

By the time I caught my breath, Jess had moved back to Ann. Who was I kidding? I wouldn't be able to breathe normally until Jess was out the front door—maybe. More than likely I'd see those captivating eyes in my dreams tonight. I knew for sure they'd be present when I relieved the tension building between my legs. After a few deep breaths, my head began to clear and I realized I was gripping the bills in my hand like a lifeline. I tossed them on the counter and rubbed my palm on my pants.

I never took my eyes off Jess. I couldn't. Not when she seductively ran her hand down her chest to dip into the waistband of her jeans. Not when she slowly slid her belt through each loop. Not when she popped the top button on her jeans. No one existed except Jess as she teasingly stripped off each layer of her clothes all the way down to a pair of tight black boy shorts.

Jess didn't ignore me, but she never got close enough for me to even think about sliding one of the crisp five dollar bills in her undies. Every time she looked at me, my pulse raced and blood pounded in my ears. It took all my concentration and willpower not to react; Jess was that good.

Finally, the music faded and the raucous women settled down. Jess went to each one and placed a light kiss on their cheek, saving me for last. Lucky for me no one was paying any attention when she stopped in front of me as close as she had the first time.

My gaze dropped to her lips in anticipation of what they would feel like against my skin. My head lifted ever so slightly, I closed my eyes and I didn't breathe. The world stopped when she kissed me. She smelled like lilac and sweat, and I knew I'd forever associate that scent with her. In an instant, it was over.

"You're right, Riley. You're not shy."

My eyes flew open. Her eyes were dark and knowing. A small frown creased her forehead as if she were trying to see deep into my psyche. I blinked to break the connection. No way was she going there. A second later, she stepped away and took her clothes from Ann.

# Chapter Two

"Where did you find her?"

"How much did she cost?"

"Does she do more than dance?"

"I need to have her at my birthday party."

"Party hell, I need her tonight. She was hot."

A variety of other questions and suggestive comments filled the room after the front door closed behind Jess.

I felt the same way I had the three times I came out of anesthesia. It was an out-of-body experience, as if I was looking down at the scene in the room. I wasn't quite all there and I shook my head to clear it. What had just happened? I had never experienced anything like that, and the way it shook me up, I hoped I never did again.

"Riley, you okay?"

Ann was beside me holding out a glass of ice water.

"Yeah, fine," I said, again too fast. "Where did you find her? By everyone's reaction, something tells me Jess will be getting more than a few phone calls." How I managed to make coherent conversation, I'll never know, but I was relieved I could. The last thing I needed was for Ann to see how much Jess had affected me.

"She was at a party I went to a few months ago, don't you remember? I told you about it. Helene got her for Joanne's birthday. You were at that conference in DC, I think."

I nodded, remembering the conversation. Ann had given me the strip by strip details and I'd commented that I was glad I missed it. Too bad I couldn't say that about tonight.

"Ann, do you have Jess's number?" Clarice asked, breaking into our conversation. Her face was flushed, her hair disheveled. I hoped I didn't look like that.

"It's on the green Post-it note on my desk. But don't take it," she added quickly. "Just copy it down."

The entertainment over, the party wound down quickly. One by one the women left, each wishing Ann a happy birthday and a promise to get together soon. We cleaned up the remnants of plates and plastic cups, took out the trash, and started the dishwasher. Ann sat by me on the couch, her head on my shoulder. "I'm exhausted."

"You should be." I kicked off my shoes and put my feet beside hers on the table in front of us. "You're getting older and you had to play hostess for your guests. All of your guests." I nudged her feet with mine.

"God, she was hot." Ann did not need to name names.

"Yes, she was."

"I hope I didn't embarrass you, too much."

I was glad to see she added the "too much" to her apology. She had embarrassed me and she knew it. "Nothing I won't get over."

"That's why I love you."

"But I am pissed that you told her I was shy. I'm not shy," I said adamantly.

"I know, I guess I just got caught up in it all. Who cares. You'll never see her again."

"That's not the point," I said.

"Then what is?"

My logic deserted me and I answered the only way a college-educated, successful woman would. "There is no point."

We sat in silence for a few minutes until I felt myself starting to doze off. "I've gotta go. I have a race in the morning."

"Why do you torture yourself like that?" Ann asked for the hundredth time.

"It's not torture if you love it."

"You need to find something else to love. Or someone," she added.

"Don't go there." It was a topic that always led to an argument. Ann thought I needed a girlfriend or, better yet, a wife. The fact that she was still single was not applicable in her mind.

"I'm too tired and too drunk to argue with you tonight. But don't think this is the end of that discussion." She lay down and curled onto her side, her feet in my lap. Ten minutes later, she was snoring, and not a ladylike snore either. Because she sounded like a broken foghorn, I refused to share a hotel room with her when we traveled together. Maybe that was why she was still single? I knew I didn't need to worry about waking her as I slid out from under her size eights.

On my way to the front door, I passed Ann's office. I backtracked to the open doorway. I looked around as if someone would see me, which was ridiculous. The last guest left an hour ago, and Ann was passed out in the other room. The Post-it note was like a green light to step out of my life. Quickly, I pulled out my phone, took a picture, and was out the front door before I could change my mind.

## Chapter Three

My hand was shaking so badly I could barely dial the number. I'd tried and failed at least eight times—either my courage ran away or my fingers hit the wrong numbers. When did dialing a phone become so difficult? When did they start making the space between the numbers so small? How did it get so late? Was it too early to call? I finally cut the excuses and dialed.

My heart skipped at the first ring. My stomach jumped at the second. My mouth got very dry at the third. The anticipation was killing me. I stopped breathing when the call connected.

"Hello, you've reached Jess. You know what to do."

A familiar beep followed her message and I listened to dead air and stared out my kitchen window. For weeks I'd rehearsed what I'd say, but at the moment I needed it the most, I forgot everything including my name. I quickly hung up, like I'd gotten caught doing something I wasn't supposed to.

If I called again, she'd see the caller ID and know I lost my nerve. How embarrassing was that? I'd bought a burner phone from the liquor store around the corner and could very easily buy another. There was no way I was going to call Jess from my own phone. I was stupid gaga about her, but not that stupid.

Several days later, I dialed again. If she mentioned my previous call, I'd tell her I hadn't wanted to leave a message. If I got her machine again, I'd simply read what I'd written on the blue paper in front of me. She answered on the second ring.

"Hello, this is Jess."

Her voice was husky and sexy, as I remembered it. It was the way I heard it in my dreams.

"Hello?"

"Uh, yes. Sorry, hello." So much for following my script. The words in front of me blurred.

"Is there something you needed?" Jess asked.

Boy, do I ever, I thought. "You, uh, danced at a party I was at a few weeks ago," I said, almost stuttering. Could it get any worse than this?

"Okay." Jess said when I didn't say any more.

"I'd like to book you for another, uh, event."

"Tell me about it."

"What do you want to know?" God, what an idiot!

"How many people will be there? What's the occasion? Where? I don't dance with men in the room and I only dance." Her voice was strong, her stipulations firm.

"No, no men," I said quickly, this time due to nerves.

"Okay," she said obviously waiting to hear more.

"Sorry, I'm a little nervous," I said. Might as well, I thought. Make fun of yourself before someone else does.

"If you've seen me dance before, you know there is nothing to be nervous about."

If it were only that simple. "It would just be one person and no special occasion." I finally answered her questions.

"Who is the person?"

Ready, set, go. "Me." The extended silence made me want to hang up and pretend this was all just a bad dream.

"I only dance," she said again, forcefully.

"That's all I want," I choked out. This was nowhere in my prepared remarks.

"Where specifically did you see me?"

"At a birthday party for a friend of mine." I heard a soft chuckle come over the scratchy line. Cheap phone.

"I do a lot of birthdays. Can you be a bit more specific? A name or maybe an address."

I gave her Ann's name and address and waited. The longer she didn't acknowledge that she remembered the party, the closer I was to hanging up. I pictured her going through a bunch of faces like she was looking through a mug book of criminals.

"Okay," she finally said and I was flooded with relief. "Where and when?"

She wasn't available the first three days I mentioned. We finally settled on Tuesday of the following week. I gave her the name of the hotel.

"I only dance. I don't turn tricks. I don't care how much you offer me. And I tell two people where I'm going and call them the minute I'm done."

"Sounds like a smart plan. And all I want is a dance, nothing more," I said.

My statement was met with another long silence. "Hello?" I said awkwardly.

"I'm here."

More silence. I was ready to hang up when she said, "Okay. What's your name?"

I knew she'd ask, and for a second I thought about making one up, but then I realized she'd know the minute she saw me. So much for anonymity.

"Riley."

I heard a quick intake of breath before I quickly mumbled goodbye and hung up.

❖

"Why are you so jittery? You can't sit still and you keep looking at your watch. Do you have some place to be? You invited me, remember?"

Ann peppered me with her questions halfway through dinner. I'd invited her in an attempt to get my mind off where I was supposed to be in ninety minutes and who I was going to see. The twelve days between talking with Jess and today had felt like twelve hundred days in hell. I couldn't sleep, my attention span was little more than a nanosecond and I could barely keep any food down.

"Sorry, no. I've just got a lot on my mind and I was hoping you'd be a pleasant distraction."

"Want to talk about it? Is it your job?"

I shook my head.

"Your parents being demanding again?"

I wish. "No. Can I play the BFF card and say I don't want to talk about it?" Ann gave me a hard look for a very long time. I tried not to squirm under her examination.

"How long has it been since you've had sex?"

So long I couldn't remember. "I've been busy" was my standard, noncommittal, bullshit answer.

"That long, huh?" Ann could always see right through me. I had to be careful.

"That's not it," I said again, trying to add more levity in my voice. "Are you still seeing Joyce?" I named the latest in a long line of women Ann dated.

"I'll let you change the subject if you promise me you're not in any trouble." She waited for my answer.

Like I was going to tell Ann I hired Jess as my private stripper. I was so in trouble. "I promise," I said crossing my heart and putting up the Girl Scout oath fingers, "I'm not in trouble." I was so very much in trouble.

## Chapter Four

I parked a few blocks from the hotel and walked, hoping to burn off some of my nervous energy. I was more anxious than when I sat for the CPA exam and the first time I had sex. The funny thing was this time I didn't have to do anything. Absolutely nothing. Nothing to remember, no impression to make, nothing. But I'd thought about practically nothing else for weeks.

Since Ann's party, I found myself looking for Jess everywhere. Anyone that looked remotely like her got more than a second glance. Every meeting with a new client was filled with apprehension that it might be her.

Ann had continued to talk about Jess almost every time we were together. Like I needed any reminders. I finally had to tell her to shut up when she started telling me, in graphic detail, the fantasy dreams she'd had the night before. Mine were much better.

Ahead of me I saw the Hilton sign lit up. The lobby was clearly visible through the windows that stretched from the ground to the second floor. Glass and chrome was the décor of choice and everything sparkled.

I was so busy looking around to see if I recognized anyone, I almost got caught in the revolving door. God, I really needed to calm down and get myself together. The hotel was on the other side of town, so the likelihood of someone recognizing me was slim. I'd thought of a valid cover story but was so nervous I'd probably forget what it was. It was nine thirty in the evening, and other than a few people in line to check in, the lobby was empty.

To my left was the lounge, and waves of cheering drifted out every time the door opened. There was probably a sports event guests wanted to watch in the company of others and not in their rooms.

When it was my turn at the counter, I was greeted by a woman about my age but fifty pounds heavier. Her name tag was imprinted with Dolly and her voice and effervescent personality were too much for my frayed nerves.

"Good evening and welcome to Hilton," Dolly chirped like I was the very first guest to cross the threshold. "Checking in?" she asked, her fingers poised over the keyboard.

I gave her my name and slid my driver's license and credit card across the counter. I'd tried to figure out how I could check in under a different name, but I didn't have any ID forgers in my contacts. So what if someone tracked it down? I could come up with a dozen plausible excuses for spending the night in a hotel.

"One key or two, Ms. Stephenson?" Dolly asked, her cheeriness and overly loud voice fraying my already frazzled nerves. Didn't she know I was meeting a stripper in my room? She needed to keep her voice down. She was drawing attention.

"Two, please, and I'd like to leave one for a friend to pick up later."

"Certainly, Ms. Stephenson," delightful Dolly said. She put the first, then the second gold card into a small box that looked like a miniature ATM machine. Her chubby fingers entered a set of numbers, and when the green light appeared on the display panel, it coughed out the card. While she was making the magic keys, I wrote Jess's name on the crisp white envelope Dolly had handed me. Without a last name, Jess's name looked as naked as I felt standing there.

Dolly handed me one of the cards, sliding the other one in the small paper pouch and writing my room number on it. I put the key for Jess into the envelope, sealed it, and handed it back to Dolly. She couldn't hide her frown when she saw only Jess's first name on the envelope. I hadn't thought about what this could look like—exactly what it was, an illicit assignation.

Dolly briefed me on the Wi-Fi code, the hours of the gym, and when the buffet opened for breakfast, none of which I was interested in. No way would I be surfing the net, exercising, or staying for breakfast. Thirty minutes after Jess was done, I'd be out of there.

Somehow, I found my way to the elevators and pushed the button to my floor. I stared at my reflection in the mirrored doors and barely recognized the woman I saw. What was I doing here? I was risking everything to sit in a chair in a hotel room and watch a woman take her clothes off. How weird was that? My boss would have a heart attack if he found out.

The door clicked open and I stepped inside. Several lights were on, so I didn't have to stumble around in the dark to find the switch. I had requested a suite and it had cost a small fortune, but it was exactly what I needed. It was tacky to sit on the bed or in the lone straight-backed chair while Jess did her thing in a cramped room.

The room had a three-cushion couch covered in a dark brown leather. Two matching throw pillows rested against each arm. A coffee table sat in front of the couch, its dark wood gleaming from a recent polish. A Queen Anne chair and an overstuffed recliner completed the seating area. The bedroom was through the doors to my right, the bathroom to my left.

I sat on the couch and in the two chairs, deciding which one offered the right view. Good God, it sounded like I was watching a basketball game or a movie. I settled on the chair. The couch was too suggestive and I'd have to move the table, which was too calculated.

If I had a dollar for every time I looked at my watch, I could pay Jess's five-hundred-dollar fee. It was now only five minutes from our agreed upon time and I was more than a little nervous. My left leg bounced up and down and my hands were sweaty. The knock on the door surprised me and I shot to my feet, almost toppling the chair over. My hand shook as I opened the door.

Jess was even more stunning than I remembered. And I had definitely remembered. She was wearing a pair of jeans, a blue shirt with buttons down the front, and the boots from Ann's house. Her smile was genuine, but half hidden by the phone she had pressed against her cheek. Her eyes darkened when she recognized me.

"Hello, Riley," she said quietly.

I remembered the sound of her voice, the husky bedroom just-woke-up quality that had often spoken my name in my dreams. She moved the phone from her face but didn't hang up.

"Come in," I said, glancing over her shoulder as she walked in.

"I'm in room seven twenty-two." She pushed an icon on the screen on her phone and glanced across the room. I could tell it met with her approval. She looked back at me before walking through each room, looking under the bed and in the closets. What was that all about?

"Yes, I'll call you in an hour." She ended the call. "Shall we take care of business before we get down to business?" Jess asked, not the least bit embarrassed by the financial transaction about to occur. This was her job, after all.

I handed her a crisp white envelope with five one-hundred-dollar bills inside. She counted them before slipping it into her bag. "No offense, but I've been stiffed before." She looked me straight in the eye.

"None taken." I stood there like an idiot because I really didn't know what I was supposed to do next.

Thankfully, Jess took pity on me. "Why don't you sit down and make yourself comfortable."

As I did, Jess pulled two small Bose speakers from her bag and set them on opposite sides of the small room. She pulled the straight-back chair from the desk and placed it in the center of the room. She touched the screen of her phone a few times and the room suddenly filled with music.

Jess turned her back to me and lowered her head as if she were saying a prayer. How weird would that be?

Tonight, her jeans were black, but she filled them out just as nicely as she had before. She shifted each shoulder back and forth a few times as if loosening the taut muscles. She did the same with her head and arms. Must be her pre-dance warm-up.

As the beat picked up, her body started to move and she walked away from me in a slow, seductive strut. I lost all concept of time and my surroundings—everything was all about Jess. It could have been minutes or hours, Jess capturing my complete attention. She turned and grabbed the bottom of her shirt. Slowly, she pulled it from her pants, its long tail falling below her ass. Gyrating her hips, she unbuttoned each of the buttons on her fly, coming closer to me with each step. By the time she was standing in front of me she had her hands inside her waistband and was starting to slide the pants down her legs.

She bent over at the waist, giving me a glimpse down the neckline of her shirt before turning around again. Her shirt just covered her ass, and a flash of black between her legs caught my attention as she shimmied out of her pants. Keeping her back to me, Jess spread her legs and threw her shoulders back. She put her hands on her ass cheeks and swiveled her ass in a circle. My heartbeat kicked up a notch.

She unbuttoned her shirt, looking over her shoulder at me once or twice. Yes, Jess, you have my complete attention. When all the buttons were opened, she shrugged and the shirt slid off her shoulders. She turned around, holding the shirt closed with one hand as her other hand disappeared under it. Her hand ran from her throat to her crotch several times as her head fell back and her mouth opened.

Coming close, she put one leg on the armrest of the chair I was sitting in. She bent her knee and, keeping her head up and her shoulders back, leaned into me. Her crotch was no more than five or six inches from my face and I inhaled her. My head started to spin. She repeated the same with her other leg and I had to clench my fists to stop from reaching out.

She stepped back and moved behind me, her fingers walking up one arm, across my shoulders, and down the other before she walked away, letting her shirt slowly fall down her back. Inch by tantalizing inch, more and more of her back was exposed. I imagined my fingers following the trail of exposed skin. When the shirt dropped to the floor, I almost moaned with relief.

Jess crossed her arms in front of her and caressed the bare skin of her shoulders. She reached around behind as if unhooking the thin black bra strap, but instead slid her hands down the small of her back, hooking her thumbs under the waistband of her boy shorts. I held my breath. She'd stripped down to her shorts at Ann's, and I wondered if she'd drop those as well in this private dance.

Jess turned around, sliding her hands up her stomach and over her lace-covered breasts. I devoured the muscles in her back, the perfect curve of her ass, her long, toned legs when she turned around. Her body was her job and, like most professionals, she wanted the best tools to work with. My eyes followed her hands as they moved over her curves and my anticipation grew as to what was next.

She pulled the chair in front of her and, standing behind it, slowly leaned over and ran her hands over the fabric. I imagined sitting in the chair, Jess behind me, her warm breath in my ear as she caressed my chest. Holding the back of the chair, Jess slowly sank down, her butt on her heels, knees apart, giving a glimpse of her crotch as she repeated the motion twice more.

When she stood again, she ran her fingertips up each arm of the chair and across the back. I felt warmth on my skin as if she were touching me. If it was possible to make love to an inanimate object, Jess was doing it. She was simulating sex, but by God, it was arousing. She walked around and turned, showing me her perfect ass. She caressed the seat of the chair, then straddled it and seductively sat down. I imagined her settling onto my face, rocking her hips back and forth. I think I stopped breathing.

Her hands moved over her stomach and breasts. Her head fell back in ecstasy. Suddenly, she threw her leg over the back of the chair and was facing me. She spread her legs apart, then together twice, using her hands to push them open and closed. She ran her hands up her stomach and she caressed her breasts.

I wasn't sure I was breathing. I knew I had to be, but I didn't think I even knew my name at that point. I was enthralled, entranced, captivated, or whatever word was listed as a synonym in Mr. Roget's *Thesaurus*. Jess had maintained eye contact this entire time and if she had been my girlfriend, she would be on her back in the middle of the bed in the next room.

This was nothing like her performance at Ann's. If I thought that was hot and sultry, this was off the charts pure, raw sexual seduction.

The music started to fade and I wanted more, but what more could she do? She was almost as naked as the day she was born and her job was done.

She ended her routine as she had at Ann's, by leaning down and kissing me on the cheek. Her breasts were inches from my hands, but I didn't try to touch them. Touching was forbidden, and I wasn't about to do anything that would sour our evening together. Or prevent another.

Again, she smelled like lilacs, and I closed my eyes and reveled in her scent. Her lips were as soft as butterfly wings. My stomach fluttered. When I opened my eyes, she was standing in front of me. Her smile was sweet and she was looking at me closely. She was probably trying to figure out what kind of weirdo I was to request her services, then sit quietly without saying a word or making any gesture to indicate I liked what she was doing. I didn't smile, whistle, or clap. I didn't reach out or flirt with her or slide money into her undies.

Jess gathered up her clothes and closed the bedroom door behind her. The click of the lock was enough to snap me back to the present. I exhaled deeply.

My body hummed with energy and tension and I felt light-headed when I stood up. Steadying myself with the back of the chair, I walked to my bag and pulled out another envelope. I pulled two bottles of water from the mini-fridge and opened one. The cool liquid felt wonderful sliding down my throat, which was parched from my shallow breathing. I didn't hear Jess come out of the bedroom but saw her when she picked up one of the speakers.

She was fully dressed and she looked just as put together as she had when she walked in. I glanced at myself in the mirror above the couch. I didn't think I looked like I'd had the ride of my life. My insides, however, were a complete and total mess.

I offered her the other bottle of water as I walked her to the door. Before I opened it, I handed her the second envelope. She glanced at it, then back at me.

"I hope we can do this again?" I asked, surprising myself. The words just came out of my mouth before I had a chance to think about them. That was so unlike me.

She frowned slightly as if she were weighing the pros and cons of my statement. For several moments neither one of us moved or said anything else. Finally, she smiled. "I'd like that."

My pulse jumped and I pretended to be calm as I opened the door. She hesitated in the doorway before turning to me. "Good night, Riley."

Her voice was seductive, and I envisioned her whispering in my ear as she snuggled behind me in bed. My stomach jumped.

"Good night." I somehow managed to say. I didn't immediately close the door, but watched Jess walk down the hall. When she got to the elevators, she didn't turn to look at me even though she had to have known I was watching her. When she disappeared in the elevator, I closed the door. It was the best thousand dollars I'd ever spent.

## CHAPTER FIVE

The next time I saw Jess was in a different hotel room, and the evening was very much like the one before. The third time, however, was completely new. The music was raw, her moves fast and hard. She was wearing a tailored men's suit with a blue shirt and red and white striped tie. She looked nothing like the men in my office. But there was no doubt she was in charge. Whoever said a woman in men's clothes was just flat-out sexy was absolutely right.

There was nothing slow or tempting about this dance. No teasing, a fleeting glimpse or a preview of what was underneath. Her moves were quick, decisive and deliberate. She unbuttoned her jacket and threw it to the floor, as if it was a claustrophobic barrier. She quickly discarded her trousers and kicked them across the room.

She danced to the heavy beat, her body moving with pure, primal sex. Her moves were aggressive and possessive, as if she were a jungle cat stalking her next prey. She yanked off the tie, wrapped it around my neck, and pulled the knot tight. Not tight enough to restrict my breathing, but enough to experience what a little bondage might feel like. Being the control freak, I never thought I'd be interested in such a thing, but I was painfully aroused by her simple maneuver.

Straddling me and sitting on my lap, Jess grabbed my hands and put them on the bottom of her shirt. With her hands over mine, she wrenched it open, sending small white buttons across the room. My pulse skyrocketed at the innuendo that I'd been overcome with desire and ripped it open, exposing the tiny red bra underneath.

If the other evenings were seductive and tantalizing, this evening was all about control, and there was more than one time I almost lost mine. Jess was dancing with abandon. It was like she was inside the music, tearing away layers to get out.

I wasn't sure how much longer I could stand the torture she was putting me through when the music wound down. Jess was covered in a light film of sweat and it was a toss-up who was breathing more heavily. My clit was hard and throbbing and demanding I do something about it. I wanted to grab Jess's hand and shove it down my pants. I wanted her to feel how wet she made me. I needed her to slide her fingers inside me, play with my clit until I begged her to make me come. I craved her body over mine, under mine, and wrapped around me.

But, of course, that only happened in my fantasy later that night, and I tried not to think about it as I walked to my morning staff meeting. I'd seen Jess three more times in six weeks and I was beginning to feel like a regular, which was a little creepy. My bank account felt the impact as well. Did she have other repeat business or was every dance new?

I stumbled and almost fell flat on my face. That would be a sight for sure. I looked behind me at the culprit and only saw the tiles and grout of the flooring. Jeez. I was tripping over nothing on the floor. That wasn't surprising. I'd burned myself twice on the iron in the last week, made coffee without putting grounds in the filter, and put a box of cereal in the fridge and the milk in the pantry. The more I saw Jess, the more unhinged I became. But I couldn't stop. Maybe I had stripper addiction. Is there a twelve-step program for that? Somewhere nestled in the woods, miles from prying eyes and temptation? I had to get it together. First, because I was not myself and people were starting to notice and, second, if Ann had any idea she'd grill me until my skin peeled.

I looked at my watch. Damn, I was eight minutes late to my meeting. I'd been late to everything lately, which was not like me at all.

I was having a Town Hall with every employee who reported up to me. At last count, that was 112, and they were all sitting in neat little rows when I walked in.

"Good morning, I apologize for running a few minutes late. I was waiting for one last piece of updated data for this meeting and it just came in."

I said a few more perfunctory comments as I walked up the center of the aisle to the front of the room. Mark, our IT guy, handed me a portable microphone. I clipped the base to my waist and the mic to my lapel.

"Let's start by welcoming our new employees since last quarter's meeting." I took the paper my administrative assistant handed me and started reading off the names. One by one, each employee stood and the room applauded.

"Dana Mason, Financial Analyst." I looked around the room and movement to my left caught my attention. A woman stood up and as my staff welcomed their new coworker, I felt the world fall out from under my feet.

❖

Somehow, I managed to finish the ninety-minute meeting without fainting, throwing up, or running from the room. I quickly figured out her real name was Dana and her stripper name was Jess, and after I saw her standing in the fourth row, I never looked that direction again. I felt her eyes on me. It was only a matter of time before my life changed forever. And not for the good.

Slowly the crowd maneuvered through the two exit doors while a few employees lingered behind to talk with me. Jon, the requisite kiss-ass, was the first and thanked me for the clear update on the company financials. Tobias, our resident doomsday predictor, asked several follow-up questions on our long-term financial stability. When I saw Dana hovering behind him, I lost my train of thought.

"Riley?" Tobias asked.

"Sorry, Tobias, let me get back with you on that." I knew I wouldn't remember. Then Dana was standing in front of me.

A woman I recognized as Joan introduced Jess, or Dana, or whatever her name was.

"Riley, this is Dana. This is her second week."

Dana held out her hand. "Thank you for making me feel welcome, Ms. Stephenson."

Her voice had the same scratchy quality in the daylight as it did at night. My eyes went to her lips remembering how they felt against my cheek. Tentatively, I reached out and shook her hand. I couldn't very well ignore it. That would be downright rude. A warm rush of pleasure floated through me.

"We're glad to have you, Dana." I almost stumbled over her name, embarrassing myself. Her face was guarded, her eyes knowing. She was worried I'd out her and she'd lose her job. I was worried she'd out me and I'd lose my job. Well, this was a cluster waiting to happen.

# Part II: Dana

# Chapter Six

There were a dozen cars parked in front of the house when I arrived. I found a spot down the street and, juggling my phone, hauled my bag to the front door. I shifted it to my shoulder and rang the bell.

"I'm here, Lou," I said. Lou, or Louise, as her mother called her, was my BFF and had tried desperately to get me to quit this part-time job. When she couldn't, she demanded that I tell her exactly where I was and when I'd be done. She also insisted on staying on the phone until I gave her the all clear.

The door opened. Light spilled out of the house and onto the porch. The woman was pretty, in a plain, wholesome way. The "Birthday Girl" hat she was wearing was a dead giveaway that I was here for her.

"Ann?"

"Jess, please come in," she said after giving me more than an approving once-over.

I cautiously stepped inside, my phone in my hand, Lou on the other end. I could tell immediately this gig was safe. I told Lou I'd call her in an hour. If she didn't hear from me, she'd call the police. Yes, a lot could happen in an hour, but it was better than nothing.

Several women were sitting on the couch, with a few more in scattered chairs and one in a bean bag. My eye caught sight of a striking woman sitting alone at the end of an island that separated the kitchen from the rest of the large room. I'd have her joining the fun in no time, I thought.

Ann handed me an envelope and I glanced inside. The correct amount of cash was inside and I slid it into my bag. I set up my speakers on either side of the room and connected them via Bluetooth to my phone. I had my songs cued up and ready to go.

Ann introduced me around, and Clarice, a woman in a red spaghetti strap top, shrieked in excitement. The final stop was the woman at the end of the island. A look of sheer panic crossed her face as I got closer. She was definitely not as into this as Clarice. She was petite, probably not more than five foot four inches or maybe five-five, and had long, blond hair. She was about ten years older than me, probably in her mid-thirties, but she was stunning. The most attractive woman in the room, by far.

"And this is my BFF, Riley," Ann said by way of introduction. "She's a little shy."

A little shy? Jeez, what a terrible thing to say about your BFF even if it were true.

"I'm not shy," Riley said firmly and, if the flush on her cheeks was any indication, quite embarrassed.

"I'm Jess." I introduced myself with my practiced sultry voice.

"Riley Stephen—" She stopped as if she were about to say her complete name. She must be a professional with a job where she meets a lot of people. Saying her full name was probably just habit.

"Hello, Riley Stephen," I said, teasingly. It reminded me of my niece Emily's kindergarten class in school where there were several Emilys. The only way the teacher could reference them was to call them by their first name and first initial of their last name. According to Emily, there was an Emily J and an Emily H, and whenever she spoke of them it was as if that was their real first name.

The instant our hands touched, I felt a spark of electricity so strong I had to look at my hand to see if it was glowing. When I looked back at Riley, her crystal blue eyes conveyed she felt it too. I'd never had this kind of reaction with a woman. I've danced in front of hundreds of women and this was the first time I felt a connection, and, yes, even an attraction to one of them. I wouldn't do anything about it because I didn't mix business with pleasure, and with Riley Stephen, that made me a little sad. When the familiar slow, steady beat started and filled the room, I decided not to think too hard about it. I had bills to pay.

My body started to move because I simply loved to dance. Any beat got my toe tapping and my blood pumping. I was still holding

Riley's hand and I kept my eyes on hers as I started to dance. Something in her face told me she had no idea I'd been hired to spend the next forty-five minutes taking off my clothes. Interesting. Everyone else in the room knew why I was there, why not her?

The women started cheering, and when I released Riley's hand, I immediately felt the disconnect.

The beat picked up in tempo and I danced around the room giving each woman several minutes of my undivided attention. I'd not yet removed any of my clothes, but each woman had stuffed a bill into my pockets.

Riley looked like she was scared to death as I made my way over to her. I approached slowly, my hips swaying to the music, my arms over my head. She swallowed hard and snapped her mouth shut. She was kind of cute when she was flummoxed. I put both hands on her thighs, slid them upward and, stepping closer, stopped inches from her crotch. I held them there for several seconds before sliding them back to her knees. I trailed my right hand up her arm and across her shoulders as I stepped behind her. I leaned in and whispered, "There's much more to come."

Before Riley had a chance to react, I stepped away and focused my attention on the woman in the green blouse. I didn't remember her name and it wouldn't have mattered if I did. She had cash in her hand, and that was all that mattered.

I started by slowly pulling my shirt from around my waist. With each tug I made sure just a hint of flesh showed, enough to give the women a preview of what was to come. I moved to the woman with the ponytail and unbuttoned the bottom button on my shirt. She placed a dollar in the waistband of my jeans right where the skin showed.

I repeated the same maneuver in front of each woman, dancing back and forth between them, encouraging them to have fun and to reward me for more skin. I had watched countless videos and had paid special attention to those that made me hot. I practiced for months before I went on my first call. I continued to do research every few weeks, perfecting my craft. I was a regular at the Candy Store, a local strip joint not far from my house. I'd sit in the back watching and surreptitiously taking notes. I'd made friends with two or three of the dancers who I still kept in contact with.

One of the women reached for me and I smoothly stepped out of her reach. I wagged my finger at her as if to say naughty girl and didn't come back around to her for several minutes. That time she behaved.

I was down to my last button, and I headed toward Riley. When she realized my intent, she looked like she was about to flee. I hoped she didn't. I looked at her, willing her to stay put.

The closer I got to her, the faster my heart beat and the shallower my breathing became. That was odd because I was in great shape and never, never out of breath. She had kept the granite island top between her and the rest of the party. As I got closer, she swiveled her chair so there was nothing between us. Her eyes held mine and I couldn't look away. Along with trepidation, I saw fortitude and couldn't help but wonder what that was all about.

I was inches from her when I unbuttoned the last button on my shirt. Her eyes darted to my hands and she looked hard at the skin that was revealed underneath. I took one step back when Ann interrupted.

"My apologies, Jess. I didn't tell Riley that you'd be here, and she never carries cash." Ann stepped away after putting a stack of bills in Riley's hands. She whispered loud enough for me to hear that Riley needed to have some fun.

"Do I make you uncomfortable?" I asked, stepping close enough for Riley to reach me.

"No," she answered quickly.

"Why didn't Ann tell you I'd be here?" I asked, suddenly curious.

"Now that she's fifty, she forgets things."

I laughed. Riley had a good sense of humor.

"Stop hogging the entertainment," someone behind me yelled. "You might not want to see more, but the rest of us do." Clapping and a few whistles followed the statement.

"Is that true?" I asked.

Riley blushed. God, she was cute. "No," she said, looking straight at my chest.

Feeling particularly naughty, I pulled my shirt off my shoulders, giving Riley the first glimpse of my breasts before turning my back to her and walking away.

I felt Riley's eyes on me as if she were touching me. I ran my hand down my chest to dip into the waistband of my jeans. I unbuckled my belt and slowly pulled it through each loop and, with one end in each hand, dropped it over Ann's head. I used it to pull myself closer to her. I didn't say anything but used my eyes to convey to Ann that she had permission to open the top button on my jeans.

The women went wild, urging their friend to do the same to the next four. I stepped out of Ann's reach and over to the woman beside her. After repeating this move with two others, I turned my attention back to Riley. I was saving the last button for her.

I would have liked to see what was in her eyes, but hers were glued to my crotch. Obviously, she wasn't as unaffected as she wanted to be. I stopped in front of her, just out of her reach. I had dressed carefully and I knew she could see the top of my black boy shorts. She sat still, the only thing moving the rapid rise and fall of her chest. When the other women reached out whenever I got near, Riley didn't. When the others whistled and made comments, Riley sat quietly. As the heavy beat vibrated in the air, I stepped closer and didn't stop until the seam of my jeans rubbed her knee.

A wave of desire shot through me and my knees suddenly felt weak. An overwhelming need to climb up her leg until I came made me see stars. Holy shit, what was going on? I'd never…What was wrong with me? I seemed to be saying that a lot tonight. As much as I wanted to continue, I knew if I wasn't careful, I might come, and that I would never do. This was business, strictly business.

"Come on, Riley, pop that last button," someone called over my shoulder. The command was repeated several more times and, as much I wanted Riley's hands on me, I stepped away. I couldn't risk it.

The music moved into another song and I was sure no one realized the transition except me. My routine was timed almost to perfection and I knew how naked I needed to be at any specific point in my set. I wasn't quite halfway finished.

I slid my shirt off my shoulders as Ann stuffed a bill into the waistband of my pants. The other women on the couch did the same as I held the front of my shirt closed teasingly. With each bill I exposed a little more. I'd done this long enough to know when enough teasing was enough, and when I sensed their mood was about to shift, I let my shirt fall to the floor.

Another five minutes and two songs later, I was down to nothing but my tight black undies. I made one last pass to each woman. The bills in my waistband were starting to itch.

I didn't ignore Riley, but I wasn't about to tempt fate and get too close to her again. Especially with only a thin layer of silk between us this time.

Finally, the music faded and the raucous women voiced their disappointment that the show was over. I went to each one and placed a light kiss on their cheek, saving Riley for last.

Her eyes dropped to my lips and I wondered what they would feel like against her skin. Her head lifted ever so slightly, a clear indication she wanted me to kiss her. I had a hard time breathing. I inhaled her scent as I leaned toward her. She smelled like sunshine and a warm summer day.

Her skin was soft and warm and I wanted to kiss her forever. Kissing the other women was chaste, but kissing Riley was the most intimate thing I had ever done. Riley leaned toward me and before my body overruled my brain, I moved my mouth to her ear.

"You're right, Riley," I said, just above a whisper. "You're not shy."

Her head snapped back and she looked into my eyes. I didn't know if she was going to slap me or drag my lips to hers. I certainly didn't want the former and would not be able to resist the latter. Instead, she blinked and the connection was lost. I couldn't be sure if I was grateful or disappointed, but the moment had passed and I stepped away.

## Chapter Seven

It was late and I was exhausted when I closed my apartment door. I'd had a grueling few weeks of classes and a higher number of dances than normal. But I didn't complain. I needed the cash.

I pulled my personal phone out of my pocket and realized I had forgot to turn it back on when I left my last gig. As it powered on, I grabbed a PowerBar and Diet Coke from the fridge. I kicked off my shoes just as the ding told me I had two missed calls and three messages. Two of the calls were from Lou, the third from a number I didn't recognize. The messages were from the local pharmacy telling me my prescription was ready, my gynecologist's office reminding me it was that time of the year, and a woman I met in class last year.

I had struggled through years of college classes and was within weeks of receiving my degree in finance. I had managed to squeeze in an internship at a local company during the days, my full-time schedule at Home Depot, and stripping two or three times a weekend. Needless to say, I was walking a tightrope between exhaustion and collapse. I'd had a final interview for a job I really wanted last week and was waiting and praying that an offer would come through. I fought back another wave of disappointment when I realized none of the messages were from the recruiter.

I flopped on the couch and my work phone launched into the air. For obvious reasons, I had two phone numbers. Jess was not my real name and I didn't want some crazy lady to have my personal number. I could always turn that one off and not miss anything important other than an opportunity to make some quick, non-taxable cash.

Picking the phone up from where it had landed on the coffee table, I saw that I had only one missed call and that caller hadn't left a message. I was grateful because I was booked for the next three weekends and I hated turning down a gig.

Most of my work was for birthdays. I'd had a few close calls with out-of-control women, but nothing I couldn't handle. My evenings at the Candy Store had taught me more than how to take off my clothes.

After finishing my dinner, I took a quick shower before opening my laptop to put the finishing touches on my last paper. I was so close I almost couldn't believe graduation day was in three weeks. Lou had convinced me to attend the ceremony, and my cap and gown were on a hanger in my closet. I had been issued eight tickets, and along with Lou and her husband, Howard, six other friends would cheer as I walked across the stage.

I was daydreaming when my dance phone rang.

"Hello, this is Jess." I waited several seconds before I repeated, "Hello?"

"Uh, yes. Sorry, hello," the voice said shakily.

"Is there something you needed?" I tried to encourage the caller to continue. Every call was money, and I needed it desperately.

"You, uh, danced at a party I was at a few weeks ago," the woman said.

"Okay."

"I'd like to book you for another, uh, event."

Event. I'd never heard my stripping described that way. "Tell me about it."

"What do you want to know?"

"How many people will be there? What's the occasion? Where?" I rattled off my standard questions, digging in my pocket for a pen. When the woman hesitated I added, "I don't dance with men in the room and I only dance." My voice was strong, my condition firm.

"No, no men," she said quickly.

"Okay." Good grief, was I going to have to drag everything out of this woman?

"Sorry, I'm a little nervous," she said.

I could understand that. "If you've seen me dance before, you know there is nothing to be nervous about." But then again, it wasn't every day that someone called for a stripper.

"It would just be one person and no special occasion."

"Who is the person?"

"Me."

It was an unusual request and it made me nervous. "I only dance," I repeated.

"That's all I want."

"Were did you see me?"

"At a birthday party for a friend of mine."

I couldn't help but laugh. Almost all of my gigs were birthday parties. "I do a lot of birthdays. Can you be a bit more specific? A name or maybe an address."

She rattled off an address I vaguely recognized, but the name Ann rang more than a bell.

A collage of faces flashed through my mind, one standing out above the rest. Maybe. No, no way in hell could it be Riley Stephen.

"Okay," I said masking my disappointment. "Where and when?"

We finally settled on Tuesday of the following week. When she gave me the name of a hotel, I immediately said, "I only dance. I don't turn tricks. I don't care how much you offer me. And I tell two people where I'm going and call them the minute I'm done." It was my security system.

"Sounds like a smart plan," she said and I thought I detected a slight smile in her voice. "And all I want is a dance, nothing more," she reiterated.

I didn't say anything for a few moments, my mind whirling with images of the women at Ann's party. I was a good judge of people and none of them pinged my creep radar. Riley, however, pinged something altogether different.

"Hello?" the woman said.

"I'm here. Okay. What's your name?" The silence on the other end of the line was so long I thought she'd hung up. How difficult was it to give me a name? Unless she was making one up. I heard an intake of breath.

"Riley."

The name took my breath away, and before I could say anything, she hung up.

## Chapter Eight

I picked up the room key from the front desk clerk, who gave me a long, suspicious look. I'd never seen her before and I'd gotten over what people thought of me a long time ago. I liked what I saw in the mirror every morning and that's all that mattered. People who judged others rarely could stand up to similar scrutiny.

The elevator whisked me to the seventh floor and I followed the signs to room 722. I pulled out my phone and pushed Lou's face on speed dial.

"I'm here."

Even though I had a key, I knocked on the door.

I would have recognized her anywhere. She was shorter than I was by quite a few inches, but when you were almost six feet tall, who wasn't? And there were other differences. She was wearing a pair of navy chinos and a green shirt that made her eyes look dark and smoky. She looked nervous, very nervous.

"Hello, Riley." I really liked saying her name.

"Come in," she said looking over my shoulder and out into the hall. Did she expect to see a familiar face? Paparazzi?

I checked in with Lou, giving her the specifics of the gig, and stepped farther into the room. It was nice, as far as hotel rooms go. At least it was a suite and not one large room with a very, very large bed in the middle.

I looked through the room, making sure there were no surprises. I'd never had any, but I didn't want to start now.

"Shall we take care of business before we get down to business?"

I'd never figured out how to ask for my payment, but this job was one where you got paid up front.

The envelope Riley handed me was thick and made of high-quality paper. No generic Office Depot, five hundred to a box envelopes for this woman. Classy.

Riley looked like she was about to pass out. "Why don't you sit down and make yourself comfortable." I pulled two small Bose speakers from my bag. I'd invested in the smallest, most powerful speakers I could afford and there was hardly a room that they couldn't fill with my music.

All set up, I turned my back to Riley and took a few deep breaths to gather my thoughts. I touched an icon on my phone. I closed my eyes and the music took over my body.

I'd chosen my clothes carefully for this evening, which was out of character. I had a standard set of uniforms for any occasion, but for some reason I'd been indecisive for this event.

You can't strip in just anything. It has to be easy to open and get out of. Nothing ruins a good strip like jumping around on one leg trying to get your other leg out of stubborn pants. I settled on a pair of black Levi's 501s. I can make opening the five buttons last close to five minutes with the right crowd.

Stripping is all about seduction, plain and simple. There were several keys to a successful, and profitable session, and I had worked my ass off to learn and to perfect them.

Layers of clothes are probably the most important element of stripping in that it gives you more to peel off. More to take off equals a longer dance, which equals more tips. Clients expect more than a fifteen-minute dance for their five hundred.

Lighting is an important component for setting the mood. This room, however, was hotel dim and much too sterile. I took several thin scarves from my bag and draped them over the lampshades.

A slow, steady beat filled the room. It had taken me months to find the right set of music. I listened to hundreds, if not a thousand tracks to find just the right mix as well as the right bridge between them. Transitioning between songs was tricky, and I was lucky I had a guy friend who was a master at it.

I stood in front of Riley, my back to her. The music began, a sultry beat and I stepped away in a slow, seductive strut. I'd always been told my ass was one of my best features and I had to agree.

Stripping is not easy. Taking your clothes off is, but dancing and looking sexy without falling over was something altogether different. The girls at the Candy Store had taught me that what you do with your hands is important. Move them smooth and lightly. Glide my fingertips up and down my body, stroking my neck and collarbone. Touch strategically; a light touch here or there is much more effective. Touch your body like you would want to be touched, they said. And they were right, it worked.

What you did with your clothes was equally important. Tug at the hem of your shirt, play with the collar, the buttons, raise your skirt a few inches to give a sense of what's coming. Use anticipation for maximum achievement. Arch your back, roll your hips, and spread your legs farther apart. Caress yourself and draw out the moment of reveal as long as you can. And never, ever rush a striptease. The slower you go, the easier it is for your audience to remember every minute.

It didn't take more than four or five minutes before it was clear that Riley was unlike anyone I'd danced for before. She didn't move to the edge of her seat in anticipation or reach out to stop me when I stepped away. There was no sign she was going to encourage me to take off my clothes or reward me when I did. With anyone else I might have felt uncomfortable and wary, but for some reason I didn't. On the contrary, it was as though I was dancing just for her, not stripping, and that made me uncomfortable. I pushed those thoughts to the side.

I ended my routine with placing a soft kiss on her cheek, just as I had before. Her skin was as soft as I remembered, and again, I was shaken with the intimacy. God, she smelled good, and I knew I'd remember her scent for a long, long time.

When I opened the bathroom door several minutes later, Riley was taking a long drink from a sweating bottle of water. Her head was back, exposing her long, smooth neck. My heart started hammering and I wanted to lick every inch of it.

She caught me staring and I felt my face flush with embarrassment. I tried to cover it by gathering up my gear but knew she'd seen me gawking at her. The tension in the air was thick, very different than any other time I'd danced. This had turned personal, very personal. I needed to get out of there now.

Riley held out another envelope before I reached the door. It was as thick as the first one but I didn't look inside.

"I hope we can do this again," Riley said, her voice shaky.

I thought about her invitation for a few moments, a thousand thoughts shooting through my brain. Do I dare? Will it be like this again? What will happen next time? Will I feel like this again? Suddenly, I wanted to know.

"I'd like that," I said and meant it.

# Chapter Nine

The third time I answered Riley's call, I was like a caged animal needing to escape. There had been hardly a night that went by that I didn't think about her. What was she doing? Was she married? Did she have a girlfriend? Did she scamper between the sheets on the hotel bed and masturbate the minute she closed the door behind me? Did she go home and do it there? Go to a bar and pick up a woman? Or was her libido bottled up so tight she was about to explode like a neutron bomb? Why did she do this? I'd stopped trying to figure out why people did the things they did. Some were so bizarre it made my head hurt to even think about them. But I wanted to know what made Riley tick, and I had a way to do that.

Early on in my dancing, one of the girls at the Candy Store told me about a movie made in the mid-nineties starring Demi Moore, appropriately titled *Striptease.* I'd watched it on Netflix at least a dozen times and had been fascinated by not only Demi's moves but her kick-ass attitude during her dances. I watched it again before heading to Riley's hotel.

I hadn't choreographed my dance, preferring to let the music take me where my body wanted to go. I was envisioning what that could be, and I almost passed the front door. That was another item on my mystery of Riley list. Why a hotel—and not a cheap one at that. The rooms had been suites, and not the Embassy Suites caliber. They would have cost a fortune if she paid by the minute it was used.

I looked at myself in the mirrored elevator doors as I rode to the seventeenth floor. I was wearing a suit with a bold patterned tie. However, no one, other than the front desk clerk, had given me a second glance. I opened my overcoat and felt my demeanor immediately change. I was sexy, sassy, and in command. I would take what I wanted.

To say that Riley was stunned by my dance would have been an understatement. Her breathing was ragged, her face flushed. She looked distressed for most of the dance. When I straddled her and ripped open my shirt, I thought she was going to take me right there. I would not have objected. But she didn't, and by the time the music stopped, I was completely spent, emotionally and physically. My hands were shaking and it took me longer than usual to get dressed. I barely made it home before relieving myself of the pent-up pounding in my clit. My dreams that night consisted of a very different ending to the evening.

## Chapter Ten

It was Monday, the second week of my new job, and I was already exhausted. I was emotionally spent, my dreams lasting most of the night. I kept seeing the look of pure, raw desire in Riley's eyes. I felt the need to get lost in something primal, something I'd never experienced before. I woke tired and emotionally drained. It was going to be a long day.

Today we were having a meeting with the big boss. Joan, my new-employee-work-buddy, was telling me what to expect as we squeezed into the crowded elevator.

"Riley is really awesome," she began explaining, but my mind had stopped thinking clearly when Joan said her name. It couldn't be, could it? Riley was an uncommon name, especially for a woman, but the world wasn't that small. Or was it? I wondered when my Riley would call again.

"She makes everyone feel comfortable and knows most of our names. I don't know how she does it."

We stopped at another floor and the people in the vestibule took one look at our sardine can and passed on getting in. Thank goodness.

"She is funny too, tells great stories. She loves to tell jokes and is really friendly. She should have been a stand-up comedian instead of a CFO."

Joan leaned in close and whispered in my ear. "And she's drop-dead gorgeous."

I glanced at Joan as if to say, you're cruising the boss? Wow, what a place.

I'd finally received the call from Allied Performance, and by the time all my paperwork was done, my pee analyzed and my background checked, it had been a week. I'd been on payroll for five days and loved it.

I didn't want to sit near the front, but Joan complained she forgot her glasses. "I want to be able to see her, not some blurry blob in the front of the room."

Joan had been a great buddy so far and I felt that there was a good chance that we could be friends. She introduced me to everybody on my floor and the ones above and below and everybody we met in the cafeteria. We were sitting with other people in my department and they were talking about the latest *Star Wars* movie when the hairs on the back of my neck started to tingle. I always trusted my gut. A voice coming from the back of the room made my pulse jump.

"Good morning, I apologize for running a few minutes late. I was waiting for one last piece of updated data for this meeting and it just came in."

My heart beat fast as the voice grew louder. I didn't hear exactly what she said after that, the roar in my ears drowning out any other sound. The woman who was the boss of my boss was none other than my Riley.

I stared at Riley as she held the attention of everyone in the room. She was absolutely stunning in a navy suit and pale blue blouse. Her heels made her legs look a hundred miles long. Her hair was pulled away from her face. I probably wouldn't recognize her if I saw her on the street.

Joan nudged me in the side with her elbow, snapping me out of my trance. "She's going to read your name and you need to stand up."

I could barely breathe and hoped my legs would work when she called my name. I was mesmerized by the way her lips moved, the way her voice sounded, the way she walked across the room for God's sake.

Joan nudged me again and I realized that Riley had called my name. She was looking around the room expectantly, but she had no idea who she was looking for. I took a deep breath and stood.

I knew the instant she saw me. She stopped midsentence and all the color drained from her face. The paper in her hand drifted to the floor. Just as quickly she recovered as if she hadn't just seen me, the woman she paid one thousand dollars a night to strip in front of her.

I raised my chin just a fraction, either in defiance or insolence, as if I were saying, I dare you to fire me. I wasn't ashamed of stripping. It was an honest job and I loved doing it. The cash was also great. My night job had no impact on my day job and was nobody's business. Until those business lines crossed.

"Welcome to Allied, Dana," Riley said, stumbling over my name.

Joan pulled at my arm as Riley continued down the list of names. "Do you know her?" she whispered.

"What? No, of course not," I said. In all the years I'd been stripping, despite the hundreds of women who'd seen me almost naked, I'd never run into one of them on the street or in Target. It would have to be Riley and it would have to be here. Just my luck.

"She sure acted like she'd seen a ghost," Joan said for colorful commentary.

"What?" I asked again, not expecting an answer. "She seemed fine to me," I said, wanting to deflect any suspicion away from Riley.

"She has lunch with all the new employees. It's on your calendar for Wednesday."

New employee lunch? I was going to have lunch with my Riley? That would be more than a little awkward and weird. Riley looked like she'd rather wrestle a porcupine than have lunch with me. Shit, this had suddenly gotten very complicated.

"Come on." Joan pulled me to my feet as the meeting broke up. "I have to introduce you. It's my job as your buddy."

I was more than a little nervous as I waited in line with my fellow newbies and their buddies. Finally, it was my turn. What in the fuck was I going to say? Hi, Riley, get home okay last night?

"Riley, this is Dana Mason." Joan nudged me forward. "She's our new financial analyst."

I held out my hand. "Ms. Stephenson." It felt odd knowing and using her full last name for the first time. "Thank you for making me feel welcome," I said. Seeing Riley again ignited my cooled libido. Who was I kidding? Dancing for her turned me on more than I wanted to admit.

My insides started twirling and that special spot between my legs came alive, demanding attention. We shook hands politely, like two coworkers would, but the energy that passed between us was anything but businesslike. As a matter of fact, it could probably power a small city. As far as first times went, this was more than a little memorable. God, I was totally rattled.

"Welcome again, Dana. We're glad to have you."

Riley's face was guarded, her eyes searching mine. I was scared to death that I'd lose this job, but tried not to show it. I'd worked my ass off going to school. This was my big break. What in the fuck was going to happen now?

# Part III: Riley and Dana

## Chapter Eleven

The rest of the afternoon crawled by, and it didn't help that Riley canceled several meetings. She was wound up and couldn't focus, and the last thing she needed was to get caught daydreaming.

She was always completely focused when she was at the office. Hell, she was always completely in tune with everything she did, including what she did for fun. The exception to that had been at her weekly basketball game last night. She'd been totally off her game and only sank the ball in the net twice instead of her usual ten or twelve times. She dribbled the ball off her foot and had it stolen from her twice. She was so worthless, she almost benched herself. She'd been thinking about seeing Dana later.

Suddenly too jittery to sit still, she needed to get out of her office. A wave of panic rolled through her and it felt like a million ants crawling over her skin.

"I'm going out," Riley said to Tina, her assistant, on her way past.

"Everything okay? You look a little pale."

"I'm fine," Riley lied. "Just going to get some fresh air." She barreled past Tina and her no-nonsense efficiency.

Riley didn't bother with the elevator. She wouldn't have been able to stand there and wait for it. She certainly wouldn't be able to stand still in the small box. She hit the exit door to the stairs.

After the first two flights, she caught her rhythm. After the next eight, her calves started to tingle. By the time she hit the ground floor, six floors later, her legs were shaking. Cautiously, Riley opened the exit door and stepped into the cool lobby of her building. A few steps later, she was on the sidewalk and turning the corner.

The midday crowds were thick and Riley slowed her pace. She was still jittery but not nearly as much as a few minutes earlier. She'd read that panic, or anxiety attacks, released a surge of adrenaline into your body. Fight or flight. Obviously, she'd chosen the latter.

The traffic light in front of her was red and she veered to her left and dashed across the street, dodging a lady pushing a dog stroller. She didn't stop to look at the high-pitched barking coming from inside as she passed. She passed two Starbucks, one Quick Copy, and any number of small restaurants and hotel entrances before she slowed down. Riley knew she must've looked a sight in her heels and skirt walking as fast as she was. She probably ran a few blocks as well.

Out of breath and out of energy, Riley collapsed on a metal bench conveniently placed under a large maple tree. Her mouth was dry and her throat ached from her harsh breathing. Her heart slowed to its normal beat and she looked at her watch. She'd been gone eighteen minutes. It seemed like only a few.

Riley looked around. She didn't recognize anything. She was on a neighborhood street with cars lining each side. She could see the street sign, but the name was unfamiliar. As her mind started to clear, she began to think. She ran a ten-minute mile, so with the traffic pedestrians and encumbrance of her shoes, she was probably less than a mile from her office.

A tall, thin man walked toward her, the Great Dane at the end of a bright orange leash walking calmly at his side. The guy looked to be a nice enough guy but Riley didn't want to ask where she was. How embarrassing would that be? They exchanged polite smiles. The head of his dog was level with hers as he passed. She could feel his hot breath. He needed a dental bone, or three.

Riley tried not to panic again when she realized she didn't have her phone or her wallet. Damn skirt with no pockets. Lyft and a taxi were out of the question. She could knock on one of the brightly painted doors. She could just see that: "Excuse me, ma'am. May I use your phone? I ran out of my office in a panic because the woman who strips for me now works for me." That sounded like a reality TV show or a Lifetime movie. The way her luck was going, she'd probably find herself being questioned by the police.

Riley retraced her steps back to the end of the block. She looked left, then right, but nothing looked familiar. She flashed back to her Girl

Scout days and looked toward the sky, then the ground in front of her. Her shadow was to her left, and since her meeting ended at ten thirty, she had to be facing north. Taking a leap of faith that her office was to the south of this neighborhood, she turned left.

Her feet were killing her, but walking and carrying her shoes was probably more suspicious than walking down a neighborhood street in a Calvin Klein suit. Two kids on skateboards almost ran her off the sidewalk. She was about to cuss at them, then thought better of it. Didn't need that kind of trouble either. Finally, after fifteen minutes she heard the sound of traffic horns, her beacon to keep moving in this direction. On the next corner was a deli that she remembered walking to one day last spring. Twenty minutes and one very large blister later, she finally saw the top of her building.

Riley stopped in the ladies' room in the lobby to assess the damage her walkabout had caused. Her hair was a wreck and her face was flushed. Some cool water and a finger comb and she was good as she was going to get. She hobbled to the elevator and pushed the up button.

## Chapter Twelve

"You need to get laid."

"I beg your pardon?" Riley said later that night as Ann handed her a wonton.

"You heard me. Unless your hearing's been affected by your lack of sex."

"I don't think one has anything to do with the other," Riley said, exasperated.

"Sex has everything to do with everything," Ann shot back. "Good sex sharpens your focus, relaxes you, and puts a glow on your face. Great sex," Ann paused for effect, "great sex makes the day brighter, the air cleaner, and people not as annoying. And you, my friend," she used her glass of chardonnay as a pointer, "you are dull and lifeless."

"Gee, thanks. With a friend like you it's no wonder I haven't put a bullet in my head already." Riley didn't need this shit from her BFF. She knew how long it had been. She didn't need reminding and she was irritated that Ann had brought it up.

Ann signaled the waiter to refill her glass. "You know I love you and I only want the best for you. I want to see you smile and look at someone with that look that says, I can't wait to get you somewhere private. When was the last time you had a simple, fast and furious fuck?"

Beer spewed out of Riley's mouth. She started coughing, not knowing how she'd managed to inhale some of the liquid at the same time.

"Whoa there, girl," Ann said, patting Riley on the back like a toddler. "You okay?"

Riley nodded as she wiped the beer off her chin and the tears from her eyes. "Jesus, you trying to kill me or something?" She coughed a few more times and blew her nose on the bar napkin.

"Of course not, just asking. A good fuck goes a long way—"

Riley interrupted, not sure how much more of this topic her body could bear. "I appreciate your concern but it's really none of your business."

"That long, huh?"

Riley coughed again, throwing Ann a dagger look, signaling it was the end of that discussion. Unfortunately, Ann missed the message.

"Seriously. When was the last time you got laid?" Ann frowned in concentration, her brows crinkling like a shar-pei. The look was not flattering.

"What is your point?" Riley asked instead. She knew she didn't want to know the answer to the question, but the sooner Ann said her piece, the sooner she'd shut the fuck up.

"My point is that you need to get out more, and I don't mean on a Wednesday night with me or your basketball games. You play with a bunch of guys. You'll never get laid that way. You need to meet someone, go on a few dates, feel that tingle of desire in your gut."

"I appreciate your concern, but I'm doing just fine."

"But fine isn't a way to live."

Riley held up her hand before Ann could say anything equally obvious. "It is for me," she said, careful to keep her voice bland, yet firm. It was the truth. She did like her uncomplicated life. It suited her, and she certainly couldn't have become as successful as she was if she'd had the conflicting priorities of a girlfriend. She had her short-term trysts now and then. They suited her and fit her personal and professional goals. As she climbed the corporate ladder she'd seen the plusses and minuses of a good spouse. One thing she'd never seen was a same-sex one. All her colleagues were married, not that they didn't have a little something on the side—or a kinky side, for that matter. But they'd kept it tightly locked in the closet, so to speak. Image and reputation, as well as competence, were critical in her world.

"You and I live in very different worlds. You're an artist, it's expected that you be flamboyant and a little wild and crazy. I'm a CFO, for God's sake. We're expected to be serious, thoughtful, and stable." God, even to her it sounded boring as hell.

"Okay, I get that nine to five, but what about five to nine?"

"My job is never nine to five, or even nine to nine." Ann had her own studio and worked whenever the spirit moved her. Riley couldn't remember the last time the spirit even came knocking on her door. Jess's face flashed in front of her and her spirit did more than knock.

"I've got to go." Riley gathered her phone and bag. "Since you insisted we talk about my sex life, you can pay." She kissed Ann on the cheek and waved goodbye as she walked away.

❖

Riley had almost canceled her monthly lunch with the new hires, but she refused to let the fact that Dana was going to be in attendance bother her. She was a seasoned, successful executive and she'd dealt with more difficult situations before. This was business, after all, and she didn't think Dana was interested in being outed any more than she was. Six people were standing around the table when she walked in at little before noon.

"Good morning." She glanced at her watch. "Or at least it is for another few minutes."

She went around the table, greeting each employee by name. She'd spent most of last night reading the bios of the four men and two women in the room. Knowing she wouldn't be able to concentrate afterward, she saved Dana's for last. She could recite it by memory.

Dana Mason, age twenty-four, graduated last month from City University with a 3.25 grade point average. She had several letters of recommendation from her professors, each stating that Dana was a hard worker, inquisitive, and sharp. Her background check was clean with only a few parking tickets, all of which had been promptly paid. Riley wondered if she got any of them where she'd been dancing. Her credit score was 783 and her bank accounts had no red flags. Some thought Allied's background checks were intrusive, but any employee who had access to financial data and systems necessitated a closer look.

She hesitated a few seconds, preparing herself before she acknowledged Dana.

"Dana, good to see you again. Is Joan taking good care of you?"

"Yes, she is, thanks."

Dana was wearing pressed chinos and a short-sleeved blue patterned button-down shirt. Riley had to stop herself from imagining her slowly opening each one.

"Good. I liked the way you spoke up in the budget meeting yesterday," Riley said, much to Dana's surprise. "We need more of that."

"Thank you." Dana was obviously unaware Riley had even been at the meeting.

After they picked up their lunches catered from the local deli, Riley spent an hour with the group answering questions and asking more than a few of her own. She found out that Dana was an only child, loved to mountain bike, and played the piano. Riley couldn't stop herself from looking at Dana's fingers after that discovery. Riley choked on her pickle when Dana said that dancing was her primary form of exercise. She dared not look at Dana as she pulled herself together.

Dana had a heart-stopping smile and a laugh that took her breath away. She talked with her hands when she was excited about something and sat quietly when others spoke. She had good eye contact and wasn't shy in front of those who were senior to her.

Riley was surprised when Dana turned the questions around to her. No one had ever asked her anything personal during these lunches, probably thinking it was none of their business.

"Well, unlike Dana, I have eight brothers and one sister." A choir of "wows" and a variety of other shocked expressions floated through the room. "I know. My mom wanted a girl so bad she kept trying until she got one, then decided that I needed a sister. Unfortunately, it took three more boys before I got one." Riley recalled the boisterous dinners as a child and the equally organized chaos of their last Christmas.

"My passion is basketball and I play twice a week and every Saturday." Her blood started to heat up as Dana's eyes moved over her body. It seemed like forever and the blink of an eye before Tina came in and started gathering everything up. It was her signal for Riley to wrap it up.

Riley thanked everyone for coming, and her excitement grew as she went around the table shaking everyone's hand again. When she got to Dana she put on her best noncommittal CFO face and extended her hand in farewell.

"We're glad to have you with us, Dana."

Dana's eyes were dark and knowing, yet nonthreatening at the same time. She looked from her outstretched hand, to Riley's eyes, and back again before taking it in her own. The same surge of electricity and connection was as strong as the first time they'd touched. Riley knew she should release her, but couldn't. It wasn't until Tina cleared her throat that she finally did.

# Chapter Thirteen

Riley paced back and forth in front of the door before finally making a decision. She slid the card into the slot, and the familiar click of the lock disengaging was unnervingly loud in the quiet hall.

For the last six days, she'd debated canceling this appointment. It was the right thing to do, and she tried to do the right thing more times than she could count. Of course, the phone rang both ways, but Jess's number never popped up on her caller ID. Riley thought it interesting that when she thought of Jess it was her body, dancing, the way she made her feel. When she thought of Dana, it was her sharp mind, her quick wit, and her grasp of their complicated business financials.

"What in the fuck am I doing here?" Riley asked as she stepped into the empty room.

"Why am I risking everything I've worked for? Why can't I stop? Nothing inappropriate happens. Unless you call an employee stripping for you inappropriate. Jesus, this sounds like daytime TV material."

Riley made the decision to leave, but just as she touched the doorknob, there was a knock. She always left a key for Jess, but she never used it, she always knocked. Would she use it this time if Riley didn't answer?

Riley wondered if Jess was having the same what-the-fuck moment about coming here. Did she care about the complete inappropriateness of this? She certainly didn't have as much to lose as Riley. Before Jess could knock again, Riley opened the door.

"You seem surprised to see me," Dana said when she saw Riley's expression.

Riley couldn't answer without sounding like a hypocrite. She'd called for Jess, the stripper, but it was Dana standing in front of her now. "I could say the same to you."

"I always keep my commitments." Dana lifted her chin a little.

Riley opened the door wider and Dana stepped inside. "But this is different." Riley suddenly felt ridiculous. Then what was she doing here?

"One has nothing to do with the other."

"Are you that naïve?" Riley asked, maybe a bit too harsh.

"No, not at all. I'm a realist."

"It certainly doesn't get more real than this," Riley mumbled. She turned and walked toward the window.

"Business is business and this isn't."

Riley spun around. "How can you say that?"

"I'm not anywhere near your pay grade so I wouldn't know for sure, but aren't you allowed to have a personal life?"

"Of course I am."

"Then what's the problem?"

Riley could think of dozens, but they all sounded tired and clichéd.

"This isn't on company time, and unless you paid for this room with your corporate credit card, this has nothing to do with your job," Dana said calmly.

"Except the potential for an above the fold headline." She used her fingers to make air quotes, "CFO caught in hotel room with employee stripper." She caught a glimpse of pain in Dana's eyes before she blinked, then it was gone.

"There is nothing illegal going on here."

"Splitting hairs, don't you think?"

"No, not at all." Dana's look was steady. "If you think there is something wrong, then why are you here?"

Dana's question knocked the breath out of her. She'd been asking herself that same question for days and still didn't have an answer.

"You think too much," Dana said quietly.

"You don't know anything about me."

I know more about you than you do, Dana thought but didn't say. She knew Riley would be here. She'd seen the look in her eyes, the tension in her body every time she danced for her. It told a very clear story that Riley might not be aware of, but one that Dana had read many times.

Chapter one was the first time Riley saw her, dancing at Ann's party. After that, every time she danced for her was the turning of a page, each one in anticipation of the next. Every time Riley's number came up on her phone, Dana knew it was the next chapter. How many more until the last page was turned? When Riley sat down in the chair at the far side of the room, Dana knew there was at least one more.

## Chapter Fourteen

That is going to be bad," Riley said to her reflection in the bathroom mirror. She'd just returned from a pickup basketball game and was even more unsettled and wound up than before she hit the court. She'd played with a couple of the guys before and they vouched for her with the other seven.

The game was strenuous and they didn't cut her any slack just because she had boobs. She'd had to concentrate and get her head in the game or risk getting knocked on her ass by the other players. For thirty minutes, she ran up and down the court with only a ten-minute break halfway through. She did her own share of pushing and shoving, her body simply taking over. A bruise just below her left eye from an errant elbow as she and one of the guys were scrambling to get a loose ball was starting to color. The blow had landed her on her ass and colorful dots had obscured her vision for a few seconds. She'd kept that fact to herself.

She'd grabbed a spot in the next game and staggered home ninety minutes later. The games hadn't cleared her mind like she hoped, and she'd expected the sheer physical exhaustion would help her sleep, but it didn't look like that was going to happen either.

Her phone was in her hand, Dana's contact info on the screen. "What in the fuck am I doing?" she asked herself again, as if this time her good angel would answer the question, giving her sage advice as to why she shouldn't make the call. Hearing nothing but the beating of her heart and the roar of her pulse in her ears, she touched the screen.

❖

"Oh my God, are you all right?" Dana quickly stepped inside and closed the door behind her. She dropped her bag on the floor and touched the bruise on Riley's face.

Dana's touch was featherlight, as if she were afraid it would cause pain. On the contrary, Riley thought. It was soothing, yet inflamed her senses at the same time.

"I'm fine," Riley said. "Nothing dramatic, just a little close contact on the basketball court." Dana's eyes were piercing, searching for the truth or a well-practiced lie.

"Does it hurt?"

Not when you touch it, Riley wanted to say. She hadn't wanted to step out of the game two nights ago to put ice on it, so her eye was swollen and the kaleidoscope of purples and reds caused more than a few heads to turn. And it did hurt like hell.

"I've had worse."

"I didn't realize basketball was such a contact sport," Dana said, her hand still on Riley's cheek.

"Only when you're not paying attention."

"Why were you not paying attention?" Dana's voice was soft, her eyes piercing again as if challenging Riley to tell the truth.

"I was trying to," was all Riley could say. She was, once again, caught in Dana's mesmerizing eyes.

"You don't seem to be the type who's easily distracted."

"I'm usually not."

"Why now? Looks like a painful result." Dana stroked the back of her fingers over the painful bruise.

"It's nothing." Riley wasn't sure if she meant the black eye or if she was trying to convince herself that her reaction to Dana's assault on her senses was nothing.

"Tell me," Dana said simply.

Riley sensed the sincerity in Dana's words, her gaze pulling her deeper and deeper into an unknown abyss. Warning bells should have been clanging in her head, but there was only the low-voltage throb low in her belly that was intensifying by the second. Her voice sounded nothing like normal.

"I can't seem to concentrate on anything these days." Dana didn't reply, the tilt of her head encouraging Riley to continue. "My mind wanders…to other things. Things it shouldn't," she added tentatively.

"Why shouldn't it?"

"Because it's not smart."

"In what way?"

Riley never voiced her concerns to anyone, not even Ann. She was a private person, preferring to deal with her own issues herself. And certainly not someone who was almost a stranger and her employee. But somehow, for some reason she didn't want to think too hard about, she trusted Dana. Her touch was too tempting and Riley stepped away, turning her back to her. "I could be hurt by it."

"Physically?"

Dana had moved behind her and Riley felt the heat of her body and the breeze of her breath as she spoke.

"Professionally." Riley tried to remember why that had been the only thing that mattered. Her thoughts were jumbled, her legs suddenly unsteady.

"How so?"

"I have a reputation to uphold. People depend on me. Thousands of people, shareholders, the board of directors." God, she sounded like a jerk—or an egomaniac.

"When did all this start?"

Riley closed her eyes, grateful Dana couldn't see her concentrate to memorize the timbre in her voice, the sound of her name, the woody scent of her.

"A few months ago."

"What happened a few months ago?"

Dana moved even closer, the tips of her breasts just touching Riley's back as she breathed. Riley's hands started to tremble. She started to slide down a very slippery slope.

"I met someone."

"Someone, as in someone?" Dana's meaning was clear.

"Yes." Riley's voice was a whisper.

"And?"

"And she's unlike anyone I've ever known before."

"How so?"

Riley struggled to find the words to describe Dana. She'd seen more of Jess than she had of Dana, way more. Jess was constantly on her mind, invading her work space, intruding in her dreams. Riley had seen Dana once or twice since their lunch, passing in the hall or in the cafeteria. They'd nodded politely like colleagues do, but didn't speak. It was Jess. It was all about Jess. She didn't even know Dana. She was pathetic. She'd fallen for a stripper.

"How so?" Dana asked again, interrupting her thoughts.

"She's younger."

"Is she over twenty-one?"

"Yes."

"Then it's not a problem."

"She has an," Riley hesitated, searching for the right word, "unusual job."

"Is it illegal?"

"No."

"Immoral?"

"Some would think so."

"Do you?"

"No."

"And all of this is a bad thing?"

Riley's body zeroed in on the word bad. Oh yes, Dana was very bad for her. "Yes."

"Because of this professional thing?"

"Yes."

"What about personally?"

Dana had moved closer, their front to back connection complete. Riley felt Dana's erect nipples through her thin shirt. "I'm not sure."

"Do you find her interesting?"

"Yes."

"Attractive?"

Riley felt her body relax into Dana's. "Yes." Her answer was barely more than a whisper.

"Do you want to get to know her better?"

"Yes." It frightened and exhilarated Riley that that was the only word she seemed capable of saying. What would Dana ask next that she could only reply yes to?

"Do your feelings for her scare you?"

"Yes." That was her answer, but this close to Dana, Riley felt safe saying it.

"Is she aware of how you feel?"

"I didn't think so." Dana moved even closer, erasing all doubt.

"And now?"

"Yes."

"What's changed?"

Riley hesitated, preparing to step out on a very thin limb. "Me."

"How so?"

"I'm here." Might as well step out with both feet.

"Do you want to kiss me?"

Riley's breath hitched when she heard the change in pronouns. "Yes." The word was almost breathless with desire.

"Put your hands on me?"

"Yes." Riley spiraled closer and closer to the edge of her control.

"Do you want me to touch you?" Dana asked, her mouth next to Riley's ear, her breath sending chills down her spine.

"Yes," Riley managed to choke out, her breathing rapid.

"In warm, wet places?"

Riley felt her body mold into Dana's. She could only nod.

"Do you want me to dance for you?"

Riley was only capable of shaking her head.

"No?" Dana asked.

"No, I only want you to dance for me. Only me."

"For your eyes only?"

Dana nipped her ear, sending rockets of shivers down her spine. "Yes."

"Are you frightened of me?"

"No." She was more afraid of herself.

"Fearful of what I may do to you?"

"No." Somehow, she knew Dana wouldn't intentionally do anything to hurt her.

"Afraid of how I'll make you feel?"

"Yes."

"Am I worth the risk?" Dana asked.

Riley started to speak but Dana stopped her.

"Don't lie to yourself."

"Yes."

"Then what's stopping you?"

# Chapter Fifteen

Riley spun around and kissed Dana like she'd never kissed anyone before. She didn't have to try too hard because Dana was all over her as well. Dana's hands were in her hair, pulling her impossibly closer, molding her body so tightly to hers Riley couldn't breathe.

The kiss pulled all the air from her lungs and the strength from her legs. She wrapped her arms around Dana's neck to stay upright, but what she really wanted to do was drag her to the bed and never get up.

Dana's hands moved insistently up and down Riley's back before cupping her ass and pulling her closer. Riley felt Dana's nipples through her thin T-shirt and she desperately wanted to touch them, pinch them, suck them, drive Dana as crazy as she was driving her.

Riley dragged her mouth away, gasping for air. Her head was spinning, her desire for Dana almost overwhelming her senses. Dana's lips were on her neck, kissing and biting with equal intensity. Riley let her head drop back, giving Dana permission as well as access to anything she desired.

Their initial coupling was frantic, their climaxes crashing. Impatient hands hurried to touch. The quick graze of fingers across skin heated with desire before it might somehow slip away. Frenzied was replaced with patience and tenderness, yet it was no less feverish. It drove Riley crazy with need. Slow and methodical, Dana worshiped her. Her body begged for more, screamed for release, but Dana ignored it. She looked at every inch of Riley, then touched the same places before her mouth finally followed the same path. Riley was seared with sensation. Every nerve was overwhelmed, the anticipation of Dana's touch, every cell in Riley's body reacting to her caress.

Riley knew she should reciprocate, wanted to, but was helpless to do anything other than feel. Dana's hands and lips and breasts cast a spell over her, and she was powerless to break it.

Somewhere after her fourth or fifth orgasm, she stopped counting. She'd always been a one and done girl, but obviously Dana hadn't received that interoffice memo. With what little strength she had left, Riley pushed Dana away. "I can't."

Unlike the other times she said it, Dana listened, but when Riley turned her back to her, Dana gathered her into her arms. Dana's body was warm against her back.

Breathless, they lay, legs entwined. Every breath sent tingles through Riley's sensitive skin.

Neither one of them spoke for a long while, the silence unbearable. Riley untangled herself and sat on the edge of the bed. Her clothes were scattered around the room, her bra and panties near the foot of the bed. She needed to get dressed and get out of here. Back to her well-organized, well-thought-out life. She started to stand up, but Dana took her hand.

"Riley."

Dana's voice was warm and inviting.

"Look at me, Riley. Please look at me, Riley," Dana said again when she ignored her.

Riley wanted to do more than just look at her. She wanted to get lost in Dana's eyes, her touch, the sensations that made her forget about everything that didn't matter. Everything except Dana.

Riley turned and faced Dana. She expected to see smug satisfaction, but didn't. She expected to see triumph, but didn't. She expected indifference, but that too wasn't there. What she did see was tenderness, kindness, and understanding. But through it all Riley saw her future.

"What do we do now?" Riley asked, afraid of what the answer might be.

Dana's eyes burned with desire with each passing heartbeat.

"We do it again."

# Opportunity of a Lifetime

*M. Ullrich*

# Chapter One

Today was the day. Luca Garner stood in a large conference room on the first floor of LGR Financial and waited to hear the biggest assignment of her career. LGR was bringing on their next five forensic accountants, and Luca Garner was excited to be one of them. Even if it meant starting out as someone's assistant.

"Good afternoon, everybody," said Marvin Howell, the temporary head of the internship program, from the front of the room. Not one person was sitting, even though the long conference table was surrounded by empty, cushy chairs. It spoke volumes of the nerves passing through each of the five new hires. "As you know, LGR brings on the top five interns from the previous cycle and gives them the opportunity to prove themselves as an integral part of our successful firm." Luca looked at the eager faces beside her and then back to Mr. Howell. The difference in enthusiasm was drastic. He let out a huff before speaking again, never looking up from the notepad in his hand. "Just like everyone else at this firm, you'll start from the bottom as someone's assistant and have the opportunity to work your way up from there. Any questions so far?" Mr. Howell bristled noticeably when someone raised their hand. "Yes?"

Luca noticed Charles, the biggest brownnoser in the group, was about to ask a question. Not surprising. "How does the selection process work?"

"Your internship was basically a six-month-long aptitude test. Anyone else?"

"How were we graded?" Charles added. Mr. Howell dropped his head, and Luca was willing to bet he hated how the responsibility of the introductory process fell on his shoulders this year. The administrator in charge of the interns was forced into maternity leave early, which left everyone ill-prepared and expected to fill in the blanks.

"The president and his top five accountants reviewed all the data from the cases the interns had input, then sent out a firm-wide survey. Moving on," Mr. Howell said, looking down at his notes. "The pairings will go as such: Andrew Jarvitz will be assisting Emmanuel Cortes, Candice Gibson will be with Howard Montgomery, Krystof W-Wy—"

"Just Kris is fine, sir."

"Thank God." Mr. Howell paused while the room filled with laughter. "You're with Karen Levy, and Charles Franklin…" He took a deep breath and adjusted his thick-rimmed glasses on his bulbous nose. "Charles Franklin and Marvin Howell."

"It's an honor, Mr. Howell," Charles said. Luca rolled her eyes.

Luca waited a beat for her name to be announced, but nothing more was said. Mr. Howell closed his notepad and appeared ready to start the rest of his day. "Okay everyone, you know where the reception area is. Head there and you'll find out where to go next."

"Mr. Howell?" Luca spoke up timidly. Of course she'd be the one to end up in this awkward spot. She felt like a kid again. The one who managed to lose their class schedule on the second day of school and not have any idea what class she should head to for first period. "Mr. Howell?" she said more loudly.

"Yes?"

"Where do I go?"

"To reception, like I just said." His patience was waning and Luca couldn't blame him.

"You didn't give me a name, the name of who I'd be working with—working for, sir." Luca tilted her head down and clamped her eyes shut, unsure of whether the words she just vomited made any sense. She heard the rustling of his notepad again.

"Who are you?"

"Luca Garner."

"Right." He tossed his notepad onto the table, reached into his pocket, and pulled out a folded note. "I got your assignment five minutes before you all arrived." Mr. Howell read slowly, his left eyebrow shooting up. "You will be assisting Stephanie Austin." A round of gasps filled the room.

Stephanie Austin was revered as the top accountant, the number one consultant in the firm, which was why she occupied the vice president suite on the top floor. But for every successful fact that floated around about her, there were less than pleasant rumors as well. She was rarely seen, usually locked away in her office or working on location with a client. Very little was known of Stephanie Austin, except her exceptional success and frigid demeanor.

"Get to work." Mr. Howell's voice broke Luca's trance.

She waited for everyone to file from the office before she asked, "How did that happen?"

"Like I just explained to my newest ulcer, data was collected—"

"No, I mean…" What did she mean? Luca wasn't sure of a tactful way to ask what she was wondering. Compliments usually worked. "From what I've heard, Stephanie Austin doesn't need an assistant."

Mr. Howell gazed out one of the large windows overlooking a small lake at the center of their corporate campus in Princeton, New Jersey. His face was lit up with a strange smile. When he looked back to Luca, she wondered why he looked so amused. "I have no doubt Ms. Austin feels the exact same way."

Luca felt his ominous tone in her gut. She swallowed her need for more information and nodded politely. "Thank you for your patience this morning, Mr. Howell. Best of luck with Charles." Luca rushed from the room and tried her best to catch up with their small group before they reached the reception desk.

"Hey," Andrew said, popping off the wall where he was waiting for Luca. "Are you okay?"

Luca gave Andrew's shoulder a gentle nudge, her way of silently thanking him for caring. They had clicked the moment they started their internship together, which was unusual amongst the cutthroat group. She knew Andrew harbored a crush for her at first, but after several mentions of the ex-girlfriend she left behind in Portland, they fell into an easy friendship. Luca was grateful to have his support.

"I'm fine. Why wouldn't I be?" Luca said, tucking a strand of her chestnut hair behind her ear. The tendril fell back out and into her face. She blew it away in frustration. Why she tried to give her pin-straight hair a curl that morning was beyond her.

"Stephanie Austin? No one works with her, Luca. Did you know most of the office calls her Stone Cold Steph Austin?"

"Like the wrestler?" Luca asked. Andrew nodded and her hands started to tremble. "I'm professional and very good at this job. No matter who I'm assisting, they're lucky to have me." Luca nodded resolutely. She'd been confident all morning, and no one was going to shake that.

Luca's confidence carried her from reception to the elevators, where she gave herself another pep talk. The calendar of motivational phrases she'd received from her mother for Christmas was paying off all in one day. Once in the empty elevator she said, "I've got this. Everyone loves me. I was the preferred teacher's pet throughout school, and even someone as eager as Charles can't change that about me." Luca straightened her posture and gave the reflection of herself on the elevator door a firm nod before the doors opened. She stepped out of the elevator and followed directions to stand just outside Stephanie Austin's office. You're hard working and a people pleaser, the perfect combination to be an outstanding assistant, she thought. Luca took a deep breath and raised her hand to the hard wood of the impressive office door. "Here we go," she said before knocking.

Her knock went unanswered.

"Are you looking for someone?" a frazzled older woman said to Luca, who stood awkwardly close to the door.

"Yes, I'm here for Ms. Austin. Is she in?" The woman's eyes widened, giving Luca the distinct feeling people rarely came looking for Stephanie Austin.

"All the executives are in a meeting right now." They stared at one another for a moment before she dragged a chair from an unoccupied desk over to Luca. "She may be a while." Her smile was polite as she left Luca alone.

Luca pushed the chair against the wall, but didn't sit. She was too nervous after seeing the shocked look in the other woman's eyes at the mention of Stephanie Austin, and knowing what so many already thought of her new boss. She swallowed back her desire to scream and run, because Luca Garner had never turned away from a challenge, and Stone Cold Steph Austin wouldn't be the first.

## Chapter Two

Stephanie Austin's latest case pile had just increased by two, and she was fine with that. She sat impatiently as the biweekly executive meeting wrapped up, still unsure as to why they couldn't address her first so she could be on her way. Stephanie had already started scribbling various notes for her new cases, all while shutting out the president of LGR's monotone voice. Gerard Witlin was satisfactory as a boss, but Stephanie really wished someone else would head their meetings. She yawned widely.

"Are we keeping you up, Stephanie?" Gerard said, smiling in her direction.

"Not at all, but you are keeping me from my work." Stephanie's lips remained in a straight line and she tapped her pen against her notepad. The five other executives around the table looked from Gerard to Stephanie and back again.

He nodded. "Very well. I'll conclude with a quick update on our staff. We have five interns taking on the role of assistants today, and while most have already been assigned to senior accountants, there's one left for someone in this room."

While everyone else around the large table perked up, Stephanie dropped her attention back to her notes. She never understood the excitement that accompanied having an assistant, nor could she grasp why the thought of having someone new replace your current assistant was so titillating. Stephanie believed in doing your own work and making sure it's done right.

"It's important to remember that the purpose of our intern to assistant program is to help groom these individuals and train them to be as successful as we are. We believe in the five interns we chose, and it's up to us to make sure they become prime LGR accountants." Stephanie circled a key word on her notepad and checked to make sure she had updated contact information for her newest client. She looked up when Gerard cleared his throat. "Stephanie, I expect you to teach Luca Garner everything you know and build her up to be as successful as you have been with LGR."

"Who's Luca Gardener?" Stephanie said, placing her pen parallel to the edge of her notebook.

"Luca Garner," he emphasized her last name, "is your new assistant."

Stephanie laughed. "No, she's not. I don't need or want an assistant."

"You have one now," Gerard said sternly, a tone he rarely took with Stephanie.

She sat forward with her elbows on the tabletop and dug them in hard. "Are you saying I need an assistant?"

Gerard's kind smile was back, though slightly hidden behind his bushy beard. He adjusted the perfect Windsor knot in his tie, a nervous habit that was often a prelude to an argument. "You know I'm not."

"Very good, then." Stephanie sat back.

"I'm telling you that you now have one. Meeting's over, everyone. Let's get to it." He knocked on the conference table and the room was cleared out, but Stephanie didn't move an inch. "There'll be no discussion," he said directly to her.

"There should've been a discussion before this decision was made for me. I work alone. I know this, you know this, everyone here knows this. I don't need some eager puppy following me around while I work my ass off to keep our clients happy. I can get my own coffee and answer my own phone calls."

"I don't think you were listening. We set these people up with experienced forensic accountants so they can learn and grow within one of the best firms on this side of the country. She's not your beck-and-call girl."

"Yes, I'm well aware considering I do sit through these meetings every year." Stephanie stood from the table, making a show of closing up her portfolio and twisting the tip of her Cross pen back into its stainless steel shaft. "Place her with someone else," she said curtly, feeling as if she were stuck in a custody battle. Except she didn't want custody of anyone.

"I'm afraid you don't have a choice in the matter, no matter how much you fight me on this. You were requested."

"By whom?"

"Someone from Marcati and Stevens. I don't have to tell you how important the cooperation between us is to our firm."

Stephanie knew very well how important good relationships between financial firms were, but she was too stubborn to admit as such. "Important enough to force one of your own into a position they're not happy about?" Stephanie waited, but Gerard didn't answer. "Who called in the favor? I want a name."

Gerard turned to the large windows lining the wall of the boardroom. The sun was shining and the sky was clear, but Stephanie knew he wasn't admiring the early spring weather. When he spoke again, his voice was low and even. "Catherine Carter."

*Dammit*, Stephanie thought. One of the most successful women in their financial world. She knew she couldn't push this too much without someone declaring a cat fight. She took a deep breath. "Gerard," she started slowly, "I would really appreciate it if you'd try to place her with someone else. Another senior accountant who can offer her just as much as I can."

"Catherine Carter asked for you, for the best, and you know as well as I do there's no one here who compares. Think about what this can do for your career." Stephanie's attention was piqued. "For you to create a protégé? Another woman who could follow in your footsteps and take the world of forensic accounting by storm. This could be the opportunity of a lifetime for you."

Stephanie was momentarily humbled, but she had to stand strong. She checked her watch. "I have a phone conference in ten minutes. We'll continue this later." She held Gerard's eye contact until she was out of the boardroom. Frustrated and distracted by her to-do list, Stephanie muttered promises of bodily harm as she walked to her office. She froze before she could manage the last twenty feet.

A beautiful, if not slightly plain, brunette stood just outside Stephanie's office door. Her brown suit and tan shirt fit a little boxy, her heels qualified as clearance section pumps, and her dark eyes sparkled in spite of her furrowed brow. She appeared to be pacing and possibly talking to herself. Stephanie knew this woman was Luca Garner, without a doubt. She was bright-eyed and very chatty, apparently. “Great,” Stephanie said to herself. She tried her best to avoid Luca as she walked to her door, which would’ve only worked if she were invisible.

“Good morning, Ms. Austin,” Luca said. Stephanie stopped with her hand on the doorknob. “My name is—”

“I know who you are.” Stephanie turned to meet Luca’s eager stare.

Luca looked slightly shaken, but persisted. “Great. I’ve heard a lot about you as well, and would like you to know that working for you, and with you, is an opportunity of a lifetime for me.”

Stephanie stared at her before asking, “Why is that phrase everywhere today? Did someone pay you to say that?”

“Excuse me?”

Stephanie shook her head. “Listen, Luca, don’t get comfortable. I don’t need an assistant and hopefully by tomorrow they’ll find you someone who does. For now, you can take that desk,” Stephanie said, pointing toward a vacant desk beside her office door. “Do whatever you want for the rest of the day.” Stephanie opened her office door.

“But, Ms. Austin?” Luca asked. Stephanie grimaced. Her phone conference was starting in a few minutes and she needed to go over her notes. But her mother had taught her to at least have manners. She looked at Luca expectantly. “I deserve to work with the best, and you’re the best.” Luca was firm, her sweet voice turning forceful, which caught Stephanie off guard.

Stephanie stepped into her office slowly, buying herself a few seconds to shake her surprise. She turned to Luca. “Then I suggest you spend the rest of this free day preparing yourself to work with the second best.” Stephanie shut and locked her office door.

# Chapter Three

Stephanie went into the office nearly an hour early on Tuesday. The appearance of Luca had caused her to become uncharacteristically distracted. She completed her phone conference flawlessly and then fell into an agitated rut. All afternoon, she could hear Luca moving about. At one point, Luca had even introduced herself as Stephanie's assistant. For all the money LGR had put into the design of their offices, Stephanie wished they had spared a few bucks on soundproofing her office.

Since she had failed to work proficiently the day before, Stephanie had no choice but to make up for the time she had wasted. Stephanie started her morning with another follow-up email to Gerard. She had already sent multiple, demanding Luca be moved and attached a list of accountants she'd fit with perfectly. Stephanie even went as far as to look for the most eligible and attractive of the staff. Maybe playing to Luca's personal prospects was a bit beneath Stephanie, but she was doing this in the name of self-preservation. She hit send on her email to Gerard and then got down to business.

The early hour flew by for Stephanie as she lost herself between old financial reports and new, lists of a company's expenditures, and employee profiles. Stephanie Austin loved what she did. She was a math geek, and being a forensic accountant gave her the opportunity to feel like a detective. If something fishy was going down within a multi-million-dollar company or between two individuals on a personal level, Stephanie would be able to trap the culprit down to the penny and guarantee a favorable outcome in court. She dropped her pen and rolled her shoulders after finishing the last notes. She considered her most recent case closed. She would email a report to the lawyers and put together a box of physical evidence to hand-deliver later in the afternoon. But first, Stephanie was in dire need of another cup of coffee.

She stood and straightened her burgundy pencil skirt before shrugging on the matching blazer. She buttoned two out of three jacket buttons and straightened the collar of her navy blouse. Stephanie checked her appearance in the full-length antique mirror she had propped against the far wall of the office. The ornate frame allowed the piece to be disguised as decorative, but it was there for Stephanie's vanity and no other purpose. Stephanie had a motto: look good, feel good, and work harder than anyone else around you. She smoothed her hands over her slicked hair and along her long platinum ponytail.

With a deep breath, Stephanie left her office and nearly collided with Luca, who was holding two cups of steaming coffee. Not one drop escaped.

"Good morning, Ms. Austin," Luca said cheerily. Stephanie gritted her teeth. "This is for you." Luca held out a mug, the mug Stephanie always used and hid in the back of the break room cabinet for safekeeping. Stephanie eyed it suspiciously. "Two and a half sugars, a teaspoon of hazelnut creamer, and a splash of one percent milk." Luca's smile was bright, perfect, and proud. "I asked around," she said with a wink.

Stephanie stared directly into Luca's brown eyes and corrected her misstep by saying, "I make my own coffee every morning." Hurt glimmered in the depths of Luca's gaze and her cheeks colored with embarrassment. In any other circumstance, Stephanie would've found such a visible reaction attractive. "I'm still waiting to hear back from Mr. Witlin about your placement, so please, leave me alone until then."

Luca placed the two cups of coffee on the desk Stephanie had assigned her and clasped her hands at her front. "Yes, ma'am."

Stephanie hadn't expected Luca to surrender so easily. She could nearly feel the argument on the tip of her tongue fizzle away. "Very good," Stephanie said. They stood awkwardly for a moment, Luca's eyes never meeting Stephanie's again. "It'd be a shame for a cup of coffee to go to waste." She reached around Luca for her coffee, catching a hint of her perfume. She smelled freshly showered and feminine. Stephanie's grip tightened around her warm mug. "I'll, um, I'll let you know when I hear from Gerard—Mr. Witlin." Stephanie retreated to her office quickly and shut the door.

Luca stood in a stupor. Her eyes went from Stephanie's closed door to her own desk. She had brought a few small plants to brighten up the surface and a monogrammed blotter her brother, Chris, had sent once news had spread. Luca moving into her new office space had been overlooked by Stephanie, someone known for her attention to detail. She thought about the email she'd received from Mr. Witlin the previous afternoon. He had welcomed her to the company once again and assured her that working alongside Ms. Austin would offer her opportunities above and beyond her expectations.

"I think it's safe to say he didn't cc her on the email," Luca said to herself, snorting. She sat behind her desk, flipping open her memo portfolio and booting up her computer. She wasn't entirely sure where to start her day. She didn't have a copy of Stephanie's cases or schedule, so her last resort was the company database, which held minimal information for every accountant.

Luca read line after line in search of Stephanie Austin's name anywhere. She made a list of other accountants within the firm who'd be able to feed her a little information. Luca felt better investigating Stephanie during her second day, as opposed to daydreaming about her like she had on her first. Her pen stilled. She wasn't daydreaming about Stephanie Austin, she was considering her for a long period of time. Which she was certain anyone in her position would also do.

Stephanie's appearance matched her tongue in sharpness. Not one of her corners was dull, and every word she spoke was pointed. And while Luca was intimidated by Stephanie, she was also envious of her. She hoped to be half the professional Stephanie was, and have a small fraction of the clientele. Stephanie Austin was a powerhouse, one Luca was determined to win over.

Luca's thought process was shattered when she heard Stephanie's phone ring through the door of her office. This wasn't the first or tenth time it had rung that morning, and Luca felt the proverbial lightbulb go off above her head. Stephanie shouldn't be answering her own phone, not while an able-bodied assistant was sitting with very little to do. Luca fished her phone from her purse and typed out a quick message to Andrew. He had dated someone in the IT department, and Luca was hoping they were still on good enough terms for a favor.

Twenty minutes and the promise of a bottle of Grey Goose later, Luca's phone was ringing off the hook. Message after message came in for Stephanie, and Luca was making a note of every company, firm, and individual, as a reminder to herself to research them later. Whether Stephanie liked it or not, Luca was well on her way to figuring out how she could help her.

Luca's progress halted when she heard a door slam shut.

Stephanie stormed down the hall, the heels of her stilettos clicked loudly against the hard floor. Luca looked around the office space from her desk, and not one set of eyes was looking up. Everyone was involved in their own business or was pretending to be, at least. The office on the far end dropped its blinds. Muted voices could be heard in the distance. If Luca had to guess, she'd say they were coming from Mr. Witlin's office. She cringed.

The click-clack of heels was approaching again, but much more quickly this time. Luca swallowed hard and contemplated hiding beneath her desk. Her plan would've worked, too, if she had acted quickly enough. Stephanie's fierce eyes trained on Luca the moment she rounded the corner.

Luca froze. Stephanie's face was red, her normally full lips pinched together in a tight frown, and wordless death threats could be seen in the depths of her icy blue eyes. "You," Stephanie said, her hard gaze trained on Luca. Luca jumped to her feet. "You will have the phones switched back before you leave today or you may as well not come back. Do you understand?" Luca nodded. "And don't you ever overstep like that again or I will make sure no one in New Jersey or the tristate area will hire you." Luca blinked, but she was so nervous even her eyelids stuttered. Luca stood a fraction taller than Stephanie, but Stephanie's deadly glare made her feel two feet tall. "It would be my pleasure to make sure you're seen as unemployable, so don't push me." Stephanie turned and retreated back into her office.

Luca fell back into her chair with a long exhale. So much for wanting to assist her new boss.

## Chapter Four

"Garner," Stephanie yelled from her office door and watched in satisfaction as Luca nearly leapt from her skin. She leaned against the doorway and waited for her assistant to approach. Stephanie stood less than ten feet from Luca's desk, but she still felt it imperative to her authority for Luca to rise and come see her.

Luca smoothed her palms along the obviously synthetic material of her ill-fitted brown skirt. "Good morning, Ms. Austin," she said, still cheery despite their first week together being anything but pleasant. Stephanie thought maybe she could make today the Friday that breaks the camel's back, so to speak. "What can I do for you?"

"I'm so glad you asked," Stephanie said, her voice toeing the line between sarcastic and professional. "All of my finished case files from last quarter need to be archived—"

"Consider it done."

"I'm not finished." Stephanie paused and shot a hard stare at Luca, letting Luca know that being cut off was greater than a simple pet peeve to her. "I'm sure you're familiar with our archives and how archaic the system is." Stephanie waited a beat and was pleased when Luca only nodded. "Alphabetical order is good, but not good enough. I'd like you to overhaul the system. You will need to sort through the files and separate them by senior accountant on the case, then put them in chronological and alphabetical order." Luca's eyes grew so wide, Stephanie wanted to laugh. "That makes a lot more sense, doesn't it?" Luca opened her mouth, but Stephanie didn't care much for her reply, so she dismissed her instead. "Have at it, Garner."

Luca slunk away just as Gerard Witlin rounded the corner toward

Stephanie's office. She smiled politely at him when he greeted her with typical morning pleasantries. But Stephanie suspected he wasn't there just to talk about weekend plans.

"What brings you to my neck of the woods?"

"I wanted to see how the situation with Ms. Garner was working out," he said, shoving his hands into his deep suit pockets.

"The situation? That's the word you decided to go with?" Stephanie led Gerard into her office. He took a seat in one of two cushy leather chairs that were in front of her wide, glass-top desk, and she sat on the edge of her lumbar-conscious chair. "The situation is still less than ideal, but judging by my many unanswered emails, you're sticking to your guns this time."

"And I'm happy to see you've decided to work with her. Any particular case or do you have her involved with your entire caseload?"

Stephanie considered the question, imagining Luca knee-deep in tattered business files. "Entire caseload."

"That's fantastic," Gerard said loudly, punctuating his excitement with a slap to his thigh. "I know Luca will be able to not only gain incredible experience with you but knowledge as well. I went back over some of the work she had done while interning here, and I have to say, she's very bright and detail oriented. You've hit the assistant jackpot with Luca Garner, and it means a lot to me to know you're finally taking it seriously." Stephanie sank back into her chair guiltily. She took a sip of water to wash away the feeling but sputtered when Gerard suggested she bring Luca to their next meeting.

She grabbed a handful of Kleenex to dry her tweed trousers. "With all due respect, that's no place for an assistant."

"My assistant is present at every one."

"Yes, but she's useful—" Stephanie closed her mouth. Gerard stared at her with an unwavering glare. "Rosie has been with the company for years. There's a level of trust and dependence established between the two of you that none of us would ever question." Stephanie's shoulders slumped. She didn't even believe that line of bullshit.

"You're not working with Luca, are you?" Stephanie didn't answer. Gerard scratched at his beard roughly and stood. "What exactly do you have her doing? And don't think about lying to me."

Stephanie hadn't technically lied in the first place, but that tidbit would remain for only her to know. "She's organizing our archives."

Gerard clenched his jaw. "We have file room clerks for that."

"Yes, but every time I told them there was a better system we could implement, they refused to make the changes. Luca was available, so I sent her down to take care of it."

Gerard pinched the bridge of his nose. "I'm disappointed in you." Stephanie flinched. She had never heard such words come from a superior. Her mother, maybe, but never a boss. "You're hurting your reputation here, and willingly toying with the success of this company, my company." Stephanie shook her head. "Don't say anything, don't defend your actions any further. I'm sure you think it's silly for me to react this way over one newbie, but some of the greatest, most successful people rose up from ground level, and it's our job to reach out a helping hand."

"Gerard—"

"Am I wrong? Or did you graduate from college and suddenly become a vice president of the greatest forensic accounting firm on the East Coast?"

Stephanie let out a long, steady breath through her nose. She felt herself getting emotional and nostalgic, both of which were unusual for her in the workplace. But she remembered the moment Gerard had confidently bolstered her own young potential like it was yesterday.

"You're right," she said quietly, a scolded child apologizing. "Of course you're right."

"I hope you take some time over the weekend to consider what you'd like to bring to my company's future, and maybe you'll have a new attitude come Monday morning." Gerard left Stephanie's office without saying another word.

Stephanie sat back and closed her eyes. She had no idea how she was going to work with Luca or how she'd manage to be the person Gerard believed she could be. The only thing Stephanie knew for sure was that she needed a drink or two.

❖

Friday nights at the Dollhouse promised many things: entertainment, drink specials, and wall-to-wall beautiful women. So driving an hour to Morristown barely caused Stephanie to bat an eye. She met her friends regularly for small social gatherings, but at least once a month they'd indulge in the best lesbian nightlife New Jersey had to offer. And after the week Stephanie had, she needed every kind of distraction she could find. A broad smile lit up her face when her friend Tina returned to their table with a round of tequila shots.

"You know what they say about tequila." Tina raised her eyebrow.

"People say a lot of things about tequila but never remember what it was," Stephanie countered before downing her shot and sucking on a wedge of lime. Her eyes were still squinty when Zoe reached across the table for her empty shot glass and called out for another round. "Be careful with this lightweight, Zoe. I have work to get done this weekend."

"When was the last time you didn't work a weekend?" asked Lee, Zoe's girlfriend of six months.

"That's not the point. The point is that I can't be getting drunk because I need a clear mind."

"Sigh." Stephanie looked at Tina, who had recently started to speak certain actions aloud. She'd been wanting to ask, but knowing Tina and her eccentric way of living, there probably wouldn't be a clear answer to give. "All you do is work with no regard for yourself. Your mental health is going to suffer."

"Funny you should say that," Stephanie said with no amusement. "I'm supposed to be spending the weekend evaluating myself."

Lee's jaw dropped. "Get the fuck out of here."

"That's great," Tina said at the same time. Tina's chipper perspective did little to inspire enthusiasm in Stephanie, but Lee's sentiment was something she could relate to.

"I'm dead serious. Gerard is second-guessing my character because I don't want an assistant."

Lee laughed. "You really don't play well with others."

"Are we talking about Stephanie?" Zoe delivered another round of shots to their table.

"See?" Lee said as she pointed to Zoe. "Everybody knows it."

"I thought I made it very clear, but Gerard is insisting I play mama bird to some fresh-faced and eager—" Stephanie froze. As she glanced across the crowded bar, a familiar set of dark eyes locked with hers. Stephanie looked away quickly and swallowed hard, trying to extinguish the uneasy feeling that shook through her abdomen. She wanted to call it annoyance, but a small voice at the back of her mind knew it was butterflies. Stephanie downed a shot to drown them.

"Maybe you should slow down." Tina sounded concerned.

Lee gripped Stephanie's shoulder and shook her gently. "What just happened? What about not getting drunk?" Stephanie reached for another shot, but Lee took it away. "Talk to us."

Stephanie cleared her burning throat and licked her lips before saying, "She's here."

"Who's here?" Zoe looked around.

"My new assistant, the puppy that I have to take care of now, the one who has Gerard scolding me and telling me I need to do some soul searching." Stephanie wanted to look at Luca again, but she was hoping Luca had overlooked her before.

"Why didn't you tell us she was gay?" Tina poked at Stephanie's stomach.

"Because I didn't know. I barely talk to her."

Zoe stepped around Lee to get a better look into the crowded bar. "Which one is she? I hope it's not the blonde, you could do better."

"Stop gawking," Stephanie said, pulling at Zoe's flowy blouse. "She's against the far wall. Black shirt, I think, and shoulder-length brown hair. Kind of plain." No one said a word. Music vibrated around them and Stephanie awaited some sort of response, but the only noise she heard came from Lee, and it was nothing more than a low hum. "What was that? What does that even mean?"

"It means that I see someone partially matching that description, so I'm not sure it's her."

"I didn't stare long enough—her shirt could be blue or purple."

"You were right about the wardrobe," Lee said. Stephanie watched her impatiently, waiting for more information, but Lee's attention was set across the room. Zoe and Tina were even fixated, but they looked a little more confused.

"That's not how I'd define plain." Tina chuckled.

Stephanie looked at her group of friends in confusion. She took a deep breath and chanced a look in Luca's direction. Luca Garner was definitely standing across the bar from her, but this was not the Luca Stephanie was used to. Gone were the ill-fitting clothes and listless hair. The Luca that was laughing unabashedly with a redhead beside her was wearing form-fitting jeans and a sleeveless shirt that showed off toned shoulders, and her hair was half up, which paired well with smoky makeup to highlight her deep eyes. Luca was smiling, and she wore that happiness better than any article of clothing. Stephanie took interest in the bowl of lime wedges on the table.

"She is prime fantasy material," Lee said in a low voice, earning Zoe's elbow to her side. "Ow, babe, think about it. Boss and subordinate?"

Zoe glared at Lee and then looked at Stephanie. "It would be hot."

Stephanie laughed loudly. "You've both clearly spent more time watching porn than ever working in an office." She threw back another shot. The alcohol was finally getting into her limbs and head. Luca being across the bar started to matter a little less, and spending time with her friends mattered a little more. She raised another glass into the air and proposed a toast. "To wonderful friends."

"You nearly drank all the shots," Lee said.

Zoe wrapped her arm around Lee and picked up the tray. "We'll get more." She pulled Lee away from the table. "You, too, Tina." Tina looked up and followed wordlessly.

Stephanie stood alone and confused, until she heard Luca's soft voice. "Hi, I thought it was you." Stephanie turned toward her. Luca smiled. She was standing with her hands tucked into her back pockets and Stephanie wondered how there was enough room in there. "You're almost unrecognizable out of work clothes."

Stephanie looked at her relaxed jeans and fitted T-shirt. Definitely a far cry from boardroom chic. "I could say the same for you," she said, the tequila convincing her eyes to roam Luca's body slowly before meeting her eyes. "This is better than the off-the-rack wardrobe you wear to work."

Luca's right eyebrow rose and the corner of her mouth twitched, hinting at a smile. "I don't put much into my work appearance."

"That's an understatement." Stephanie downed the last shot.

"Because I like to be judged on my work performance, not whether or not my ass adds anything to the office atmosphere." Stephanie was very interested in what Luca had just said but was incapable of fully concentrating on it. She shook her head. "What brings you here tonight?" Luca asked.

"Just a night out with some of my friends."

"You have friends?"

Stephanie leaned back from the table and shot her a look. "Yes, I have friends."

Luca covered her mouth for a moment before saying, "I'm sorry. I can't believe I said that. Of course you have friends, everyone should have friends, even—"

"Even who, Luca? Even me?" Stephanie felt her skin heat and chest tighten in that coiled, ready to unleash sort of way that always led to mean words and name calling. She watched as panic and embarrassment played across Luca's face.

"No. That's not what I meant. You're just so independent." Luca's features contorted in what appeared to be pain as she pieced together the excuse. Stephanie's tequila-infused spirit wanted to laugh, but she remained stoic. "I just imagined you working through the weekends and always focusing on being the absolute best at what you do. How else do you impress so many powerful people on such a regular basis? I'm just shocked that you have time for friends, that's all."

"Garner?"

"Yes?" Luca spoke more to her folded hands than to Stephanie herself. She hadn't met Stephanie's eyes since the beginning of her haphazard apology.

"I think you should head back to your friend now."

Luca perked up. "Oh, she's not my friend. I was set up on a blind date by a family friend. I don't think it's going to work out." Stephanie glared at Luca, jolting her into action. "But I'm going to head back. Enjoy your night, Ms. Austin."

Stephanie relaxed the moment Luca turned around. Zoe was beside her immediately, handing her another shot. "So that's the assistant?" Zoe said as they continued to watch Luca.

"She's shocked I have friends." Stephanie tried to use the same glare on Zoe when she laughed at her, but it had no effect on her old friend. "I'll get rid of her, mark my words." Stephanie threw back her final shot of the night, and it definitely tasted like regret.

# Chapter Five

Luca rearranged the folders on her desk for the tenth time that morning. She had been fifteen minutes later than usual, which was still early for the workday, but it meant she'd missed her opportunity to make Stephanie's coffee for her. After seeing Stephanie at the bar on Friday, smiling and laughing like a normal person, Luca couldn't get her out of her head. She couldn't stop wondering if this new common ground would open the door for an amicable work environment or whether she'd shot herself in the foot by approaching and speaking to Stephanie. But Luca couldn't help it. The moment their eyes locked, she'd felt drawn to Stephanie, and the closer she got, the more relaxed Stephanie looked, warmer than Luca ever expected her to be. Luca felt she was being handed the opportunity to improve their relationship.

Boy, was she wrong.

The sound of Stephanie's office door opening jarred Luca to attention and she stood. "Garner," Stephanie said with her eyes on her phone screen. "Why aren't you down in archives?"

"Mr. Witlin had the clerks take over, and I was told to return to my duties." Luca's explanation went unacknowledged as Stephanie typed out a message on her phone. "Ms. Austin, I want to apologize for the other night."

"I've already forgotten about it."

"I was just surprised to see you at the Dollhouse." Stephanie's thumbs stopped moving and she looked up. Luca had a feeling she was poking at a sensitive topic, so she treaded lightly. "If you're not out at work, I want you to know you can trust me. I won't say a word."

"I don't mix my personal life with my work life. It has nothing to do with being in or out of the closet; it's about being a respected professional. So, yes, I'd appreciate it if you kept our social run-in between us." Stephanie continued with her message. Luca started to sit but stopped halfway when Stephanie added, "I need you down in reception."

"Of course." Luca started to gather her phone and to-go coffee. "What do you need me to do?"

"Wait."

"Wait? Wait for what exactly?"

Stephanie sighed like this explanation was the most inconvenient part of her day. She made a show of locking her phone screen and pinned Luca with a hard stare. "I'm expecting a very important certified letter and would like you to be there when it's delivered so I don't have to wait for the receptionist to bring it. Do you need any more information before you do as I ask?" Stephanie said with a tilt of her head.

Luca knew the question was rhetorical, but she shook her head anyway. "I'll have my phone if you need anything else."

"A green monster salad from the vegetarian place on the corner. After you get the letter, of course. Bring them both to my office when you have them."

"Yes, Ms. Austin." Luca waited for Stephanie to retreat to her office before rolling the tension from her neck. She gathered her things and walked to the elevator. The short ride down offered Luca a moment to calm herself. She felt a little foolish for having any hope her situation would improve after an awkward run-in, or at all. She took a deep breath as the elevator doors slid open.

The reception desk was always a hive of activity. Clients lined up for directions, employees lined up for messages that hadn't come in yet, and the phone never stopped ringing. Luca often wondered why the firm invested in installing a tranquil water feature beside the reception desk. You could never hear it, let alone enjoy it.

"Good morning, Luca. What brings you down to the hubbub hub, hon?" Millie laughed at herself, much like she did every time she gave Luca the same greeting. Luca found it endearing and adorable.

Why couldn't she run into Millie at the Dollhouse? Luca rolled her eyes. Because she's as straight as they come, she chastised herself.

"Good morning, Millie. Has the mail arrived yet? Ms. Austin is waiting for a certified letter."

"No mail yet," Millie said, lifting her index finger to Luca to wait as she lifted her phone receiver to her ear. "LGR Financial, how may I direct your call?" Millie made a show of yawning at the phone, causing Luca to chuckle. "Of course, we're always taking on new clients. Let me transfer you to our client care department and we'll get you set up. Have a wonderful day."

Luca stood amazed. "How do you do that?"

"Do what?" Millie's big blue eyes never left Luca, but her hands manipulated the buttons to transfer the call, and she picked up her morning coffee to take a sip.

"You speak with such cheer, like you're wearing a smile when you're not."

"I've never really thought about it. I guess I'm just a people person."

Luca rested her elbow on the high reception counter and leaned in. She wanted to indulge in Millie's kindness for a little longer. Her cute, curly blond hair and vibrant smile didn't hurt either. "Have you always worked with people?"

Millie's attention left Luca when an older woman approached the counter. Without missing a beat, Millie greeted her. "Good morning, Mrs. Rosenberg, lovely to see you again. You can head straight up to the third floor. Everyone is waiting for you in boardroom C. And yes, I made them put on a pot of French vanilla coffee for you," Millie said sweetly.

"Still swooning over the unattainable?" Andrew's voice startled Luca from behind. She spun around and punched him in the shoulder. "Ow, dammit." Andrew held his arm. "Not cool, Luca, I could never get away with doing something like that to you."

"If I ever sneak up on you like that, you're welcome to hit me." Luca turned back to Millie and looked expectantly between her and the large glass front door. "Millie, what time does the mail usually come?"

"Usually by noon."

Luca looked at the modern clock hanging on the wall. It was nearly ten. "That's not too bad."

"But no later than three," Millie added. Luca's head dropped.

"Expecting an important package?" Andrew asked with a boyish smirk.

Luca stared at him long and hard before responding. "Men shouldn't be allowed to say the word 'package,' and Ms. Austin is expecting a letter. It's my job to be here when it's delivered." Luca watched Millie hand three different files, from three different stacks on her desk, to two different accountants. Millie was trusted with more important work than she was. "And I have to get her a green monster salad."

"Oh, those are good," Millie said, nodding to Luca.

Andrew grabbed Luca's arm and pulled her into the corner by the water feature. The bubbling sound was quite relaxing when she could hear it. "How's everything going? We haven't had a chance to talk much since we were divided up."

Luca stared as water moved down a stone surface and considered the question. How could she sum up the first week of working with Stephanie Austin? She looked into Andrew's concerned eyes. "She doesn't want me around, which has been made very clear, multiple times a day, since the moment I was assigned to her. But the positive is that I haven't been fired." Luca frowned and added, "Yet."

"She can't just fire you because she doesn't want you around."

"Are you sure? This is Stone Cold Steph Austin we're talking about."

Andrew laughed. "You know the laws just as well as I do. You're not going anywhere as long as you keep being the kick-ass rookie accountant I know you are. You've always been the most professional one in our flock, and if worst comes to worst, ask to be switched with Charles. Ms. Austin will be screaming to have you back."

Luca started to laugh along, feeling a little lighter than she had. She thought back to Friday. "I may have done something uncharacteristically unprofessional."

"Did you give her the finger?" Andrew asked hopefully.

"No, but I'm surprised she didn't give me the finger when she saw me this morning. I saw her out Friday night and I said hi."

"No way. Where?"

"The Dollhouse. She was out with a group of friends and they were laughing and she seemed approachable, almost warm even. So I thought it'd be a good time to smooth things over and let her see that I'm on her side and want to work with her."

"The Dollhouse? The gay bar you talk about?"

Luca's eyes closed at her slipup. She'd forgotten ever mentioning the place to Andrew, and now she had broken the small promise she had made to Stephanie. Her stomach dropped with guilt. "The ladies' bar and yes, but please keep that between us. I don't need her finding out I've been blabbing about her personal life. I already made the mistake of talking to her outside of work." Luca cringed at the memory. "I basically told her I was surprised she had friends."

Andrew's eyebrows shot sky high. "Luca, you didn't."

Luca let out a long exhale. "Oh, Andrew, I did."

"You were speaking for the rest of us, too." Andrew patted her back reassuringly. "Don't worry too much about it. Things can't really get worse for you, can they?"

"Please don't tempt fate or karma or any of that crap."

Andrew let out a soft laugh and looked at Luca warmly. "You look different today, but I can't put my finger on how."

Luca touched her hair self-consciously. As she readied herself that morning, she'd considered the way Stephanie appraised her at the bar. So she chose to put in more effort by shaping her hair with a blow dryer instead of letting it air dry into a limp mess. She even applied a hint of eye makeup. Luca was taking Stephanie's advice and putting a little more care into her work appearance for herself. Not to re-experience the thrill of Stephanie's attention falling on her once more.

"Luca?"

"Yeah?" Luca looked up at Andrew.

"Are you sure you're okay?" he asked with a skeptical tone and matching eyes.

She waved off his concern. "I'm fine, really, just another Monday."

"If you say so. I have to get back upstairs, but we should do lunch soon."

"Definitely." Andrew was gone before Luca finished the word. She took a seat in a small plush chair next to the reception area and sipped at her coffee. She was glad she had the foresight to bring it along with her. Luca was in for a long wait.

The mailman arrived closer to one thirty than Luca cared for, but it was better than two. She bid Millie an almost flirtatious farewell and rushed to the corner deli to pick up Stephanie's salad along with multiple beverage choices. Stephanie didn't ask for a drink, but Luca felt it was better to be safe than sorry. She stood outside Stephanie's office door with bags and certified letter in hand and knocked once, then twice. Luca couldn't hear a sound coming from inside Stephanie's office, so she decided to open the door slowly and take a peek inside.

Stephanie's computer screen was bright. No screen saver danced about, so Luca gathered she hadn't been gone for long. No purse or blazer hung beside the door, leading Luca to believe Stephanie had stepped out. Luca backed out of Stephanie's office and stared at the bags in her hands.

"Is there something you need from my office, Garner?" Stephanie said with an icy tone.

Luca near choked. "No, I have your lunch and I knocked, but you didn't answer."

"So you thought it'd be best for you to let yourself in?" Stephanie's eyebrows were perfectly shaped into a sharp arch, a point that became deadly when raised or furrowed.

"Again, no," Luca said slowly, giving herself a moment to choose her next words wisely. "I have the certified letter you've been waiting for. Considering its importance, I wanted to be one hundred percent sure you weren't here to receive it before I held on to it for another minute. I didn't go any farther than six inches into your office. It wouldn't be my place to do such a thing." Someone like Stephanie had to enjoy self-deprecating talk.

Stephanie held out her hand for the letter, which Luca handed over immediately. She used her index finger to slice the envelope open in one smooth motion. Luca flinched at the sound of paper ripping. Stephanie looked over the letter and said, "You're right. It's not your place and you should remember that, but you made the right call this time. This letter is the first piece of physical evidence that links my client's business partner to embezzlement."

"Why send it in the mail? Wouldn't hand delivery be safer?" Luca was bright with excitement because Stephanie was finally sharing professional information with her.

"Hand delivery is safer but could also appear suspicious. Do you know how many certified letters come and go daily? A lot. No one would suspect such a crucial bit of information to be sent through the post office."

"Who's it from?" Luca had to know; she needed to be involved, and now was her chance to ask questions.

"My client, Raymond Farnsworth, fired over thirty employees two years ago, citing major layoffs due to financial issues. Common in this day and age unfortunately, but his business partner never seemed concerned about their company's well-being. Raymond was clearly shaken, and after a year of constant stress, he hired us to figure out what was going wrong with his company."

"And you found out exactly why the stress was one-sided."

A sly smirk spread across Stephanie's face. The small smile reached her twinkling eyes and Luca held her breath as she held on to the moment. "He did hire the best. I started small and followed the trail up to the top. This," she held up the envelope, "is the final nail in the coffin."

"Wow." Luca looked at the raised envelope with awe.

"Now I'll be here until midnight preparing my report, but it'll be worth it."

Stephanie's excitement was contagious. Luca licked her lips before speaking. "I can stay, if you need me."

Stephanie looked at Luca. All her liveliness dropped away and she turned to stone once more. "That won't be necessary." She walked to her office. "I don't need you."

Just as Stephanie was about to shut the door, Luca called, "I have your salad and few options to drink."

"I already ate." Stephanie shut her office door, leaving Luca with a meal she couldn't stomach if she tried.

# Chapter Six

Our first quarter results blew last year out of the water. We've not only closed more cases, but we've done so effectively." Stephanie watched as Mr. Witlin regarded his top employees proudly. "When I started this company, it was no more than a few desks in an office space with one window, and a slew of people who had no idea what forensic accounting was. I owe my success, and gratitude, to each of you and your predecessors."

Stephanie looked around the table, and everyone shared the same confused look. Gerard Witlin was a gracious man, one who never hesitated to show appreciation for everything his employees did, but his current display was a little out of the norm. Stephanie's stomach sank with worry. Were they closing? Was Gerard retiring? "Is everything okay?" Stephanie dared to ask.

Mr. Witlin smiled brightly and said, "Everything is better than okay. I'm ending our meeting with an announcement. We're expanding. I've just signed a deal for an office in the heart of Chicago." Stephanie sat back in relief. "My time will be split between the two offices for now as we set up and hire worthy candidates. Some of you may be asked to travel, but it won't become a habit, unless you request it." Gerard looked directly at Stephanie and winked. Odd, but not altogether out of character. Stephanie wondered if he'd consider her to head the new office. Chicago wasn't the worst city to live in. "There'll be more information available about the new office in weeks to come, but until then, get out of here and get to work."

Stephanie hung around an extra minute, as customary, to share a moment alone with her boss. "This is exciting news." She gathered her pen and portfolio.

"It is. I'm very proud of what we've accomplished here and I believe we'll be just as successful with this expansion."

"Do you have anyone specific in mind for the new office?"

Gerard looked Stephanie in the eye when he responded. "Yes, I do. Once we're ready to move forward, I'll make the formal announcement."

Stephanie's face lit up. "Very good. I'll get to work, then."

She rushed from the boardroom with an extra bounce to her step. Stephanie hadn't felt this kind of anticipation and excitement in quite a while. No grand projects or big changes had found their way into her life recently, and she felt ready to tackle it all. That excitement fizzled away to confusion when she turned the corner to find her sister-in-law, Kathy, with her four-year-old son, Mitchell. Stephanie didn't like unexpected guests. She looked for Luca, a sharp reprimand ready on her tongue, but she was nowhere to be found.

"Your secretary went to get Mitchell a snack," Kathy said.

"She's my assistant and a junior accountant here," Stephanie said, clarifying that Luca's job was more than generic secretarial duties. Why the misunderstanding mattered to her at all was something Stephanie would have to evaluate at a better time. "What are you doing here?"

"I tried to call you seven times, but you never answered."

"I was in a meeting." Stephanie looked from her fidgeting nephew and back to Kathy, waiting for an explanation.

"Your assistant told us that and said we could wait here. Rick has appendicitis."

Stephanie's eyes went wide. "Oh my, is it bad? We both know how delicate he is." Her joke fell flat when Kathy's face remained stiff.

"He's being rushed into surgery. They have him scheduled for noon. That's why I've been calling you." Stephanie looked at her watch and was surprised to see it was nearly eleven thirty. "I need you to watch Mitchell."

"What?"

"Here you go," Luca announced loudly, gaining Mitchell's attention. "Do you like animal crackers?"

"I like el'fants." Mitchell's mumble made Luca smile, but his charm was lost on Stephanie. "They're my favorite."

Stephanie pulled Kathy just inside her office, leaving Mitchell and Luca to sort through a cardboard zoo of edible animals. "I can't take him, I'm working," Stephanie said in a hushed tone, as if Mitchell would know she was trying to pass him off.

"I don't have a sitter available, my parents are on a cruise, and I don't think your mother will make it up from Florida in under an hour." Kathy crossed her arms over her chest.

Stephanie took a deep breath. She and Kathy rarely saw eye-to-eye, but Kathy took good care of her brother and was a wonderful mother to Mitchell. Stephanie looked out her office door and caught Luca blowing air past a Post-it she had placed over her lips. Mitchell found the fluttering sound of the paper hilarious and was red-faced with laughter. She smiled. "I'll figure it out, but you better get out of here. Rick is probably in a panic that you're not back yet."

"Here's a bag full of toys and activities to keep him busy." Kathy pulled Stephanie in for a quick, awkward hug. "I'll call you when he's out." She ran from the office, leaving Stephanie with Luca and a child, and no idea of what to do with either.

She'd spent very little one-on-one time with Mitchell, not because she didn't love the little boy but because she didn't know how to act around a child. Mitchell was the first baby to come along in her family since she was born—that gave her very little confidence when it came time to interact with children. Stephanie didn't realize she was standing still, holding the bag of Mitchell's belongings and staring at him in a panic, until Luca spoke up.

"Ms. Austin? Is everything okay?" Luca was seated behind her desk with Mitchell on her lap. He pressed at the buttons of her phone, absolutely giddy over the sounds they made. Luca looked so concerned with her big, innocent brown eyes shining at Stephanie. "He can stay with me. It won't be a bother."

Stephanie ignored Luca. "Mitchell, come into Aunt Stephanie's office. I have your toys," she said, looking into the stuffed canvas bag. "And your coloring books." Mitchell stared at her wide-eyed, his chubby fingers still running along the phone, and made no move to leave Luca's lap. He had clearly made a new friend. "I can't have people thinking I run a babysitting business while I'm here."

Luca stood and placed Mitchell gingerly on his feet. She walked him into Stephanie's office and offered him a high-five. "Remember my name?"

Mitchell's face scrunched up. "Luca."

"That's right." Luca gave him another high-five. "If you need anything, or if your aunt needs anything, just call me. Okay?"

"Stay here," Mitchell said while playing with one of the buttons on his polo shirt.

Luca looked up at Stephanie. She was biting her lower lip and Stephanie wondered if Luca knew how to say no to a kid. "Luca has a lot of work to do today, so it'll just be the two of us for now." She could handle her nephew on her own. How dare anyone doubt that? He'd have a great time.

"Later, bud." Luca ruffled the dark curls on the top of his head. Stephanie considered their quick bond to be cute—children were usually great judges of character—but it was time for Luca to go. She didn't have to see just how awkward Stephanie was around the small being that shared her DNA.

"Thank you, Luca." Stephanie dismissed Luca and waited for her office door to shut fully before looking at Mitchell again. "What would you like to do? Color? A puzzle?"

"Will Luca come back?"

Stephanie sighed. So much for conversation. "Luca's busy. Would you like to color her a picture? I bet she'd love that." Mitchell nodded enthusiastically. Stephanie pulled over a small table she had tucked into the corner of her office and set up Mitchell with his coloring books, blank paper, and every crayon and marker in his bag. He climbed up onto her cushy armchair and Stephanie prayed he wouldn't fall. The last thing she needed was to be the cause of a daddy-son day at the hospital. "Got everything you need?"

"Yes." Mitchell didn't even look at his aunt before reaching for a red crayon.

"Great." Stephanie reached out, ready to mimic Luca's earlier playful touch, but she stopped herself. Would Mitchell be as receptive to her playing with him as he was Luca? She didn't want to experience that kind of rejection. She clasped her hands together and turned away awkwardly.

She settled behind her desk and opened the first of many unread text messages and emails she had. Many were panicked messages from Kathy, which Stephanie was quick to delete, and another was from Lee, asking how her assistant was doing. Movement from Mitchell's direction drew Stephanie's attention away. He was rolling his crayons off the table and laughing as each hit the floor. She didn't move, deciding that if Mitchell wanted crayons to color with, he'd pick them up himself.

Stephanie opened an email from the state police with an attachment. A document loaded and she read through pages of banking documents related to a fraud case she'd been handed the previous morning. She could've obtained the documents herself, but the New Jersey state detectives were eager to help her as much as possible. Their cooperation made Stephanie's job easier, which she appreciated and would miss once she was in Chicago. She glanced up to find Mitchell holding a sheet of paper to his face, trying his best to make the same noises Luca had made with the Post-it. Stephanie relaxed. Maybe she could handle babysitting after all.

Less than an hour later, Stephanie regretted her earlier confidence. Mitchell was fifteen minutes into a temper tantrum, completely dissatisfied with every activity she had to offer. He had tried to rearrange her binders to his liking, fallen from the chair not once, but twice, and even tried to add his very own piece of art to her gray walls. She tried her best to explain why red crayon was meant for paper, not walls, but the waterworks started the moment Stephanie said no, and hadn't stopped since.

"Please, will you just tell me what you want?" Stephanie asked desperately. She was staring her red-faced nephew in his watery eyes, trying hard not to gag at the trail of snot that had run into his mouth. "Are you hungry?" He cried louder. "Tired? Please tell me you're tired." Mitchell continued to cry, not answering one of Stephanie's questions. She grabbed her phone and searched how long an appendectomy should take.

"Ms. Austin?" Luca poked her head into Stephanie's office.

"Luca." Stephanie rushed to the door, grabbed Luca by her forearm, and tugged her into her office. She shut her door and locked it. "He's been crying since I told him he couldn't write on the walls and hasn't stopped. I don't know what to do."

Luca smiled reassuringly and nodded to Stephanie before walking over to where Mitchell had thrown himself onto the floor in hysterics. She folded her legs beneath her the best she could while wearing a skirt and lounged casually beside the combusting child. "Why so glum, chum?" Luca poked at Mitchell's back.

Stephanie scoffed at Luca soft words. "He can't hear you over his—" Mitchell stopped crying suddenly. Her ears were still ringing from the noise, but her office was finally silent. "Cries."

Luca looked up and shot Stephanie a wink. "You seem really upset. Is there anything I can do to make you feel better?" Luca mouthed for Stephanie to go and nodded toward her desk. "Do you want to help me draw a picture?" She rubbed soothing circles on Mitchell's back, visibly calming him. Stephanie felt a pang of jealousy for an instant, before it melted away into awe.

"Luca," she whispered daringly. "This isn't your job. You don't have to."

"I don't have anything else on my to-do list. The least I can do is make sure my boss gets her work done." Luca reached into Mitchell's bag for the half-eaten box of animal crackers and popped one into her mouth.

Stephanie ducked her head guiltily and nodded. She returned to her place behind her desk and resumed her work. Every now and then she'd spare a glance to Mitchell and Luca when they'd share in a moment of laughter. Stephanie wasn't in on the joke, and still she couldn't help but laugh along.

"Who's your favorite princess?"

Mitchell thought long and hard before answering. "Snow White."

"Why?"

"She's pretty," Mitchell said shyly.

Luca nodded. "I always liked Aurora, she has beautiful hair." Luca seemed to think hard for a moment before adding, "I guess I always preferred blondes."

Stephanie shifted in her seat and cleared her throat. She subconsciously fingered the end of her long, platinum ponytail. She stole a long look at Luca.

Luca looked right at home on the floor beside a small child, acting gleeful when she did something as simple as color a cartoon character blue all over. She didn't care when Mitchell dotted the tip of her nose with a black marker, but she punished him with a tickle attack until he begged her to stop. They even shook hands when they reached a peace agreement. Stephanie tried her best to put her attention on the total reports in front of her, but her eyes kept wandering back to Luca's smile and relaxed position on the floor of her office. Once Stephanie's eyes fell to Luca's creamy thighs, becoming more and more exposed by her climbing skirt, Stephanie forced them back to her computer screen. She even went as far as sinking lower into her chair to obscure her view. Noticing such a thing was inappropriate.

Stephanie's phone rang, offering her sweet relief from her warring attentions. Kathy's name lit up the screen and she answered quickly. "Hey, Kathy. How's the patient?"

"Out of surgery. Everything went perfectly. The doctor said his appendix was 'ripe for picking,' which put an awful visual in my mind." Stephanie laughed and cringed at the same time. "How's Mitchell doing? Is he behaving himself?"

"Things were a little touch and go for a bit, but we've got everything under control now."

"We? Did you pawn my son off onto your assistant? I won't blame you if you did. He seemed to really like her."

"I tried my best, but he prefers Luca." Stephanie checked on the duo again. Mitchell was nearly lying across Luca's lap as she showed him how to draw something.

"Don't be offended. That child almost always chooses the person he's not related to. He does it every time we have a get-together. He'll ignore Rick and me for hours."

"Good to know. This wound should heal faster, then." Stephanie laughed.

"I'll be by soon to wrangle him." Kathy's voice was slightly muffled by the sounds of hospital announcements ringing out. "Rick will probably come home after recovery. Once I get him home and settled, I'll come by."

"No rush," Stephanie said, surprising even herself.

"I'll call you when I'm on my way."

"I'll have him ready at the curb with a 'free to good home' sign." Kathy laughed out loud and Luca looked at Stephanie with wide eyes. She shot Luca a playful smirk, one that was quickly returned.

Stephanie ended their call and announced it was lunchtime. Mitchell must've been hungry because he jumped up and cheered.

They quickly agreed on takeout from a local burger place, Mitchell declaring a "chee-burger" was needed. Luca offered to get the food, but Stephanie waved her off immediately. She didn't want to risk another meltdown in Luca's absence. Their lunch was delivered pretty quickly and they ate in silence. Stephanie felt indulgent for the California-style cheeseburger she was devouring, but once they had started to talk about burgers, a salad just didn't hold any appeal.

Stephanie ate alone at her desk, while Luca ate alongside Mitchell at the table across the office. She felt like an outsider, and in a sudden swell of courage, she decided to change that. Stephanie partially wrapped her burger and picked up her drink, phone, and fries, carrying them carefully to the table. She pulled up another chair and sat. Luca looked at her curiously and Stephanie shrugged. "Even I'm entitled to a lunch break," she said with a soft smile. "What are you working on, Mitchell?"

"I'm coloring sweepin' beauty for Luca. She's her favorite."

"Sweepin' beauty?" Stephanie said and Luca nodded. "That's what I used to call my cleaning lady." Stephanie knew her joke was terrible, but it went over Mitchell's head and Luca chortled. The sound made Stephanie grin. "You're really good with kids," she said to Luca.

Luca took a bite of her burger and nodded enthusiastically as she chewed. She waited until she was finished to speak. "I love them. I have a niece, Mackenzie, who's a real fireball. She's going to be eight at the end of the summer. And Daniel is my six-year-old nephew. They're the reason I moved back to Jersey."

"Where were you?"

"I went to UCLA and then followed my ex-girlfriend up to Portland for about a year. She was an artist, kind of like Mitchell here." Luca split her attention between talking to Stephanie and Mitchell, which kept him in place.

"I hope she used a broader color palette." Stephanie tried for a second successful joke, which was uncharacteristic for her while she was at work. The joke barely earned a smile from Luca.

"She was actually a sculptor," Luca said wistfully. "I was the bookworm and she was the artist—classic case of opposites attract."

Stephanie felt uncomfortable with the personal subject matter, but she couldn't tamp down her rising curiosity. "Opposites make for a good balance, no?"

"I suppose it could, but not in our case. Here's the yellow." Luca handed a crayon to Mitchell. He grabbed it and got busy on the princess's hair. "I was missing my family, so when we split, I packed my things and practically ran back to Jersey."

"Do you miss that life?"

"No." Luca's dark eyes locked on Stephanie's. "I have family here, great friends, and a job I'm working really hard at succeeding in." Stephanie felt that dig in her chest. "I feel at home here."

Stephanie kept her questions to herself from then on, too scared of what else she'd learn about Luca, and subsequently about her own poor choices. They cleaned up lunch and watched as Mitchell dozed off in the big armchair. Before either woman noticed the time, Kathy was calling to let Stephanie know she was on her way. Stephanie left the task of waking Mitchell up to Luca, not wanting to face him if he grew grumpy. Naturally, Mitchell didn't mind being woken by Luca. Luca could do no wrong.

They stood outside together, the late afternoon breeze holding a chill unique to springtime. Stephanie held one of Mitchell's hands while Luca held the other. Kathy pulled to the curb, a genuine smile spreading across her face when she waved to her son.

"Thank you so much, both of you, for watching him. He would've been a handful in a hospital."

"That's what family's for." Stephanie let go of Mitchell's hand so he could go to his mother. She was surprised when he turned to hug her first. She gave in to the temptation, and ruffled his hair. "See you soon, Mitchell."

"What about Luca?" Kathy frowned down at her son when he ran over to hold her legs next. He burrowed his face into her. "Why are you suddenly shy? Give Luca a hug." He shook his head.

"It's okay." Luca waved it off.

Kathy bent to pick up Mitchell and rested him on her hip. He whispered in her ear and Kathy laughed. "He thinks you're pretty like Snow White," she whispered. Mitchell hid in her long hair.

Stephanie laughed outright and said, "You should see her when she's not dressed for work." She froze and thought, my God, did I really just say that? She cleared her throat harshly. "She's missing the singing birds."

Kathy hitched an eyebrow at Stephanie. "Thank you both again. I owe you." Stephanie didn't hear a word; she was too busy trying not to die of embarrassment. She chanced a look at Luca and noticed a faint blush coloring her cheeks. Dammit. "We'll talk soon, Steph. Nice to meet you, Luca."

They exchanged generic goodbyes as Kathy loaded Mitchell into her car and Stephanie watched as they drove off. When she turned back to Luca, she felt a renewed wave of discomfort rise in her chest. She said the first thing that came to mind.

"You've done enough. Go home." The dismissal was curt and Stephanie was ashamed of herself. She tried to fix it but only dug herself deeper. "Now I'll have to stay late to make up for the work I missed." She rushed past Luca and back into the building.

She wasn't lying that she had to catch up on her work, but more than anything, she needed space.

## Chapter Seven

Stephanie had left early Tuesday morning for her trip, and felt relieved to know she'd be away from Luca for three days. She'd be able to think clearly and breathe. Those plans didn't pan out as well as she had hoped. Stephanie phoned the office multiple times a day to retrieve messages from Luca, even when one phone call would've been sufficient. At first she convinced herself Luca needed to be monitored, but that excuse fell away. Luca had proven herself to be incredibly reliable. Stephanie eventually surrendered to the truth after her third phone call on Wednesday afternoon—she called to stay connected to Luca. She found very little rest after that realization. Even the pampering of her hotel's spa did little to wash away the unnerving truth.

Soon after, she had emailed Marvin Howell with a request for Luca's internship file and a few cases that Luca had been an integral part of. He was curious, of course, but he knew better than to question Stephanie. He sent them to her in record time, and she spent the evening going over every detail several times. Stephanie felt like a fool because Luca was brilliant and her attention to detail rivaled some of the top forensic accountants Stephanie had met. Luca had been responsible and dependable, and didn't hesitate to take charge of unexpected situations as they arose—a list of traits that made every one of Stephanie's arguments about not wanting to work with her irrelevant. Warring emotions tore Stephanie apart. Luca was not only an excellent employee deserving of Stephanie's attention but someone Stephanie feared could become a very important person in her life. She hadn't grown comfortable with either fact by the time she returned from her trip and had to return to work that Friday morning.

"I've been very unfair to you, Luca," Stephanie started confidently. "I disregarded your talent and professionalism because I was blinded by my own pride. I'm better off working on my own, but if I'm going to be forced to work with someone, I'm glad it's you." Stephanie stared at her reflection in the foggy mirror before dropping her head and breathing deeply. "I'm terrible at this." For the first time in her career, she was going tell someone she was wrong. Stephanie looked at herself again and squared her bare shoulders. Water droplets still clung to her freshly scrubbed skin. "Luca, I'm headstrong and bullish at times, but that doesn't mean I fail to recognize potential or when someone deserves to be treated better."

Foreboding filled Stephanie's belly as she dressed for her return to the office. No one likes to admit they're wrong, especially while they stare into doe eyes. But Stephanie's turmoil had nothing to do with Luca's eyes, or perfect smile, or her long legs. Stephanie swallowed hard as she buttoned her blouse. Professionalism, that's what Stephanie's troubles boiled down to. She grabbed her navy blazer and headed to her car. As she started the engine, Stephanie decided she wasn't starting to like Luca as a person. Not one bit.

The drive to the office was surprisingly traffic-free, which Stephanie viewed as a blessing and a curse. She made her way up to her office, replaying the short speech she had prepared in her head, and was only slightly disappointed to find Luca's desk empty. Stephanie figured she had made it to the office first. She went about her usual morning routine, but this time, she left her office door open.

She breezed through emails in her inbox from clients, saving her boring company emails for after lunch. Stephanie started to worry once half of her coffee was gone and Luca still hadn't shown up for work. Stephanie picked up her phone and dialed the receptionist.

"This is Stephanie Austin," she said curtly.

"What can I do for you, Ms. Austin?" Millie's voice was as chipper as always.

"Have you seen my assistant, Luca Garner, at all today?"

"No, ma'am."

Stephanie sat back and frowned. "It's not like her to be so late," she mumbled more to herself than to Millie.

"Not at all. Luca usually arrives twenty to thirty minutes early every day."

Stephanie was unsettled. "Thank you for your help, uh…"

"Millie, my name is Millie, Ms. Austin." Stephanie cringed at the change in Millie's tone. She was noticeably deflated. By Stephanie's approximation, Millie had been with the firm for nearly three years. She should know her name.

"Thank you, Millie." Stephanie hung up the phone and returned her attention to Luca's desk. The small personal effects Luca had brought into the office were still there—a note holder shaped like a cat, a large mug with *Fabulous!* scrawled across the front served as a pen holder, and a tall, single orchid. The purple and white of its petals caught Stephanie's eye every time she walked past Luca's desk. Clearly Luca hadn't quit. Stephanie scratched at her forehead, then ran her fingers through her hair. Luca could be sick. Stephanie slapped her desk in a eureka moment. All she had to do was check in with whomever Luca would call in sick to. Stephanie's eyes closed and she dropped her head.

Luca would call her superior, Stephanie Austin, the one person who made herself as unavailable as possible.

Stephanie opened her emails again, hoping that Luca had reached out. An unread message from LGRstaff.garner sat boldly in Stephanie's inbox. The time stamp for the email read 12:38 a.m. Luca had taken the time late at night to let Stephanie know she'd be absent. Panic and worry started to set in as Stephanie began to read.

*Ms. Austin,*

*I will be unable to make it into work today and will likely not be able to return until Wednesday of next week. I just received news that my grandmother has passed away. This wasn't a complete shock, as she has been unwell for quite some time, but my family is hurting nonetheless. I apologize for the sudden and short notice.*

*Regards,*

*Luca*

Stephanie sat back with her hand on her chest. Her heart was breaking for Luca, but the impersonal email didn't clue Stephanie into whether Luca would want to hear from her. Customary procedures in the workplace would be to send flowers to the funeral home and a sympathy card to the employee. Beyond that? Stephanie was clueless. She picked up her phone and dialed the first person who came to mind. Thankfully, Lee picked up after only one ring.

"This is weird. We've never spoken on the phone."

Stephanie laughed. "I know it is, and hello to you, too."

"Sorry, you caught me off guard. What's up?"

"I need some advice," Stephanie said before taking a sip of her room temperature coffee.

"Please, please, please tell me this has something to do with your hot assistant." Lee's excitement shined in the high volume of her voice. A spirited Lee was a loud Lee.

Stephanie tilted the phone away from her ear slightly. "It does, but it's not—"

"Yes." Stephanie could hear Lee clapping over the phone. "I knew it, just ask Zoe. I called it the moment I saw you two giving each other the look."

Stephanie scoffed. "What look?"

"You both had this 'I can't help that I find you attractive, but I'm going to hide it' look. It was great. I told Zoe you'll have your assistant in bed by the end of the month."

"I don't know what Zoe sees in you." Stephanie pinched the bridge of her nose. "Anyway, can you be serious for one minute?" Stephanie heard nothing but a faint buzz in the line and took that as a positive answer. "Luca's grandmother died."

Lee sighed heavily into the phone. "No shit. That's sad. Were they close?"

"I have no idea. This is the first I've heard of her grandmother."

"Still not opening up to her?"

"I am…a little." Stephanie thought briefly of their day spent with Mitchell and how she'd opened up to Luca, only to close back up after. "I'm trying." Lee laughed. "I really am. I came to work today with a whole speech prepared to tell Luca that I'm now completely dedicated to teaching and training her to be the best forensic accountant there is. After me, of course."

"Of course."

"And now she's not here. And I've never directly been someone's boss before. I have no clue how to handle the death of an employee's family member. I know standard procedure, but that's it. Should I do something more?"

"If you care about Luca, you should," Lee said. Stephanie was quiet, giving Lee an opportunity to pounce on her. "You totally care. Holy shit, mark this day on the calendar."

"Make sure you mark it as the day I started to care and the day I kicked your ass. Lee, please, help me. I didn't call you for insults."

Lee was silent for a moment. "Why did you call me?"

Stephanie almost snorted at the fair question. "Out of everyone I confide in, you're the most levelheaded, believe it or not. In spite of your teasing and inability to focus on the severity of a situation, I know your advice will be sound whenever you decide to grace me with it."

"Imagine for a moment that you're closer to Luca. Say, I don't know, you actually opened up to her from day one, how would that affect the situation today?"

Stephanie considered the question. If she had worked with Luca from the first day assigned to her, surely a personal connection would've been forged. Stephanie would've learned about Luca's ill grandmother in the fashion she had learned of her bubbly niece and nephew. "She would've told me herself, not through some company-addressed email."

"And what would you do?"

"Whatever she needed," Stephanie said, answering without thought. "But the reality is that Luca has no idea that I'm a decent human being."

"Don't be so hard on yourself, most people don't know that you're a decent human being."

"I hate you."

Lee laughed. "Email her back. Let her know she's in your thoughts."

"That seems too simple."

"You underestimate the little things."

"Thank you for your help, I guess." Stephanie glanced at her watch. "I've wasted enough time on this. I'll email her and talk to you later." Lee didn't respond right away, no witty remark or farewell. Stephanie wondered if the call had been dropped. "Lee?"

"There's more to life than work, and I'm worried you don't realize that." Lee let out a breath into the phone. "We will talk later, but for now, try to be more human. Goodbye, Steph."

"Bye." Stephanie disconnected the call and stared at her phone. The background picture was still the factory set image of a starry sky. Of course there was more to life than work, but what Lee failed to realize was that the risks Stephanie took for her clients were the only risks she felt comfortable taking.

Stephanie stared at the email on her screen for a while, planning out a proper response. Keeping the email simple seemed smartest, but she dared to make it more personal.

*Luca,*

*I'm very sorry to hear about your grandmother. Share my deepest condolences with your family, and don't hesitate to reach out if you're in need of anything over the next few days. Take as much time off as you need. I'd like the details of the planned services to share with the staff, as it's come to my attention that you're well liked.*

*With sympathy,*
*Stephanie Austin*

Stephanie looked at her name and the blinking cursor that danced beside it. She made a quick edit, signing it simply but with meaning: *Stephanie*.

## Chapter Eight

Luca fingered the lily's leaves gently. Her coworkers had sent such an elegant arrangement to the funeral home and the gesture touched Luca deeply. Truth be told, the flowers that lined the room offered her the perfect distraction, a short getaway from the constant stream of people. Even her own family was overwhelming her. Luca had spent most of Thursday night crying until she fell into a fitful sleep. Her heart had never known such mourning. Losing her granny was the first major loss she had experienced as an adult. Luca would have preferred to grieve alone, bask in her sadness solitarily, and show a strong face to those outside her own little world. But she couldn't, so she went around and read each card attached to the flower arrangements. The full vase from LGR was by far her favorite, and she knew her grandmother would appreciate the simple elegance of lilies as well.

Once Luca was out of flowers, she began pacing in front of the doorway to their private room of the funeral home. She hated being around dead bodies, especially when the one on display belonged to a woman who helped raise her. She was uncomfortable with the idea of a viewing before a funeral and just wanted the evening to be over. Almost every person that had approached with condolences was a stranger, save for a few close family friends. Luca was about to slip outside for some fresh air when she heard her name being called. She turned around to find her sister-in-law, Alice, waving her over. Her short ebony hair bounced with the motion.

Alice stood beside a gorgeous redheaded woman and someone Luca recognized immediately, even if her relaxed demeanor didn't match Luca's memories of her. "Catherine," Luca greeted Alice's best friend with a warm hug. "I haven't seen you in forever."

"Not since you were in college. I'm so sorry about your grandmother. Bethany was such a wonderful woman." Luca simply nodded, no longer able to come up with words of gratitude for people's sympathy. "How have you been otherwise?"

"Pretty good," Luca said, looking from Catherine to the woman fidgeting beside her. "I heard you've been doing pretty well for yourself."

Catherine shot the woman at her side a smile dripping with affection. "Luca, I'd like you to meet my fiancée, Imogene. Imogene, this is Chris's sister you've heard so much about but have yet to meet."

Imogene reached for Luca's hands. "I lost my grandfather a couple of years ago. I know everyone's words start to sound the same after a while, but I am truly sorry for your loss." She held Luca's hands gently and looked into her eyes as she spoke. Luca would've found it alarming, if Imogene's eyes weren't such a calming blue.

"Thank you."

"I've heard so much about you from Chris and Alice, I feel like we've already met. The Valentine's Day fundraising banquet is my favorite night of the year thanks to you." Luca looked at Catherine, who was blushing, then eyed Imogene curiously. Imogene giggled. "It's a long story."

Alice cleared her throat. "We should have dinner soon," she said directly to Catherine and Imogene, and then to Luca. "I hope the three of you can make it. Mackenzie has been asking for you, Cat." Catherine beamed with a million-watt smile. "And Daniel is missing his aunt."

"I'm missing Daniel, too. I was just talking about him last week. My boss's nephew—"

"Stephanie Austin?" Catherine asked abruptly.

"Yeah," Luca said with a small smile at the mention of Stephanie's name. She looked at Catherine and tilted her head. "How did you know?"

Catherine pointed to the entrance. "Stephanie Austin is here."

"What?" Luca spun around and the sight of Stephanie made her teeter on her feet. After gaining her physical and mental balance, Luca stared for a moment, taking in Stephanie's fidgeting form. Stephanie's usual confident air eluded her.

"That was nice of her to stop by." Alice broke Luca's trance. "Go say hi, we'll hang back." Alice nudged Luca.

Luca took a deep breath and approached Stephanie, who appeared to visibly relax once Luca was in front of her. "You didn't have to come," Luca said quietly.

Stephanie stared at Luca, cool blue eyes scanning her face slowly. "Of course I did." Stephanie's face was void of any outward emotion. "Your email sounded sad, and although I don't doubt you have a strong support system, I felt it was important that you know I'm here—"

Luca was struck by the unexpected act of kindness. She threw her arms around Stephanie and held her tightly. Not one person that night had managed to shake her emotional strength, but one small, warm admittance from Stephanie severed every tether holding her control in place. Luca shed her first tears of the evening on Stephanie's shoulder.

"I'm sorry." Luca started to pull back, but Stephanie's arms wrapped around her waist to hold her in place.

"Don't be," she whispered into Luca's ear. "Sometimes we all need a moment of weakness to remind us of how strong we really are."

Luca sank further into Stephanie's hold. The softness of the moment was unusual. She took a deep breath to calm herself but focused on Stephanie's floral scent instead. Her perfume was neither sweet nor musky, but instead light and fresh. Stephanie smelled the way sunshine would during an afternoon spent in a garden. Luca stepped back, realizing an embrace could only go on for so long before Stephanie would deem it inappropriate. She was afraid to look into Stephanie's eyes, fearful the warmth she saw earlier had slipped away. Surprisingly, Stephanie was smiling at her.

"Tell me something about your grandmother." Stephanie looked around the crowded room and added, "She was obviously very loved."

"She was," Luca said proudly. "She was a member of every church group within a ten-mile radius and never missed mass. She also loved romance novels and buying jewelry from QVC." Luca laughed and dabbed carefully beneath her eyes with a tissue.

Stephanie's small smile had yet to fade. "Tell me more." Her request sounded soft, smooth, and personal. "What's your favorite memory of her?"

"Baking Christmas cookies. Every year we'd spend an entire day baking batch after batch of Italian cookies and chocolate chip. And then she taught me how to wrap a gift perfectly, crisp corners and everything. It's an art, you know."

"I do know because I'm terrible at it, but that's for lack of trying. I love the ease of gift bags." Stephanie shrugged.

The topic, nostalgia, and Stephanie's personal confession lifted Luca's spirits slightly. She felt her sadness fade to manageable grief once more. She squared her shoulders and looked Stephanie in the eye. "One day, I'll blow your mind with my wrapping skills, and you'll be begging me to teach you." Stephanie didn't respond, but the challenging glint in her eye spoke for her. Luca laughed and gripped her elbow. "Come on, let me introduce you to some of my family. My parents disappeared, but my brother and his wife are right over here." Luca led Stephanie to where she had left Alice earlier. "They've heard a lot about you." Stephanie pulled away and Luca looked back to find her with a panicked look on her face. "Stephanie?" The use of her first name came naturally during such a personal moment.

"I'm sorry. I'm sure they're not my biggest fans after how I've been treating you at the office. This is about celebrating your grandmother's life and I don't want to distract anyone from that." Stephanie looked past Luca to the flowers at the far wall. Luca was stricken by Stephanie's change of face. The worry lines between her brows deepened, and her lips thinned out into a near grimace. Luca felt something shift within herself. Never had she expected to see Stephanie Austin worry so much about other people's thoughts.

"You have nothing to worry about." Luca grabbed Stephanie's hand. "I've said all good things."

"How is that even possible?"

Instead of answering, Luca tugged at Stephanie's hand and walked her over to Chris and Alice. "Everyone, this is my boss, Stephanie Austin." Alice looked at their joined hands and back to Luca curiously. Luca dropped Stephanie's hand and cleared her throat. "This is my sister-in-law, Alice, and my brother Chris."

"Thank you for coming," Chris said. Stephanie shook their hands and offered her condolences before turning to Catherine and Imogene.

"Catherine Carter, as I live and breathe." Stephanie gave Catherine a professional hug before pulling back to stand beside Luca.

"It's nice to see you again, Stephanie," Catherine said with a kind smile. "I just wish it were under better circumstances."

"Me too, but this gives me a chance to tell you how right you were about Luca," Stephanie said. Luca looked at Catherine, whose eyes went wide. "She's as brilliant as you said and I'm fortunate you requested I take her on."

"You had me placed with Ms. Austin?" Luca asked. Stephanie shifted uncomfortably beside Luca, mirroring Catherine's stance. "You called in a favor, didn't you?"

"I knew where you were working and I wanted to make sure you worked with the best." Catherine's explanation was awkward.

Luca pinched the bridge of her nose. She felt Stephanie's hand rest on her shoulder. "I thought you knew."

"No, I didn't." Luca took a deep breath. Did this mean that she hadn't earned her position? "I did think it was a little weird for an intern to be assigned to you, Ms. Austin. That was a first and I couldn't figure out why it was me." Luca stared at Stephanie, hoping to hear anything that'd make her feel a little better.

Stephanie opened her mouth to speak, but Catherine spoke first. "Because you deserve an opportunity to thrive in this business, and that'll never happen if you're not taught by the right people."

"Catherine's right." Stephanie nodded. "You could've been placed with a male fossil who'd treat you like another woman trying to make it in a man's world. You're smarter than that, you're better than that, and you deserve a fair shot to show off how successful you can be." Luca's heart sank, as if it were trying to meet with her flip-flopping stomach. "I've caused a commotion at a very inappropriate time and I'm sorry." Stephanie clutched her purse tighter against her side and looked to Chris. "Again, my condolences to you and your family." Stephanie took off for the door. Luca was frozen as Stephanie walked out.

Stephanie rushed across the parking lot of the funeral home. "Stupid, stupid, stupid," she said to herself as she fumbled through her overstuffed purse for her phone. She wanted to tell Lee just how terrible her advice was, that this funeral and Luca's personal life were no place for her, but deep down she knew blaming her friend was unfair. She dug herself into this rut. If she had been more open from the beginning, Catherine's input wouldn't have been a secret and Stephanie's own presence tonight wouldn't have been so awkward. Stephanie let her head fall back and she stared up at the night sky. She breathed deeply, letting the fresh air cleanse the scent of roses and lilies from her nose.

"Why did you say those things?" At the sound of Luca's voice, Stephanie jumped. She turned to find Luca right behind her. "Were you just trying to appease Catherine? If that's the case, I can tell you right now she's not that kind of person. You don't have to lie to her."

"I wasn't lying," Stephanie said with a shake of her head. She looked back to the sky, far from Luca's dark eyes that were no less intense in the shadows. But Luca's eyes and the stars sparkled like one and the same. Stephanie spoke to the heavens. "Every single accountant you worked with last year wrote glowing recommendations for you. When I spoke to each of them, they all jumped at the chance to add to their praises. You were rated top of your class, have the top statistics of your intern group, and are not at all cocky about it." Stephanie looked at Luca, whose mouth formed a small *O*, and laughed. Stephanie was tired of holding her head high, so she let her rigid, professional façade fall away. "You're incredible."

Luca stared back at Stephanie, expressionless, until she shook herself back into the moment. "You read up on me," she said with a hint of wonder.

Stephanie nodded. "While I was away I had a lot of time to think about all the ways I've been doing wrong by you. It wouldn't benefit either of us if I didn't take the time to help you grow." Luca stood motionless. Stephanie couldn't blame her skepticism. "Can you keep a secret?"

"Of course."

"Witlin is opening another office in Chicago, and he's going to ask me to head it." Luca looked at her for longer than a moment without a response, forcing Stephanie to explain further. "Once I'm gone, you could be transferred to one of the aforementioned fossils or someone without the kind of experience you'd truly benefit from. We need to make the most of the time we have left together."

"Wow, um." Luca looked away and Stephanie followed her eyes to watch a couple walk from the funeral home hand in hand. "That's really great for you, congratulations."

Stephanie watched every nuance of Luca's face as she spoke. Her words were positive, but her eyes were sad and her smile strained.

Stephanie glanced back at the building. Of course Luca was sad, she was dealing with the passing of her grandmother and Stephanie was keeping her from the services. Embarrassment flushed across her face. "I'm so sorry for keeping you."

"Who are you?"

"Excuse me?"

"Who are you?" Luca let the question hang between them before shooting Stephanie a bright smile, one Stephanie felt in her knees. "You're not the same Stephanie Austin I left at the office on Monday."

Without hesitation, Stephanie grinned to match Luca's. "I suppose you're used to me talking while my head is up my ass." They laughed together at the truth of the statement. "When I'm wrong, I say I'm wrong." She screwed up her mouth and bopped her head from side to side. "Maybe not in the best of ways or in the nicest of terms, but I do, and I'm saying I was wrong with my entire approach to you being my assistant." Stephanie reached out and placed her hand gently on Luca's forearm. "Take your time grieving, get some rest, and be prepared to work your ass off when you get back to the office."

"I will, Ms. Austin."

"And please, call me Stephanie from now on." Before Stephanie knew what was happening, Luca stepped into her and wrapped her arms around her neck. After a second of hesitation, Stephanie relaxed and returned the hug.

Under the star-filled sky, Stephanie hoped that the embrace was as comforting for Luca as it was for her.

# Chapter Nine

Luca returned to work Wednesday of that week. She still felt sad and was all too ready to throw herself back into her job. She stepped off the elevators and approached her desk, a desk she no longer recognized. Stacks of files cluttered the normally tidy surface and two more boxes were stacked off to the side. Luca looked at the coffee in her hand and wondered if there'd be any room for it.

"Luca." Andrew's loud voice carried across the office. He was carrying another box of files.

"How long have you been here for?"

"I just got in," he said, setting the box atop the growing tower. "Before I did anything I was told to bring this up to you. What's going on?"

"I'm not sure." Luca barely finished her sentence before the door to Stephanie's office opened.

Andrew looked up in fear and turned to Luca. "Text me later." His retreat would've been funny, if Luca wasn't so confused by everything else around her.

"Ah, I see you've received your assignment just in time." Stephanie's voice had returned to the monotone drawl Luca was used to. The warmth and personable tone she had witnessed at the funeral home was either long gone, or just a dream. "I hope you brought your lunch with you today because you'll be working through it." Stephanie's eyes were on her phone, and not once did she peek at Luca, who still stood holding her coffee. "I need you to review every one of these files."

"Every one?" Luca asked with wide eyes. There had to be sixty files on the desktop alone.

Stephanie took a paper from a file she had tucked under her arm. "Every single one. We're looking for connections between these companies and individuals, and any activity outside of the norm. We have to check every number—we may even need to check them twice." Stephanie handed Luca the paper but didn't let go right away. When they looked at one another, something fierce danced in Stephanie's eyes. "This is a big case. Are you up for the challenge?"

"Absolutely." Luca tugged at the paper. She smiled when Stephanie let go.

"If you come up with a system, let me know. There's more boxes in my office." Stephanie started her retreat.

"Are any of these archived on the computer?"

Stephanie turned back with a smirk and said, "No, and where would the fun be if they were?" She stepped into her office and shut the door.

Luca approached her desk slowly, looking at the boxes and noting the years written on the exterior. They spanned over half a decade. Stephanie wasn't just teasing when she told Luca to prepare for working her ass off. "Wow," she whispered to herself. She found a clear area to set her coffee down and pulled out her chair. A small note on the seat caught her eye. Luca unfolded the paper and read aloud. "Look in your top drawer." She followed the instructions and found an unwrapped box with a small card on top.

*Good luck on your first day. You're going to need it.*
*—Steph*

Luca ran her thumb along the cursive, smirking at each word in turn. Her breath caught when she opened the box. Inside was a sleek silver pen with a filigree clip. Luca examined the pen, feeling the weight of it in her palm and spinning it between her fingertips. The light caught the polished metal just so, highlighting an engraving along the side: *Wrongfully Underestimated.* Luca chuckled and fought against the tears she felt stinging her eyes.

She didn't expect Stephanie's acceptance or her willingness to work side by side, but Luca was truly ill-prepared for Stephanie's kindness. Stephanie Austin was a workplace drone, one that was determined to be the best and perform her best at all times. Failure had no place in Stephanie's world, whether it was her own or someone close to her. But Luca had seen a new side of Stephanie. She was warm and kind and funny. Luca couldn't help but think if she'd have met her at a bar, she'd find herself pining after the gorgeous blonde. But Stephanie was, in reality, Luca's boss, and completely out of Luca's league. One of life's cruel twists.

Luca looked to the small card again, this time with sadness. She took the small note and tucked it away in her purse. She wanted this version of Stephanie for herself—partially for selfish reasons and also to protect Stephanie. Her workplace persona was built after many years of hard work. Luca didn't want to be the one to break it all down now.

The first three hours of Luca's day were spent cross-referencing names and companies with detailed financial reports that cluttered her desk. She had barely made it through one stack by the time her stomach growled, signaling lunchtime. Luca recalled Stephanie mentioning working through lunch, but without Stephanie popping from her office again, Luca wasn't sure if that was truly the case. She opened the bottom drawer of her desk, the designated snack drawer, and fished around for something to satisfy her angry, grumbling stomach. Every nutritional morsel was gone—no more granola bars or trail mix packs were tucked to the back. Luca's only choices were chocolate, sour straws, and one lonely pack of Yodels. The cream-filled devil's food snack cake would have to do.

Luca unwrapped her snack impatiently, tearing at the cellophane as if it were biting her back, and shoved three-quarters of chocolate-coated roll into her mouth. Stephanie chose the moment before Luca's teeth sank in to open her office door. Luca froze. Her eyes were on Stephanie, her mouth was full of cheap cake, and her fingertips were sinking into the melting chocolate of the small piece that couldn't fit in her mouth. She could feel her cheeks warm when Stephanie smiled coyly.

"I was about to ask if you'd be interested in venturing out for lunch today, but I see you've already eaten."

"I camff—" Luca's eyes widened. Talking with your mouth full showed poor etiquette. She chewed quickly and threw the remaining Yodel in the trash. She swallowed, cleared her throat, and looked at Stephanie before continuing. "I can go for something a little more filling."

Stephanie's smile broadened and she said, "Grab the files that are labeled July 2013 and we'll head out. I'll brief you on exactly what we're doing once we get to the diner."

"The Atlantis Diner?" Luca said, hope filling her voice and eyes.

"Of course. No one goes to the dive across the street." Stephanie spoke a true statement. Diners were everywhere in New Jersey—some sat face-to-face on opposing streets—but just like Philly with its cheesesteak stands, there were good, and then there were the best. Stephanie stepped back into her office and reappeared with her briefcase and blazer. She wore a cobalt pencil skirt that matched the blazer. The color did wonders for her eyes. "Ready?"

Luca had yet to move from behind her desk, but luckily she knew right where 2013's folders were set. She lifted the small stack and looked back at Stephanie. "I'm ready to get down to business and eat a lumberjack breakfast."

Stephanie tilted her head. Luca noticed the way her left eyebrow had a higher natural arch than her right. "Pancakes or French toast?"

The question caught Luca off guard, so she blurted the first thing that came to mind. "Are you making me choose?"

"No," Stephanie said, laughing quietly and looking around. Luca wondered if she worried about breaking the office's expectations of her. "I'm just curious."

"I like them both equally. Pancakes are versatile, but making the perfect French toast is an art form."

"Can't argue with that logic." Stephanie ushered Luca to the elevators, and once they stepped inside, she looked at Luca. "I'm happy with either, as long as they're served with a good cup of coffee."

Luca felt she should write this information down, but she knew her memory would never be faulty enough to let any information about Stephanie Austin slide. "A good cup of coffee makes everything better." The elevator dinged their arrival to the ground floor.

Stephanie stepped out first and looked back at Luca. "Agreed."

Luca was a bundle of jittery nerves during the short, silent ride to the Atlantis Diner. She hadn't expected Stephanie to drive them both, but she definitely wasn't surprised by Stephanie's sleek new Audi. Luca's stuttering heart hadn't begun to settle until after she had placed her food order. She smiled at Stephanie when she placed an order for the same breakfast feast.

"You inspired me," Stephanie said with a wink.

Odd, but nice, Luca thought as her belly quivered slightly. "So, what's the lowdown? What's this big case that'll have me up at all hours?"

Stephanie stirred half of a creamer into her coffee and tapped her metal spoon against the ceramic cup three times before looking at Luca. "It's a secret." Luca's eyes rolled as far back as they could. "But not from you, just everyone else. Hence why I waited until lunchtime to fill you in. We needed to be out of the office."

"Does Mr. Witlin know?"

"No. Only I knew, and now you."

Luca pushed aside her silverware set and napkin and leaned forward on the table. "Why so top secret?" The fluttering in her chest was back, but this time Luca was excited.

"Because I'm taking it upon myself to investigate the one who initiated the investigation." Stephanie's eyes never strayed from her coffee as she spoke, drawing Luca's attention to her long lashes. Stephanie looked up, her eyes fierce and sparkling. "This goes a lot deeper than a simple investigation," Stephanie said. She laid her hand upon the stack of files. "I'm grateful that I'll have your assistance on this case, Luca."

Luca was taken aback by Stephanie's sincere expression. Things had actually changed. "I'm grateful for the opportunity, Ms. Austin."

Stephanie laughed and sat back from her coffee. "You really need to stop with that—as lovely as it may sound. Stephanie is fine, but feel free to call me Steph if you'd like. Just keep that one to a minimum in the office." Stephanie lifted her index finger to her lips in a mimicked shush. Luca watched with rapt attention, entranced by the way Stephanie's full lips puckered. Why were beautiful women so goddamn distracting?

"Two lumberjack breakfasts with pancakes, white toast, wheat toast, and one chocolate chip pancake." The waitress set the meal down and waited a polite second for any further requests. "Enjoy."

"Why the extra pancake? I wasn't going to ask before, but my curiosity got the best of me." Stephanie went about spreading a hint of butter on her pancakes, far less in comparison to Luca's slathering.

"I like to have dessert with all of my meals." Luca grabbed the syrup and poured it across her entire plate. "You've been with LGR for some time now, why are you still so protective of your reputation?"

"As much as I'd love to talk about myself, we're here for more important things."

Luca felt thoroughly scolded. "Of course. I'm sorry, Ms.—Stephanie."

"I'm not withholding," Stephanie said, reaching out and placing her hand on Luca's. Luca almost dropped her knife. "Later, I'll tell you all about my early career and how I achieved my position. I promise, because I want you to follow in my footsteps." Luca looked at Stephanie's hand on hers. Their skin tones almost matched, but where Luca had olive undertones, Stephanie was pure alabaster. Stephanie drew her hand back abruptly. "Back to business."

"Yes, business." Luca shoved an obscenely large bite of pancake into her mouth.

Luca ate and listened as Stephanie outlined their entire case for her. Luca asked few questions, not wanting to interrupt Stephanie, but there were times when Stephanie would speak too quickly for her to keep up. Her excitement was contagious and Luca found herself falling into the adorable display. Once their plates were clean and Luca had stopped picking at her dessert pancake, Stephanie looked at her expectantly.

"Thoughts?"

Luca laughed outright. "You just told me the CEO of a million-dollar marketing outfit fired his business partner for skimming from the top of the business's funds, and now you've discovered the CEO is the one who may be guilty in all of this." Luca scratched at her forehead. "I have a lot of thoughts, but not many of them stray far from holy shit and what a can of worms. I am curious why you're keeping it a secret, though."

"Because these are big accusations, and I think it'd be in our best interest to uncover and collect as much evidence as possible before we involve anyone else. I'm never wrong; now we just need a stack of hard facts to keep my streak alive." Stephanie sat back with a smug smile and crossed her arms over her chest. "Are you worried?"

"Worried? No. I'm actually pretty excited." Their waitress stopped by and placed the check on the table between them.

"Why's that?" Stephanie said, snatching the check from Luca.

"Because you have no real idea what I'm capable of, and I finally have a chance to show you."

"I really didn't think you were the cocky type. I guess I was wrong."

Luca leaned forward and said, "Does it count as cockiness if you really are that good?" She stood and stretched her legs. They'd been at the diner for too long. Luca's backside hurt from sitting on worn padding, and the air-conditioning must've been getting to Stephanie because when Luca looked back to her, she shivered.

# Chapter Ten

Stephanie was amazed at how quickly three weeks had passed. Three weeks of late nights, hushed investigating, and white lies between outside coworkers. Three weeks of isolating themselves in Stephanie's office. They started work before nine in the morning and made a habit of staying well past seven—giving Stephanie the opportunity to enjoy almost every meal of the day with her assistant. All this time spent with Luca helped make Stephanie feel a little less alone than she normally would while working around the clock. And she enjoyed every minute of it.

She had learned so much about Luca, like how almost anything could trigger a random memory from Luca's childhood or how Alice wasn't her number one fan after their first disastrous meeting at a family barbecue. And in turn, Stephanie found herself opening up more easily than she had in the past. She spoke lightly of her parents' divorce and the older of two brothers who turned his back on their family years ago. Stephanie would've hesitated, but Luca's eyes were so kind and gentle, encouraging even at their darkest. She was going to miss those eyes once she was living in Chicago, but she had them now, along with Luca's smile that left her utterly powerless. Which is why when Luca pulled a small bottle of tequila from her purse on Friday night, Stephanie couldn't help but laugh.

"I don't normally drink, especially not at work, but I felt like we needed to celebrate a little since we're nearing the end of this case." Luca unscrewed the top and poured two fingers' worth into two glasses. "I wasn't sure which brand you liked, so I went according to the cashier's recommendation. Now that I think about it, I'm not even sure they were old enough to drink."

Stephanie took her glass and swirled the golden liquid around. "How do you know I even like tequila?"

"You were drinking it at the bar."

Confusion washed over Stephanie before realization set in. "Ah, yes. Now I remember." Stephanie sipped at the tequila, not wanting to cloud her mind.

"I shouldn't have approached you that night, but I'm terrible at handling awkward situations. As it turns out, I handle them by making it more awkward for everyone involved. Your friends probably thought I was a loon."

Stephanie held her glass to her lips and looked at Luca over the rim. Luca had grown more beautiful to her as time passed. Where she was once average, Stephanie noticed lovely traits beneath, like the way her hair remained silky straight even on humid days, or the arch of her eyebrow and the angle of her jawline. Not one bit of Luca was average, just covered up to appear so. But her brilliance was truly her most exquisite feature, the one that kept Stephanie up at night, craving her conversation.

"My friends actually thought you were pretty hot and teased me about fulfilling their boss/assistant fantasies." Stephanie wasn't entirely sure why she shared that bit, but Luca's widened eyes made her happy she did. Something about knowing the Chicago office announcement was coming and the taste of tequila on her tongue bolstered Stephanie's bravery. Luca revived a once-forgotten feeling in Stephanie.

"That seems to be a very popular fantasy." Luca cleared her throat. "Do you have the expense reports from the first half of this year?"

Was Luca speaking about herself? Her own fantasies? Stephanie shook her inner questions away and shuffled through the many folders and papers she had on the tabletop. "Right here." She handed the file to Luca and stood. She walked to her desk for a highlighter, but also to escape from under Luca's gaze for a brief moment. Subtle flirting was one thing, but the more time she spent with Luca, the less subtle she felt.

"I don't see anything recently that looks out of the ordinary," Luca said from behind her.

"Because he got smarter after he fired his partner. Notice the direct deposits that go into two different accounts every week." Stephanie marched back to the table and stood behind Luca. She bent over her and pointed to a series of numbers on the page. Luca's hair grazed her arm and Stephanie prayed Luca wouldn't notice her goose bumps.

"There's nothing unusual about that. I have my pay deposited into two accounts, one for spending and one for bills."

"Very common indeed, but considering the fact that this guy's being investigated, I dug a little deeper into the details of those accounts." Stephanie opened another folder and stood back to watch Luca scan the pages. Every once in a while, Luca would take her bottom lip between her teeth as she concentrated—a very distracting move. "What do you see?"

Luca ran the fingertips of her right hand over the print, making Stephanie imagine the way her touch would tickle her skin. Get a grip or get laid because this is getting out of hand, Stephanie thought.

"There are two people on this account," Luca said quietly, her voice taking on a shy quality. "Every other account we've looked at, even his personal accounts, have only had his name on them."

Stephanie nodded. "His wife is attached to this account, and if we take a look at her other accounts…" Stephanie slid one last folder to Luca with a smile.

"Jackpot?" Luca asked with bright eyes and a slight tilt to her head.

Stephanie pulled her chair closer to Luca and sat. She leaned forward slightly so her next whispered words would be heard loud and clear. "I wouldn't know. I just had that folder delivered to me before dinner."

"And you've been hiding it," Luca said in a near squawk.

Stephanie sat back laughing before pushing the folder to Luca again. "I want you to be the first to look through it."

"Why?"

"Because over the past three weeks you have proven to be one of the most intelligent investigators I've ever worked with, and you've earned the right to be the name stamped on this case." Stephanie took a deep breath. "I want this case to go on your record, on your résumé, so when I'm not here anymore and if you start to look elsewhere for employment, you'll get hired by one of the best."

Luca's eyes shone with an odd weakness, a moment of emotion

Stephanie had only seen at her grandmother's funeral. Luca was genuinely touched. But that vulnerability was washed away by a smirk. Luca leaned forward slightly and said, "You think you're that important, huh? If you go, I go?"

Stephanie set her shoulders, ready for a challenge. "I do, and I know that no one else here is capable of helping you reach your true potential."

Luca looked at her tequila before downing the rest and looking back at Stephanie. Her eyes were watering slightly. "What is my true potential?" Luca's voice had turned husky.

Stephanie followed Luca's lead and swallowed the rest of her drink, but her eyes never strayed from Luca's. She licked a lingering droplet of alcohol from her lip before shifting into Luca's space further. This flirtatious, playful element between them sparked a neediness within Stephanie that shocked her. A foot separated them, and Stephanie was unsure that she'd have enough strength in her voice to carry her words to Luca.

"I, uh, I think that with the right training you'd be able to—"

"Top you?" Luca said with unwavering confidence and Stephanie could swear her eyes grew a fraction darker. Stephanie looked at Luca's lips for a brief second before she pulled back into her chair, needing to feel the solidity of it beneath her.

"You're capable of topping all the best investigators out there. You could top this whole firm and then some." Stephanie cringed at her own joke. Luca wore a polite smile as she studied Stephanie for a moment. Instead of bringing any further attention to Stephanie's discomfort, she opened the file. Stephanie sighed in relief.

"Holy shit." Luca's exclamation startled Stephanie.

"What is it?" Stephanie asked from her safe space, pressed against the back of the chair.

"Let's just say our guy used up all of his smarts early in the game."

"Smoking gun?"

Luca looked up from the paperwork with a brilliant smile. "The whole armory is smoking."

"Great." Stephanie stood and stretched. "Take that home with you and highlight each and every transgression. We'll write our final reports and call the lawyers on Monday." Stephanie headed for her desk, picked up her briefcase, and started to pack up for the night.

"Wait. That's it?"

Stephanie looked up in confusion to stare at Luca, who was now standing on the other side of her desk. "That's it. Enjoy your weekend, do something fun. You earned it."

"Let me buy you a drink." Stephanie's eyebrow quirked up. "To celebrate closing this case. After all, this may be the only big case you and I get to work on together." Stephanie thought Luca's offer over and over. It wasn't unusual to have a couple drinks after a case, and the night was still early. "Meet me at the Dollhouse tomorrow night around eight. What do you say?"

The Dollhouse? Saturday night? That didn't sound like a couple of coworkers grabbing a drink after a tedious few weeks. That sounded like a date. What was Stephanie supposed to say?

"I'll see you tomorrow at eight."

## Chapter Eleven

Luca questioned herself again and again as she drummed her fingers on the bar top. The beautiful, androgynous bartender had offered to get her a drink several times, but Luca insisted she was waiting for someone. She wouldn't be surprised if Stephanie didn't show, but it was only a quarter past eight and Luca held on to hope. Hope that Stephanie wouldn't stand her up, hope that this was more than celebratory drinks, and hope that the uncontrollable flirtations meant more to Stephanie, just as they did for Luca. Working beside Stephanie had opened Luca's eyes to a world she'd never imagined. There was someone out there, a brilliant woman, who shared in so many of Luca's interests and who could share in the misery and the joy of her profession at the end of the day.

But Luca wouldn't allow herself to get lost in those dangerous daydreams. Stephanie was her boss, a devout professional, and was moving to Chicago in the near future. Yes, long distance could work, but Luca was the kind of woman who craved physical attention at the end of the day, nearly every day, when she was in love. In love? Luca signaled for the bartender, her throat suddenly very dry, and asked for vodka cranberry.

"Getting started without me?" Stephanie's voice came from over Luca's shoulder. Luca jumped. She turned to find a very casual version of Stephanie standing shyly behind her. She wore a simple black V-neck shirt, the neckline cut distractingly deep, and skinny jeans. She had never looked more beautiful to Luca. Stephanie's platinum hair fell loosely around her shoulders and caught the light in such a way that caused every tendril to nearly glow. Stephanie shifted and said, "Sorry

I'm late, I've been a bit sluggish all day. Do you want to stay at the bar or grab a table?"

Luca shook herself into action and nodded. "A table sounds great. What would you like to drink?"

"A Yuengling, please."

"No tequila?" Luca said, her lips turning up slightly.

"Maybe after my first beer."

Luca went about ordering and paying for Stephanie's drink. She led them to a small table off in the corner of the bar, far from the crowds and in just enough of a secluded space to be able to be heard over the music. On this Saturday, they played hits from the '80s and '90s. Luca watched Stephanie take the first sip from her bottle, her bottom lip looking more plump as it sealed around the glass. Stephanie had very few wrinkles across her fair skin, but the lines by her mouth and the creases on her forehead held Luca's attention. She wanted to know all about the times Stephanie had laughed with wild abandon, and what had caused her to worry so. Who helped Stephanie Austin create her professional outer shell, and how many people were privy to what was beneath?

"You're staring. Why are you staring?" Stephanie squinted one of her eyes as she looked at Luca with suspicion.

"I want to know more about you," Luca said, confessing so much in very few words.

Stephanie laughed. "You already know more than most."

"Is that your favorite beer?"

Stephanie looked at the bottle in her hands. She rolled it between her palms and picked at the label before answering. "No."

"Then why do you drink it?"

"It was my mom's favorite beer, so we'd always have it in the house for special occasions." Stephanie took another sip and her face remained passive. "This beer reminds me of simpler times. Why are you smiling?"

Luca hadn't realized she was grinning until then. "I'm sorry, I just don't hear of many moms being beer drinkers. Wine, vodka, rum? Of course."

"Only the cool moms prefer beer." Stephanie winked.

"I'll drink to that, and to our shared success." Luca tapped the rim of her glass to Stephanie's bottle.

"Well, well, well. Look who it is," a faintly familiar voice called out. Lee approached their table with Zoe in tow. Tina followed closely behind as she chatted with a young butch girl. "Hey, guys."

"Hi." Stephanie looked at Luca in unspoken apology, but her face had panic written all over it. "Lee, Tina, Zoe, I'm not sure if you remember my assistant, Luca."

"Hi, Luca." Zoe reached out to shake Luca's hand. "It's very nice to see you again." Luca shook Zoe's hand briefly and returned Tina's halfhearted wave. Luca was sure Tina missed the gesture because her attention was on her conversation partner's beefy biceps.

Lee reached out next. "I've heard so much about you, Luca. Sorry about your grandmother."

Luca looked at Stephanie curiously, but she couldn't see around Stephanie's hands covering her face. She was curious how often Stephanie had spoken about her to her friends. "Thank you. Would you like to join us?" Luca asked. Stephanie peeked between her fingers.

Lee was ready to pull up a chair, but Zoe tugged her arm. "We don't want to impose."

"You're not. We're just celebrating the end of three grueling weeks at work." Luca wanted Stephanie all to herself, but maybe Stephanie would prefer to have her friends around as a buffer. For all Luca knew, Stephanie could've asked her friends to drop by. Stephanie's face gave no indication of what she wanted. "Steph?"

"Head up to the bar," Stephanie said to Lee. "We'll meet you in a few." Stephanie watched the short train of her friends leave. "I'm sorry."

"No, I'm sorry. I shouldn't have just invited them over like that, but I want you to be comfortable, and I thought having your friends here would help that."

"Why wouldn't I be comfortable?"

"Because it's just you and me."

Stephanie slid her beer aside and leaned forward. Her features turned soft, the way Luca was used to seeing them toward the end of a long day or when they'd leave the office for lunch. "Luca, I've spent more time with just you than I have with anyone recently." Luca wanted to argue how Stephanie should spend time with her friends if she had been monopolizing her time, but Stephanie reached out and grabbed her hand, effectively shutting down every voice in Luca's head. "If I thought I'd be uncomfortable tonight, I wouldn't have come." Luca sat stunned, her eyes never leaving the pale hand that grasped hers. "And now I've made you uncomfortable," Stephanie said, withdrawing her touch.

"No, you didn't. Not at all." Luca placed her hand back on the table top, palm up, but pulled it back immediately. She sat back nervously, unsure of what to say or do next.

"Come on, Luca, you have so much bravado in the office. Where is it now?" Stephanie's eyes glittered as she teased and her smile was positively wicked.

"Back at the office, undoubtedly." Luca wasn't always the brightest when it came to women showing interest in her, but right now she felt completely brain-dead. Stephanie's touch could've been innocent, or she could've purposely sparked the fire Luca felt on her skin. She looked over her shoulder to catch Lee and Zoe watching them. "Do you want to step out onto the back patio for a bit? Get some fresh air?"

Stephanie stood and started toward the back of the bar. Luca followed wordlessly into the crowds of people that stood by the exit in preparation for their next cigarette break. The night air was humid, typical of New Jersey summers, but the season was still too early for the heat to suffocate. Lightning bugs danced off in the distance. The Dollhouse had a small wooden deck with a few chairs and an outdoor sofa. Strings of old-fashioned glass bulbs lined the space, making an average night feel magical and romantic. Luca's breath caught when Stephanie turned back and looked her in the eye.

"Why did you ask me here tonight?" Stephanie's blunt question took Luca by surprise.

Luca felt like she was being tested. She responded slowly. "To celebrate…"

"But why here and why tonight? We had tequila in the office. We could've stopped at any bar last night after we left. Why did you choose this?"

Luca's heart began to hammer as she registered Stephanie in her personal space. Luca smelled her perfume, even her shampoo, as Stephanie stood with her arms crossed over her chest. Fear drove the next words from her mouth. "I think we both earned a night out."

Stephanie sighed and her head fell. "I deal with a lot of people every day, but you, Luca Garner, confuse the shit out of me."

"What?"

"One minute you're assertive and confident, then the next you look like you're about to crawl out of your skin. You invite me here, order me a drink and tell me you want to know more about me, then you invite my friends to join us. You're sending a lot of mixed signals."

Luca wanted to curse, or at least whine, at her own behavior. She closed her eyes and took a chance on the truth. "Unless we're talking about a case, you scare me. And, let's face it, you scare me a little bit then, too."

Stephanie reached out to hold one of Luca's hands between her own. "Why do I scare you?"

"A combination of things, really." Luca laughed awkwardly. Stephanie's hands were incredibly warm, but dry, highlighting the softness of her palms. "I sort of think you're perfect." Luca swallowed thickly. Her lips felt tight with trepidation as she continued to speak. "But what I know is you're my boss, and way out of my league."

Stephanie stared at Luca, unblinking. Luca swore she saw a hundred different thoughts swimming behind Stephanie's vibrant blue eyes, but no words left her lips. She dropped Luca's hand and put on a plastic smile. "You should think more highly of yourself, Luca. And I'm far from perfect. As a matter of fact, from where I'm standing, you're way out of my league." Luca was speechless, but even if she had a comeback prepared, Stephanie wouldn't allow it. "Let's go back in to meet up with Zoe and Lee."

Luca watched as she walked back inside. She felt like she was spinning and the voice in her head was screaming to pull herself together. Stephanie needed to know that Luca wanted her for exactly who she was. Luca rushed through the small crowd of people outside in order to catch Stephanie before she got too far into the bar, before she met up with people who'd extinguish the bravery swelling within. Once she was close enough, Luca reached out and grabbed Stephanie's wrist. Stephanie turned and eyed Luca curiously, but that confused look didn't stop Luca from stepping close and bringing their lips within a whisper of each other.

"I'm scared and shy around beautiful women, but more

importantly, brilliant women make me dumb. You do all of these things to me, and I invited you here tonight in hopes of getting over myself and telling you that I really like you and I'm constantly imagining what it'd be like to kiss you." Luca took a breath and waited for Stephanie to respond. Stephanie's face split into a radiant grin. "May I kiss you?" Stephanie nodded and Luca pressed forward. Her heart stuttered at the feeling of Stephanie's lower lip fitting perfectly between hers.

Luca unconsciously grasped Stephanie's hips and pulled her closer. Now that they had made it to this point, Luca no longer wanted any space between them. She reveled in the suppleness of Stephanie's mouth, waited to dive in deeper. This shallow introduction was perfect, a perfection she wasn't ready to break.

Stephanie, on the other hand, didn't hesitate to weave her fingers into Luca's hair and hold her in place as she opened her mouth for their first tentative taste. Luca could've sworn flames engulfed her on the spot. The tip of Stephanie's tongue teased hers before traveling along the bow of her upper lip. Luca's knees started to give, but she pressed on and deepened the kiss, not wanting Stephanie to gain the upper hand. A small moan escaped Stephanie, and Luca froze. They were standing in the middle of a bar. Not exactly where Luca had imagined rounding first base with this woman, and Luca had imagined many different versions of that scenario.

Luca stood in wonder as she noted how sexy Stephanie Austin looked when disheveled. Stephanie was breathing heavily and her face was lit with a pleasant blush. "That was…"

"Unexpected," Stephanie said.

Luca smirked. "I did ask first."

"No, not the kiss," Stephanie said, laughing softly. Luca had never heard that particular laugh before, and she felt herself fall further into Stephanie. "We work very well together, both professionally and, well, not so professionally. A first for me."

"You were unexpected for me." Luca traced Stephanie's jawline with her fingertip.

A rowdy patron bumped into Luca, jarring her mind enough to force the many questions she had for Stephanie away. But when she looked back into Stephanie's eyes, she saw open honesty and desire.

The night was still young, and there was no way Luca was about to give up this opportunity to get closer. “Want to get out of here?”

“Are you sure you don’t want to spend more time with my friends?” Stephanie covered her mouth with her hand, obviously hiding a laugh. Luca wasn’t prepared for many of the things life was throwing at her, and Stephanie’s sarcasm was definitely at the top of her list.

## Chapter Twelve

As Stephanie drove along toward home with Luca following in her car, she went through a mental checklist. Her cleaning lady had stopped by the day before, so her house was in order. Stephanie had followed her usual self-grooming ritual as she showered before heading to the bar, and she felt ready for whatever would happen once they arrived at her house. But no amount of preparation calmed the war raging between her heart and mind.

She was moving to Chicago soon, a fact she kept repeating to herself. She had searched for apartments and saved the most promising prospects. The advancement of her career would exceed any expectations she had in place. But where did Luca fit in all of this? Stephanie pressed her fingertips to her lips. She recalled just how soft Luca's mouth was, and Luca's strength as she gripped her hips. She looked in the rearview mirror to make sure Luca hadn't changed her mind and pulled a dramatic U-turn to escape. Right there in the reflection was Luca, loyal as always.

Stephanie couldn't remember the last time she had craved someone like this, body and mind. She had spent a few years searching for this feeling, but work had taken over and Stephanie never felt the loss. Stephanie would've overlooked Luca, too, if she hadn't been forced to work with her. The irony wasn't lost on her.

She pulled up to her house. One lamp beside the front windows was on thanks to a timer. Her nerves kicked in full force as she parked and turned off her car. Bringing Luca home was likely to be a mistake. Even if the night was perfect, that'd do nothing but spark the beginning of heartbreak. Then Stephanie felt her body flood with warmth at the thought that the night might be perfect. She climbed out of her car and waited for Luca to do the same. Luca looked nervous as she shut her car door and looked around Stephanie's neighborhood. The night was quiet, only the wind rustling trees filled the silence.

"Cute house," Luca said. The ranch-style home was big enough for Stephanie to live comfortably, but not too big that she'd feel lonely.

"Thank you, it's a nice escape from occupational chaos." Stephanie wanted to say how much she'd miss her little house once she moved to Chicago, but bringing up her transfer would be a mood killer. They walked together to the covered front porch and Stephanie caught herself wanting to share with Luca that it was her favorite spot. But something inside her, an indulgent, romantic side of her that she'd all but forgotten about, hoped she'd be able to share that with Luca as they drank their coffee together the next morning. "Would you like something to drink?" she asked as they stepped inside. "I don't have much, but I may have a bottle of wine."

"I'll just take a water, thank you." Luca stood no more than three feet inside Stephanie's entryway and looked around. Stephanie was a little self-conscious of her house, thinking it could be warmer or more colorful, but she loved clean lines and neutral colors, and loathed clutter. "I wasn't kidding when I said I rarely drink, but my nerves got the best of me tonight."

Stephanie smiled. "Me either. I drink socially, and I'm not social very often."

Luca snorted. "I want to tease you, but I won't." Luca didn't look up, and for all the amusement she held in her voice, her body language screamed nervousness.

Stephanie stepped toward Luca and rested a hand on her forearm. "Luca, relax." She stepped closer. "And please, tease me if you'd like," she added in a purr. Luca didn't move or say a word, leaving Stephanie to wonder just how nervous she was. Concern set in. "Are you okay?"

Luca's eyes flew to her. "Yes, I'm definitely okay, I promise. I'm just not very good at this." Luca grabbed Stephanie's hand and interlaced their fingers.

Stephanie led them to her sofa. She sat as close as she could while keeping a comfortable distance. "What aren't you good at?"

"The awkward first steps, making the first move."

"You did pretty well in the bar."

"That was before I was in your house, surrounded by everything Stephanie Austin."

"I still intimidate you?"

"No." Luca inched closer to Stephanie on the couch. "It's like being a kid again and finding out you're going to Disney World—hard to believe it's really happening and very afraid it'll be taken away at the last minute." Stephanie placed her hand on Luca's thigh and reveled in the firm muscle that jumped beneath her touch. Luca laughed and placed her hand atop Stephanie's. "That was from excitement, not fear."

"I hope I don't scare you anymore." Stephanie ran her fingertip along the bend of Luca's jawline and enjoyed the shiver that jolted the other woman. "You know my deepest secret."

Luca's breathing had become shallow. She turned to face Stephanie fully, causing their legs to press together. Their faces were only six inches apart. "What's your secret, Steph?"

"That I'm not at all who I appear to be. That I'm nothing more than a tequila-drinking softie with loud friends and a quaint home in the suburbs. Hardly what anyone would imagine for Stone Cold Steph Austin." Stephanie was highly amused by Luca's cringe.

"You knew about the nickname?"

Stephanie chuckled. "Of course I did," she said, running her fingers through the ends of Luca's chestnut hair. Not one knot stood in protest. "No one is particularly quiet in the office, but Mr. Witlin is the one who told me—after he had stopped laughing for nearly fifteen minutes."

"I always did like Mr. Witlin."

"He and I are both confounded by the name. What do I have in common with a wrestler?" Stephanie looked at Luca with a genuinely perplexed expression. She thought maybe her assistant could clue her in to the underground workings of the office and the hottest gossip, but Luca's lips were on hers a second later. Surprise settled into divine indulgence as Stephanie welcomed Luca's lips, teeth, and hands all over. Way better than office secrets.

Stephanie turned and sank into her couch cushions, pulling Luca to lie atop her. The weight of Luca's body pressed against hers drew a quiet moan from Stephanie. Her lips were still parted and puckered when Luca pulled away, flushed and smiling.

"Now I know your other secret," Luca whispered, running her lips along Stephanie's exposed neck. She ran her hand up Stephanie's rib cage and grazed the side of her breast. Stephanie moaned again.

"What's that?"

"You're a total bottom. No one would ever expect that."

Stephanie looked up into Luca's dark eyes and fought against her growing smile. "You caught me." She tugged at the hem of Luca's simple shirt and dipped her hands beneath. She felt along the soft skin of her abdomen, pressed her fingertips into the firm muscle beneath, and dragged her short fingernails along the waist of Luca's jeans. "And I'm willing to bet no one would suspect you'd be the one to top me."

"I know I didn't." Luca lowered herself into a searing, yet gentle kiss, making Stephanie feel like she was melting into the furniture. Luca sat back slightly and grasped both of Stephanie's hands. She raised them and secured them above Stephanie's head in a firm grip against the couch cushions. Stephanie tested Luca's strength and was equal parts impressed and turned on by it. "Don't move," Luca whispered harshly before bringing her lips to Stephanie's neck once more. Stephanie had no intention of moving. Why would she want to? The only movement she made was spreading her legs to welcome Luca into her body further.

Stephanie's head fell back at the feel of Luca's free hand snaking beneath her top. Feeling Luca's fingertips dancing along her skin was overwhelming in the best way. It had been so long since someone had touched her with unhurried care. Stephanie felt as though every touch of Luca's was executed with precision and determination, like she wanted to make sure the sensation was never forgotten. If that was her plan, Stephanie knew Luca would be successful. Stephanie whimpered as Luca pinched her nipple through her sheer bra.

"You're driving me crazy," Stephanie said in a near whine. She was being tortured, exquisitely so. Luca held Stephanie's face and kissed her deeply before sitting up fully. Stephanie was already panting when Luca removed her shirt. Stephanie's mind nearly short-circuited. She should've known something marvelous hid beneath the off-the-rack suits. Stephanie swallowed harshly and tested Luca's earlier command by reaching out to touch the tempting olive skin before her. Luca allowed it.

Stephanie's eyes were glued to her own hands as she traced along Luca's soft abdomen with featherlight caresses. Luca's torso was engulfed by goose bumps. Watching them come and go was hypnotic. Just as she reached for the button on Luca's jeans, the familiar buzzing of her phone filled the silence. Stephanie stopped moving.

"I'm sorry," she said shamefully. Luca shot her a warm smile and sat back. Stephanie scrambled about, trying to remember where she had set her purse. She answered the phone as soon as she found it. "Kathy? Is everything okay?" She looked at her watch, concerned by why her sister-in-law would be calling after ten at night.

"Of course, why wouldn't it be? Oh shit, I'm sorry it's late. When you have a kid, you completely forget what living during normal hours means." Stephanie looked over her shoulder to Luca and mouthed an apology. Luca remained shirtless and sprawled casually across Stephanie's couch. She pressed her thighs together, teasing the throbbing in her clit with the promise of pressure and friction to come. The desire to hang up on Kathy was overwhelming. "I'm calling because your brother had the brilliant idea we should have an impromptu family barbecue tomorrow afternoon."

Stephanie laughed. "Last minute as always."

"Yes, and since he likes to announce but not plan, I'm calling everyone to invite them. If you're free tomorrow, you should stop by for a bit. My parents and brothers will be there, and honestly, I could use a buffer." Stephanie's eyes were still on Luca, fixated on the way she was twirling her hair around her long index finger. "Steph?"

"Yeah?"

"Yeah, you'll be there?"

"Would it be okay if I brought someone?" she said casually. Luca's hand stilled and she stared.

"Sure, and I do hope you mean Mitchell's best friend, Luca. He's been jabbering about her constantly."

Stephanie turned away from the woman in question and lowered her voice. "Don't mention anything to Mitchell because I don't know if she's free—"

"I'm free," Luca called out, loudly enough for all sets of ears listening to hear.

"Oh my God. She's there?"

"We'll see you tomorrow," Stephanie said, ignoring Kathy and shooting a glare to Luca. "Can we bring anything?"

"Just yourselves and some details."

"A very noisy toy for Mitchell, got it. Goodbye, Kathy." Stephanie hung up as Kathy started to threaten her well-being. "We're going to a family barbecue tomorrow." Stephanie reclaimed her spot next to Luca but refrained from climbing onto her lap. She wasn't entirely sure if a familial interruption and invite to spend time with family was a mood killer.

Luca rested her head in her hand and sat with her elbow propped on the back of the couch. She reached out and fingered the ends of Stephanie's hair. The gesture was small, but one that spoke volumes of their mutual need to touch and be touched. "I love barbecues and would love to see Mitchell again. But I have an important question, and I'm a bit worried it'll make me sound presumptuous." Stephanie's heart started to beat faster in the pit of her stomach. "If I didn't feel comfortable on your couch anymore, where might I find your bedroom?"

"You're not being presumptuous," Stephanie said with a quiet laugh. "But you are very sexy and a bit of a psychic, apparently." Stephanie stood and grabbed Luca's hand to pull her up.

As they walked hand in hand toward the bedroom, Luca said, "I actually have a funny story about a psychic. Remind me to tell you about it when we're in the mood for talking."

"That probably won't be for a while." Stephanie pulled her shirt over her head and kicked her shoes off. She had never felt as sexy as she did in that moment, under Luca's intense gaze.

"I'm okay with that."

❖

They lay spent in one another's arms an hour later. The sweat on their skin had just begun to dry. Stephanie nuzzled the nook of Luca's neck sleepily and lost herself in the scent of sex that surrounded her. Luca drew lazy circles on Stephanie's shoulder blade, which was as good as a lullaby.

"I don't want to ruin the moment…"

Stephanie sat up slightly. Despite the slight twinge of fear she felt at those words, her focus remained on the delectable feel of her bare breast pressed against Luca's skin and the way her swollen lips still tingled. This was the kind of moment that clung to your heart forever. "You really need to work on your introductions."

Luca laughed lightly. "I'll take that into consideration, boss." Luca kissed her gently. "You're amazing, this is amazing." She ran her fingers along Stephanie's collarbone and down to the peak of a pink nipple. "But my mind keeps wandering to what's next. I can't do casual with you. You're not just any woman, and I don't think I'll be able to convince my heart of that lie."

Stephanie's throat tightened and her eyes burned with unexpected tears. She felt the same way about Luca, and as obvious as it was every day, she'd tried to keep her growing affection buried. She placed her palm on the center of Luca's chest and focused on her heartbeat, rapid after her confession.

"I feel the same way. It's not every day that someone waltzes into my life like this. I'd be a fool to think you're ordinary." She pulled the sheets down Luca's body and nearly lost her thoughts in the way her pale lilac sheets contrasted with Luca's dark nipples. "You are far from ordinary, Luca Garner, and I believe you came into my life for a reason." Stephanie didn't bother to fight off the waver in her voice. For the first time in a long time, she felt her heart open courageously.

"So, what do we do?"

"We take our time. There've been no formal announcements yet, which gives us time to explore this. Let's take this time to really figure out what we want. You may not even like me after spending so much time with me." Stephanie pinched Luca's side, drawing out a deliciously girly giggle.

Luca swatted Stephanie's hand away. "I wholeheartedly doubt that, and I know you won't give up Chicago."

"I won't—"

Luca placed her finger against Stephanie's pink lips. "And I'd never ask that of you."

"I'll fight to make this work." Stephanie spoke against Luca's finger before kissing it gently. "But I do think it's in our best interest to focus on the now." Stephanie drew Luca's leg between her own and pressed her center against Luca's thigh. She was still wet from Luca's earlier manipulations. Stephanie's body had forgotten all about its fatigue and was now listening to her heart. Spending every moment wrapped around and filled by Luca was exactly what she needed. Sleep be damned.

## Chapter Thirteen

"As much as I love everything you're doing right now, we really need to get out of the car. I don't want your brother coming out here to find us like this." Luca laughed at Stephanie's exaggerated whine. They had been parked out front of Stephanie's brother's home for over twenty minutes. Every time Luca reached for the door handle, Stephanie would pull her in for a kiss. Luca wasn't about to complain, but she was beginning to worry about the quality of her first impression with Rick.

"I can't help myself," Stephanie mumbled between kisses. "Your lips are amazing."

"Every inch of you is amazing, but there are people waiting for us and I really want a hot dog."

"We spend one night together and you're already choosing hot dogs over me," Stephanie said with exaggerated disgust.

"Food is a necessity that gives me energy, and I'm pretty sure you prefer me to be energetic." Luca got out of the car just as Stephanie reached for her. "Barbecue now, touching later." Luca went to grab Stephanie's hand as they walked up the front walkway leading to Rick's house but wasn't entirely surprised when Stephanie pulled away. "Are we not out while we're here?"

Stephanie frowned at her. "It's been a very long time since I've brought anyone to meet my family. I guess I forgot proper etiquette."

Luca stepped into Stephanie's space on the doorstep. She smiled softly, pouring as much affection into the gesture as possible. "How long are we talking?"

"Years. I didn't even bring my last serious girlfriend around because my family never really seemed interested in meeting her." She shrugged. "Maybe I didn't seem all that interested in her, either."

"And me?" Luca intertwined their fingers again.

"I'm very interested and I know Kathy is—" The front door swung open.

"Kathy's what? I heard my name." Kathy looked between the two women as she dried her hands on a dish towel.

"I was just saying how happy you are that Luca could make it," Stephanie said. Kathy's eyes dropped to their joined hands and her face lit up. "And how happy I am that she could make it, as well."

Kathy smiled triumphantly, like she was responsible for the two who stood together at her door. "Come on in," she said, stepping aside. "There's a bouncing little boy running amok in the backyard waiting for you two."

"For Luca," Stephanie said, correcting her quickly. Kathy and Luca looked at Stephanie. Thick silence followed.

Luca's face dropped. "Steph, you're his aunt. He's definitely excited to see you."

"He's crazy about you and I totally get why." Stephanie pulled Luca even closer. The small confession cut through the tension that had filled the entryway.

Kathy clapped her hands together. "Well, all right then. This has become too cute for my liking. Let's head out back."

Luca waited for Kathy to be a few steps ahead of them before pulling Stephanie in for a brief but hard kiss. When she pulled back, she grinned at how shocked Stephanie was. "Crazy about me and interested in me? Watch out, I'm going to start thinking you like me."

"Shut up."

Luca laughed all the way to the backyard as Stephanie pulled her along. They stepped onto the large deck together. The day was sunny but not too hot, making it the perfect day for a barbecue. Luca stood still for a moment, soaking up the feeling of the warm air and Stephanie's hand in hers. Life had definitely taken an unexpected turn for the better. Stephanie tugged her hand.

"Are you ready to meet my brother?"

"I am. Which one is he?" Luca surveyed a group of men standing both by the grill and a cooler. One man with shaggy blond hair and stubbly face jumped out. Luca was sure she had won the guessing game, so she stepped away from Stephanie and walked right up to him. "Hi, I'm Luca. It's great to finally meet you, Rick." Luca thrust out her hand and waited for him to take it, but Stephanie swept in and redirected Luca's offered hand to someone else entirely. A dark-haired gentleman with even darker eyes and a blinding smile winked at Luca. He was the polar opposite of Stephanie in appearance, with a skin tone closer to Luca's and considerably taller. You'd never think they were siblings.

"Luca, this is my brother, Rick. Rick, this is Luca, my—"

"Something special enough to bring to a family barbecue. No need to label it anymore. Come here." Rick pulled Luca into a tight bear hug. His warm first impression was definitely opposite of his sister, too. "It's great to meet you." He pulled away from Luca and looked at his sister, who was red faced from laughing so hard. "And to think, my sister hated you in the beginning."

"Rick." Stephanie punched his upper arm. Rick genuinely looked pained for a second, but it wasn't long before he broke out into a deep, animated laugh. Stephanie looked at Luca with earnest eyes. "I never hated you."

Luca drew Stephanie into her body with an arm around her waist. "You didn't hate me, but you did hate the idea of me. And that's okay because I got to prove Stephanie Austin wrong. How many people can say that?" Rick raised his large hand and Luca high-fived him.

"I like her, Steph. Feel free to bring her around any time."

"That's it? No intense big brother interview?" Stephanie huffed.

"Nah," Rick said with a shake of his head. He turned his attention back to the grill. When he opened the lid, Luca's stomach growled at the smell of charred burgers and hot dogs. She saw one nearly black hot dog to the back with her name on it. "The thing with Steph is that she's so hardheaded that by the time she figures out she even likes a girl, she's known her forever. Thereby doing the screening process for me. My son was a big help with screening, too."

"Speaking of," Stephanie said. She looked around the yard. "Where is Mitchell?"

"After we promised him for the thirtieth time today that Luca was coming, he insisted on changing into a new shirt. Maybe I do need to watch out for you." Rick pointed at his eyes and then at Luca. "Everyone else in my family is smitten with you. Kathy may be next."

"It'll never happen," Kathy said from behind Luca. When Luca turned around, Mitchell launched himself into her arms. "No offense, Luca, but you're not my type. I like burly and hairy." Kathy patted Rick's cheek and scratched at his thick black beard.

"I'll come back for you in the winter, then." Luca winked at Kathy. She yelped when Stephanie pinched her backside. "Fine, I won't come back for her in the winter."

"I'm pinching you because I don't like hairy and burly."

"So high maintenance."

"Hi!" Mitchell yelled directly into Luca's ear. Her mistake for not acknowledging him right away.

"Hey, Mitchell. How have you been?" He buried his face into her neck. She looked to Kathy, who mouthed that Luca made him shy. "Your aunt and I are very happy to see you again. What's that on your shirt?"

Mitchell leaned back and picked up the front of his T-shirt. "El'phants."

"Aren't elephants your favorite?" He nodded so emphatically that Luca's grip almost faltered. "Do you know what your aunt's favorite animal is?" He shook his head and batted his large eyes. "Me either. Let's ask her." They both turned to Stephanie, who looked shocked by such a question.

"I guess I like peacocks." Mitchell looked unimpressed by her answer, so Luca silently encouraged her to pick a better, more child-friendly animal. "I like giraffes."

"Their necks are so long." Mitchell reached up over his head, almost smacking Luca's forehead in the process.

"So long." Luca agreed and added, "And they have long, long legs, just like Aunt Stephanie." She shot Stephanie a wink. Stephanie's cheeks colored instantly. Warm thoughts of kissing up those legs that morning made Luca's cheeks light up, too. She cleared her throat. "You hungry, bud?"

"Very," he said dramatically. "I could—I could eat a giraffe!" Luca and Stephanie laughed loudly and shared in Mitchell's sentiment. They had only managed a small breakfast together before Luca had to rush home for a change of clothes. Which, of course, took place after a long shower together.

Stephanie wrapped her arm around Luca's waist and leaned in to whisper, "I think the food's almost done. I'll sneak up and grab some. You two go get us some seats. Deal?"

"Deal," Mitchell and Luca said simultaneously. Luca watched Stephanie sneak off like a thief in the night. She played it up to entertain Mitchell, and Luca couldn't believe this was the same woman who initially seemed so awkward around kids. Maybe Luca had helped chisel away at that barrier a bit, maybe she hadn't. All Luca knew was that the blonde who was snatching up burgers and hot dogs was surprising her more and more every day. Mitchell wiggled in her arms, which were straining to keep him up. She set him on the ground.

"Okay, Mitchell, lead me to the best seats in the house." Luca followed Mitchell, and it wasn't until they were halfway up the stairs that led off the living room that she grabbed his shoulders and turned him around. "Maybe we should stay out on the patio where the rest of your family is."

"But the best seat in my house is my room."

"I bet it is, kid, I bet it is."

Once Luca and Mitchell rejoined Stephanie and the growing crowd in the backyard, the barbecue was in full swing. Luca tried her best to keep up with introductions and random conversations. The entire afternoon was a great success. Every one of Stephanie's family members, whether blood or by marriage, was welcoming and warm. She sat with her arm across the back of Stephanie's chair and Stephanie's hand resting on her thigh. Luca felt the small gesture in her chest, warm and significant.

The sun was beginning to set and Stephanie had not so discreetly checked her watch multiple times. They were gearing up to leave when Luca's phone rang. She lifted it from where it sat facedown on the table and frowned at the screen. The caller ID read "unknown number" and Luca declined the call. She shrugged at Stephanie, who looked concerned and turned her attention back to Kathy's best friend, Rita.

"Our date was terrible, horrible, and the kiss at the end of the night was even worse, but he was persistent."

"I would say so, considering you've now been married for ten years." Kathy laughed and swallowed the rest of her chardonnay. "We all married pretty young, except Stephanie here."

"To be fair, I wasn't able to legally marry until recently."

"How old are you, Stephanie?" Rita's question was met with a cold moment of silence. Luca shifted uncomfortably.

Stephanie twirled the singular ice cube in her glass of sweet tea twice. "I'm thirty-seven."

Rita leaned forward on her elbows with a mischievous grin. She looked directly at Luca and said, "Please tell me she's a cradle robber."

Luca's phone buzzed with a new voice mail. She picked it up and waved it around. "Saved by the bell. Excuse me while I go check this." She kissed the side of Stephanie's head and left the table.

"She can't be more than twenty-two. No way," Rita said, undeterred by the interruption.

Stephanie watched Luca pace as she listened to her message. She looked a bit rattled and made a phone call immediately afterward. Stephanie sipped her iced tea and took an ice cube into her mouth to chew it, releasing a bit of her nervous energy. "She's twenty-six." Rita started to cheer, but Stephanie raised her hand to stop her. "I don't care about age, and honestly, she's more mature than most women I know." She glared at Rita, earning a laugh from Kathy.

Kathy looked over her shoulder and back to Stephanie. "How did this happen? I mean, I knew you had a thing, it was so obvious, but how did it become a real thing?"

"We spent a lot of time working together and we sort of evolved from there." Stephanie started to twirl the ends of her hair as she thought of a way to describe the progression of her feelings for Luca. "We worked side by side, day in and day out, for weeks and didn't grow tired of one another or annoyed with one another. That speaks volumes of a partnership, besides the fact that she's absolutely gorgeous."

"She does have a bit of that girl next door, Sophia Bush and Rachel Bilson thing going on." Stephanie and Kathy both looked at Rita.

"Who?"

"*The O.C.*? *One Tree Hill*?"

Kathy scratched her forehead. "No clue."

"Nope, me neither," Stephanie said with shake of her head. She laughed lightly and looked back to where Luca was, only to find her charging back toward the table. "Luca? Is everything all right?"

Luca was pale and refused to make eye contact with anyone. "I have to head out. Will someone give you a ride home?"

"I can leave with you—"

"No, you stay. I insist." Luca's behavior was unlike anything Stephanie had ever seen.

Kathy offered. "I can drive her home. It'll spare me from most of the cleanup." Luca didn't acknowledge the joke and barely offered up a curt thank-you before heading out of the yard.

Stephanie sat confused and stunned for a moment before springing to her feet and chasing after Luca. She nearly had to sprint to catch up and met Luca just as she reached her car. "Wait," she said, reaching out for Luca's hand, but was dismayed when Luca pulled away forcefully. "What's wrong?" When Luca turned back, fierce redness colored her cheeks and tears filled her eyes.

"That phone call was from Mr. Witlin." Stephanie's stomach sank. "He wanted to call me himself to share the exciting news before it was formally announced tomorrow. Guess who's shipping out as soon as possible to be taken on as a rookie forensic accountant at LGR's Chicago branch?"

Stephanie's head was spinning and she took a deep breath to help collect her thoughts. "He must've noticed how great a team we are and decided to send both of us."

Luca let out a bark of artificial laughter. "I'm so dense, I thought the same thing. I even went as far as saying it. But you're not going to Chicago, Marvin is. After about the fifteenth time I asked why, Mr. Witlin finally admitted that he was filling your request. You wanted to get rid of me so badly that you didn't care if I was shipped to another state."

Stephanie felt the blood drain from her face. She grew unsteady on her feet. When had she made such a stern request? *I'll get rid of her, mark my words*. The promise came flooding back powerfully. She closed her eyes and could taste the burn of tequila from that night. She'd gone home after their run-in at the Dollhouse and drunkenly demanded Luca be sent anywhere, to anyone, without a care of where she landed. "Shit," she said under her breath. "Luca, this was never what I wanted."

"Yes, it was." Luca stood yelling on the sidewalk. "From the moment you met me you wanted to get rid of me. I just didn't know the lengths you would go to." Luca turned to get in her car, but Stephanie reached out and grabbed her.

"Please—" Stephanie's voice broke as tears welled in her eyes. "I'll fix this. I'll make it right."

"There's nothing you can do. I already quit my job."

"You what?"

"I quit. I'm not going to Chicago. You know how I feel about being away from my family, and I'm definitely not going after a job I'm being forced into because of someone who couldn't bear to work with me. God, did I earn any of this on my own?" Luca took a deep breath and scratched her head. "I really thought you had changed. No—" Luca stopped herself. She shook her head and gave Stephanie a sad smile, a sight Stephanie knew her heart would wear as a scar. "I thought you were finally allowing yourself to be the person you always were but kept hidden."

"I am that person, you have to believe me." Stephanie grasped desperately onto Luca's arm, trying to pull her close, as if that could shake her into a changing her mind.

Luca stepped up to her and held Stephanie's face in her hands before pressing a brief, delicate kiss to her lips. Stephanie's tears felt hot between their cheeks. Luca pulled away and said, "Whether I believe you or not won't change what you did. Goodbye, Stephanie."

Stephanie stood on the sidewalk, her hands on her hips and her head thrown back. She tried desperately to rein in her emotions as she stared blankly at the stars. Not ten or a million twinkling lights would make her feel any less like her own little world had just fallen apart.

## Chapter Fourteen

Stephanie called out sick for the first time in over a year that Monday. She couldn't face Mr. Witlin or Marvin, for that matter. She felt betrayed by her entire team, the group of people she had grown with over the years, but deep down she knew that was irrational. She knew her emotional turmoil, the nausea that kept her up, and the tears that made her eyes puffy beyond repair were completely her fault. Stephanie's stubbornness tore her newfound happiness away before she even realized it was there. Life was cruel. Stephanie was even crueler.

She dragged herself out of bed on Tuesday morning and moved sluggishly through her morning routine. She didn't care if her hair wasn't perfect or if a few wrinkles still marred her dress shirt—her day was already doomed, why did a few minor details matter? She threw random pieces of fruit into a brown bag to bring with her, and hated how a banana reminded her of the morning she spent with Luca. She needed sliced banana in her corn flakes, and there was just no settling for anything else. Stephanie teased her all morning about it, laughing openly and easily like she hadn't done in a while, until Luca shut her up with kisses. Stephanie smiled sadly and left the banana on the counter.

LGR's building had yet to fully wake up by the time Stephanie arrived. The hustle and bustle hadn't fully ignited, and the phones were surprisingly tame. As Stephanie walked to her office, she felt multiple sets of eyes follow her. None of them were accompanied by a friendly smile, not even the fake ones she had grown used to. She didn't dare remove her dark sunglasses until she was in the safety of her office. She silently thanked herself for having the foresight to grab coffee from an outside coffeehouse on her way to work. There'd be too many people crowding the break room.

Stephanie shut her door and felt compelled to lock it but refrained in the name of professionalism. She set her briefcase down and hung her linen blazer on a hook beside the door. She packed her sunglasses into their case. A green folder caught her eye from her desk. The folder was easily recognizable because she had handed it to Luca only three days prior. Stephanie took a seat and reached out, her hands shook lightly as she flipped the cover open to reveal a small handwritten note. Luca's crisp, feminine handwriting would haunt Stephanie for some time to come.

*Ms. Austin,*

*My findings were abundant and will more than likely be a surprise, even to you. You've stumbled onto something bigger than either of us expected. Not only do you have solid evidence against all parties involved, you have the beginnings of a multi-million-dollar laundering scheme. Read through this file carefully, and check my notes in each highlighted section.*

*I wish you all the best with this case and every one that finds its way to you in the future. Thank you for taking the time to help me grow as a forensic accountant, and for showing me what can be accomplished with hard work and dedication. My experience with LGR has been invaluable.*

*Regards,*
*Luca Garner*

The formality of Luca's final letter tore deeply into Stephanie, so she did the only thing she was capable of: work. She sifted through page after page, finding Luca's little notes to be her only reason to smile. But the deeper she got into the reports, the wider the web of inconsistent totals grew. Stephanie came across new reports on new businesses that Luca must've acquired on her own, leaving Stephanie to wonder when she had done all of this work. All of Stephanie's regrets hit her in that moment. She'd not only lost a wonderful person who had come into her life, she'd also lost one of the best employees she had ever worked with. Stephanie's own bullish stupidity had affected her personal and professional life.

"Son of a bitch." She checked her watch and counted the free minutes she had before her nine o'clock meeting. Stephanie grabbed the file and ran off in the direction of Mr. Witlin's office.

She hoped she'd get there before anyone else and have a moment alone with Mr. Witlin, but she arrived to a line forming outside his door. Accountants were waiting to speak with him, and Stephanie was willing to bet it was about senior positions in the Chicago office, even though she had missed the formal announcements. Stephanie didn't give a shit about Chicago, not anymore. Stephanie practically elbowed past everyone and came to a standstill before Mr. Witlin.

"Good morning, Stephanie," he said cheerily. "I hope you're feeling better today—"

"Why Luca?"

Mr. Witlin's face fell into confusion. "Excuse me?"

Stephanie decided to slow down and try again. "Why Luca?" He narrowed his eyes slightly, as if still trying to see the meaning within her words. "Why would you choose to send Luca Garner to Chicago?"

"Wait a second," a younger gentleman interjected from just outside the office. "You chose an assistant over me?"

Mr. Witlin closed the door and turned back to Stephanie, who was at his toes. "I expect you to explain yourself."

"I expect you to warn me before you transfer my assistant." Stephanie felt herself getting heated and knew she should take a breath and calm down, but too many emotions were clashing within her. She couldn't contain them all.

Mr. Witlin's jaw tensed firmly enough to be visible beneath his beard. "Do not forget your place, Ms. Austin. While I appreciate your ferocity at work, I think it would be in your best interest to take a step back immediately."

Stephanie did just that. She put a little distance between her and her boss and tried her best to tamp down her anger. She gritted her teeth and tried again. "Why did you choose Luca to transfer without talking to me first?"

"I didn't think I had to." He straightened the perfect knot of his tie and smoothed his crisp collar. "I was giving you what you wanted. Honestly, I expected a thank-you this morning. It worked out perfectly that things wrapped up in Chicago and we're ready to go live. Ms. Garner showed incredible potential and was recommended by Catherine Carter—seemed like a no-brainer to me. The transfer got her off your back, but she'd still be employed by a prestigious firm. Apparently Ms. Garner didn't care much for the idea. And if this is displaced anger over not being named to my Chicago roster, your behavior regarding Ms. Garner spoke volumes of you as a person and an employee."

Stephanie rubbed small, firm circles on her temples. Stephanie was no longer focused on her own reputation. "I need you to give me permission to hire her back."

"First you needed me to get rid of her for you, and now you need me to allow you to get her back? I sure hope you have more to say than that."

"She's an asset to this company. I realize now that I should've said that earlier. I had multiple opportunities during our meetings and every run-in we had in the hallways. That's my fault, all of this is my fault. Luca shouldn't be without a job because I'm an asshole." Stephanie tugged at the cuffs of her shirt and stood tall. "If you do not allow me to bring Luca back onto our team, you can consider this my resignation."

"You're going to quit over an assistant?" Mr. Witlin gawked at her.

"No, I wouldn't be quitting because of Luca, I'd be quitting because I've dedicated years of my life to this firm and have proven time and time again that I'm a trustworthy asset. If you tell me I can't hire her back, then you're telling me you don't trust me when I say having her will allow us to continue being the best firm on the East Coast, and eventually one of the best in the country." Stephanie felt light-headed by the time she finished her tirade, the reality of her ultimatum kick-started her heart rate. She tried her best to keep her breathing even and her eyes unblinking as she stared down her boss, but all she wanted to do was put her head between her knees to keep from passing out.

"I suppose this is when I tell you whether your next phone call will be to Luca or to unemployment?" Stephanie nodded. Mr. Witlin smiled softly. "Do tell Ms. Garner that I'm happy to have her back."

"Happy will be an understatement after you look at this." Stephanie slid the green folder toward him on the table. "We had to keep this case under wraps for a bit while we collected enough evidence. Luca found this, and all I did was give her one crumb to follow." Stephanie knew she was beaming with pride.

Mr. Witlin took the folder from Stephanie and tucked it under his arm. "For the record, I didn't want to let Luca go."

"Furthermore for the record, I was a terrible person for strong-arming you into that decision." Stephanie turned for the door, but was called back.

"May I ask you something that borders on personal?"

Stephanie tilted her head. "Of course."

"Should I assign Luca to work with a different senior accountant?"

Stephanie knew he was keenly observant, but that didn't soften the shock she felt. "If you're worried about conflict of interest, Gerard, I assure you I'll come to you at the first sign of an issue. But for now, I believe we're both professionals and you won't have a problem." Stephanie didn't need to say the implied aloud. She saw the glint in Mr. Witlin's eye that told her he already figured out more than she'd ever share willingly. "Let me know when you finish going through that." Stephanie pointed to the folder. "You're going to want to assemble a team, and Luca and I will be heading it." Mr. Witlin nodded and Stephanie made her way back to the office.

She had two meetings scheduled for the afternoon and knew she couldn't have this conversation with Luca over the phone. Her intentions being misinterpreted was the last thing Stephanie wanted. She'd have to wait until after work, which was probably for the best. She'd have time to collect her thoughts and figure out how to apologize for something so extraordinarily awful. How do you apologize for something you never thought yourself capable of? Yes, extra time to think and plan was a good thing. A young man who Stephanie recognized as a former intern walked past her door and shot her an evil look.

Stephanie just hoped she'd survive the workday. She could practically smell the torches burning and see the pitchforks in the distance.

## Chapter Fifteen

Luca turned off the TV after cycling through the channel guide for the hundredth time. Not one good show or movie was on, no worthwhile program was on her list to stream, and she didn't care to talk to anyone from the outside world. Luca had already ignored one call from her brother and four from Alice. Andrew had called multiple times and Charles even sent a message asking if Ms. Austin would be interested in taking him on. The only call Luca answered was from Catherine, and she was flattered when she was offered a job. But being a financial advisor was never part of her plan because forensic accounting was in her heart. Even if Stephanie had stained Luca's dream career with a bitter aftertaste. She threw the remote on her cluttered ottoman and went to the kitchen for a snack. She barely lifted her feet as she walked, allowing herself to glide along on her white socks. She had worn the same old flannel pajama set for two days, even putting it back on after showering because she could count on its comforts. Luca had always reasoned that as long as you didn't sweat or have sex while wearing them, pajamas never really got dirty anyway.

She groaned in dismay when she opened her empty fridge. A carton of orange juice sat beside a bottle of ketchup and a package of bologna. Hardly anything worth getting up for. Luca's stomach growled in complaint, desperate for something more than the handfuls of dry cereal she had choked down that morning. She considered delivery, but when her stomach growled again, Luca knew what was needed.

"Taco Bell," she said to herself as she grabbed her keys and made her way out. She was shocked to find Stephanie standing on the other side of the door, phone in hand, looking like a deer in headlights. "How long have you been standing there?"

"Not long. I was just about to call you." Luca looked Stephanie up and down, noting the creases in her shirt and pants, and the way her hair was pulled back without care. She must've just come from the office. "Twenty minutes."

"What?"

"I've been standing here for twenty minutes trying to decide if I should call, text, or just knock. I decided that calling would be my safest bet."

Luca crossed her arms over her chest, painfully aware of her unkempt state. "What are you even doing here?"

"I want to talk to you about a few things. Can we go inside?" Stephanie asked. Luca hesitated. "This is more of a professional visit than anything else, I promise."

Luca stepped aside and let Stephanie in. At least her nerves made her hunger go away, saving her a trip. "My place is a bit of a wreck right now, so excuse the mess." Luca watched as Stephanie floated about her apartment, looking at anything and everything her eyes could fall on. By the time Stephanie had made it to her bookcase, Luca cleared her throat to get her attention. "You're not talking."

"Sorry. There's so much more in your place than mine. It's very distracting."

"Yeah, well, we are very different people." Luca plopped down on her worn sectional sofa.

"Are we?" Stephanie sat on the sofa, too, but at the farthest point from Luca. She looked at Luca intensely, in the kind of way Luca always felt beneath her skin.

"You came here for a professional discussion." Luca needed to remind Stephanie, because she was not willing to welcome anything else.

"I'd like to offer you a position with LGR."

Luca laughed outright. "You've got to be kidding me." Luca despised playing games, and career tug-of-war was topping the most hated list right now.

"I'm very serious. You can be placed with another senior accountant if you'd like, but I came here specifically for you to be on my team of investigators set to work on the money laundering scheme you uncovered. This is essentially your case, Luca, no one else should be working on it."

Luca saw the earnest look in Stephanie's eyes and believed every word, but that didn't change the past. "How am I supposed to work with you now? I'd be second-guessing my every move and wondering if you'll have me cut from the team without warning."

"I mistreated you before. I handled everything so poorly from day one up until the moment I realized how vital you'd be to LGR. What I did was wrong and completely out of line. You have my word that I won't do anything like that again." Stephanie sat prim and proper, her back pin straight and her hands folded neatly on her lap. Her face remained stoic. She reminded Luca of the Stephanie she'd met on her first day.

"What do you think your word means to me now?"

"I spoke to Gerard Witlin directly about your worth to his company. I made it very clear that we will not remain at the top of our game if he didn't agree to hire you back. Mr. Witlin trusts my word, and I think you should, too."

"Mr. Witlin and I are not the same, especially not in this situation."

"You'll be able to see more clearly if you separate personal from professional," Stephanie said matter-of-factly, like Luca's feelings were just another bit of business for her.

The small piece of advice cut the cord of Luca's emotional control. "I can't do that." She popped up from the couch to stand and pace. "I'm not like you, Stephanie. I think, feel, and act with my heart." She pounded the center of her chest with her fist. "I'm not calculated and cold. I can't sit and talk business with someone when I can still feel them against my skin, when I still ache because of them." Stephanie's head dropped. "I can't turn off my feelings just because I have to go back to work."

Stephanie sniffled. "I can't either," she said quietly, barely above a whisper. Luca stumbled back a step in disbelief. "I'm not calculated and cold. I'm professional and guarded. I think things through before I act, and I keep the people I work with at arm's length because I've had to." Stephanie looked up at Luca with watery eyes. "I've worked with horrible people in the past. Men who've harassed me, women who took advantage of me, and so many more who acted like I was invisible."

"Steph—"

"I am the way I am today for many reasons, and I thought you'd find them all out as we got to know one another. It's not because I'm heartless or that I like being a bitch, it's because my heart has no place in my professional life." Stephanie wiped her face and moved to stand before Luca. "I've done nothing but think, feel, and act with my heart since you managed to get through to it. Yes, I fucked up early on and I'm very sorry, but that doesn't change the fact that we make a great team—in and out of the office. I forgot about the email I sent to Mr. Witlin because I sent it the night you approached me in the bar. I wanted you gone then because I was drunk and I knew you were dangerous."

Luca laughed loudly and then covered her mouth. "I'm sorry," she mumbled between her fingers. "No one has ever called me dangerous before."

"You were to me, because I knew that if I let you in, I'd be a goner."

Luca reached out and wiped away a tear from Stephanie's cheek. "And how do you feel now?" Luca stepped closer, closing the distance between their bodies.

"Oh, I'm definitely a goner." Stephanie laughed. "I threatened to quit LGR if he didn't hire you back." Luca's mouth fell open. "I really do care and I missed you so much." Her chin started to quiver again. Luca pulled her into a hug and buried her face into the crook of Stephanie's neck. She could feel her own tears start to rise. "It was only two days, but they were the loneliest two day for me."

Luca kissed Stephanie's neck and then her ear. She kissed her wet eyelids and the tip of her nose. "I was so mad at you." Stephanie tried to pull away, but Luca held her chin and didn't allow her to escape. "But I still missed you and your stubbornness. I really, really like you, Stephanie Austin."

"I really, really like you, too. And I'm so sorry for everything I've done."

Luca saw nothing but sincerity in Stephanie's eyes. She licked her lips in preparation for the kiss she had been craving since their last goodbye, but she stopped herself short. "Can you promise me something?"

"Anything." Stephanie's eyes were already closed and her full lips were pouty.

"If you find that at some point you've stopped liking me, do you promise not to have me moved halfway across the country?" Luca asked. Stephanie slapped at her shoulder lightly.

"You're being mean. That's not funny—" Luca cut off Stephanie with a kiss.

Their lips melded together perfectly, just like they had during their first kiss, and just as they would for many kisses after that. Luca felt along Stephanie's arms and shoulders, reveling in the solid presence of the woman who had made her way into Luca's heart without warning. She weaved her fingers into Stephanie's hair and held her close as she deepened the kiss. Stephanie's hands gripped Luca's waist with an exquisite intensity. They worked together so well, even in intimacy. Luca's partnership with Stephanie was sure to surprise her every day, both inside and outside the office.

## One Year Later

Stephanie never wanted the music to stop. "I haven't danced this much in years," she shouted to Luca, who was dancing along with wild abandon. Stephanie twirled once more before shuffling toward Luca on the dance floor. A crowd had formed in the center of the floor, all shaking and bopping around the newlyweds. Stephanie practically jumped from excitement when Luca had received an invitation to Catherine and Imogene's wedding, and even more so when she read the small note inside stating how honored Catherine would be to have both Luca and Stephanie as witnesses on her special day. Stephanie had never been a big fan of weddings, but this celebration felt nothing like any wedding she had ever been to.

"Are you having fun?" Imogene asked from over Stephanie's shoulder. She was swinging from Catherine's arms, her long red hair flowing about.

Stephanie's broad smile matched Luca's grin. "I'm having a blast. You really know how to throw a party."

"Try telling that to Cat. She thinks I went overboard."

Stephanie looked around the rustic winery and took in the colorful displays of flowers and romantic paper lanterns that hung everywhere. Once upon a time, she would've thought the decorations to be a bit flamboyant, but now she saw things with her heart before her mind could pass judgment. "The space is lovely and you're both gorgeous." Imogene smiled radiantly and pulled herself into Catherine more tightly.

"Not as gorgeous as you," Luca whispered into Stephanie's ear.

"No one is supposed to be more beautiful than the brides on their wedding day," Stephanie chastised. She wrapped her arms around

Luca's neck and pressed their hips together. "Except you. You're the most breathtaking woman in the world."

Luca chuckled. "You're a smooth talker, Ms. Austin. Are you looking to get lucky tonight?"

"I wouldn't hate it if we snuck out a little early." Stephanie brought her hands to rest on Luca's chest, left bare by the neckline of her black dress. She scratched her skin lightly with her short nails. Luca's breath hitched. "This wedding is making me think about how much I love you and this dress." She slid her index finger beneath a thin strap and toyed with it. "I'd love nothing more than to be able to show you what I'm thinking."

"Want to know what I'm thinking?" Luca's eyes were intense and Stephanie felt her heartbeat jump.

"I'm going to slow it down for a minute." The DJ interrupted the moment. Stephanie let out a disappointed groan. "But I want all the couples to stay on the floor." The singles and bashful couples scattered. Stephanie remained in Luca's arms. "I'm going to play one of the brides' favorite slow songs, and as it plays, I'll ask couples who've been together, either married or dating, for a certain amount of time to leave the floor. Eventually, we'll be left with the couple who's been together the longest, and if they don't deserve a round of applause, none of us do." The crowd cheered.

"This'll be quick." Luca laughed.

"At Last" by Etta James started playing. Incredibly clichéd, but no less romantic. Stephanie held Luca tighter. The DJ let the song play for thirty seconds before he started the elimination. "Any couples together for less than one month, please leave the floor. Marriage cancels out dating, so let's have the newlyweds step off the dance floor." He waved as Catherine and Imogene stepped aside, all smiles, and everyone continued to dance. His six-month announcement knocked a few more couples from the floor.

Stephanie stared into Luca's eyes as she swayed to the music. "You didn't tell me what you're thinking." She played with the fine hairs at the nape of Luca's neck.

"Every couple that has been together for a year or less, please step aside."

"That's our cue." Luca pulled Stephanie off to the perimeter of the dance floor.

They stood together silently, Stephanie standing with her back resting against Luca's front. Luca's arms were loosely around her waist. Stephanie felt safe and loved, two things she never thought she'd grow used to or become dependent on. She closed her eyes and let her head fall back onto Luca's shoulder. The five-, ten-, and twenty-year-old relationships joined them as Stephanie lost herself in the moment. Luca's lips grazed her ear and a chill crept along Stephanie's skin.

"I was thinking about how I'd like to marry you one day." Luca's whisper was raspy and low, just as it always was during their most intimate moments.

Stephanie stiffened briefly at the unexpected confession. They had spoken of their relationship and the future of their coupling, but this was the first time marriage was mentioned. She turned to face Luca as the crowd celebrated the final couple that danced in the middle of the floor. She searched Luca's face and found nothing but adoration and sincerity. "You would?"

Luca nodded and brushed a piece of Stephanie's hair behind her ear. "Of course we have a little ways to go before then, but I see a forever with you. A stubborn, hectic forever," Luca said with a high-pitched laugh. Stephanie knew she was nervous talking about this; her chest was splotchy and voice louder than usual. "But a forever I know I'd be happy in."

Stephanie wanted to say so much, but the music had died and she knew there were better times than that moment to discuss her daydreams with Luca. She kept her reply simple. "I see the same forever as you."

"Come on." Alice rushed up to them and grabbed their wrists. "Time for the bouquet toss, and you're both unmarried women." Her grin was alarming, as was the crazy and amused look in her eyes.

Stephanie stood beside Luca as all the eligible women gathered for the bouquet toss. Stephanie always considered the tradition to be silly, but if Luca was lining up, so was she. Everyone counted in time as Imogene stood in front of them, her infectious laughter filling the room. On three, the bouquet of bluebonnets and wildflowers went up into the air. Stephanie's mind flashed with images of a life lived alongside Luca, and as her hands filled with the soft petals of the bouquet, her heart filled with love and an understanding that Luca was right all along. Working together had truly been the opportunity of a lifetime.

## About the Authors

**Julie Cannon** (JulieCannon.com) divides her time by being a corporate suit, a wife, mom, sister, friend, and writer. Julie and her wife have lived in at least a half a dozen states, traveled around the world, and have an unending supply of dedicated friends. And of course, the most important people in their lives are their three kids, #1, Dude, and the Divine Miss Em.

Julie's novel *I Remember* won the Golden Crown Literary Society's Best Lesbian Romance in 2014.

**Aurora Rey** grew up in a small town in south Louisiana, daydreaming about New England. She keeps a special place in her heart for the South, especially the food and the ways women are raised to be strong, even if they're taught not to show it. After a brief dalliance with biochemistry, she completed both a BA and an MA in English.

When she's not writing or at her day job in higher education, she loves to cook and putter around the house. She's slightly addicted to Pinterest, has big plans for the garden, and would love to get some goats.

She lives in Ithaca, New York, with her partner, two dogs, and whatever wild animals have taken up residence at the pond.

**M. Ullrich** has always called New Jersey home and currently resides by the beach with her wife and boisterous feline children. After many years of regarding her writing as just a hobby, the gentle yet persistent words of encouragement from her wife pushed M. Ullrich to take a leap into the world of publishing. Much to her delight and amazement, that world embraced her back.

Although M. Ullrich may work full-time in the optical field, her favorite hours are the ones she spends writing and eating ridiculously large portions of breakfast foods for every meal. When her pen isn't furiously trying to capture her imagination (a rare occasion), she enjoys being a complete entertainer. Whether she's telling an elaborate story or a joke, or getting up in front of a crowd to sing and dance her way through her latest karaoke selection, M. Ullrich will do just about anything to make others smile. She also happens to be fluent in three languages: English, sarcasm, and TV/movie quotes.

## Books Available From Bold Strokes Books

**A Call Away** by KC Richardson. Can a businesswoman from a big city find the answers she's looking for, and possibly love, on a small-town farm? (978-1-63555-025-2)

**Berlin Hungers** by Justine Saracen. Can the love between an RAF woman and the wife of a Luftwaffe pilot, former enemies, survive in besieged Berlin during the aftermath of World War II? (978-1-63555-116-7)

**Blend** by Georgia Beers. Lindsay and Piper are like night and day. Working together won't be easy, but not falling in love might prove the hardest job of all. (978-1-63555-189-1)

**Hunger for You** by Jenny Frame. Principe of an ancient vampire clan Byron Debrek must save her one true love from falling into the hands of her enemies and into the middle of a vampire war. (978-1-63555-168-6)

**Mercy** by Michelle Larkin. FBI Special Agent Mercy Parker and psychic ex-profiler Piper Vasey learn to love again as they race to stop a man with supernatural gifts who's bent on annihilating humankind. (978-1-63555-202-7)

**Pride and Porters** by Charlotte Greene. Will pride and prejudice prevent these modern-day lovers from living happily ever after? (978-1-63555-158-7)

**Rocks and Stars** by Sam Ledel. Kyle's struggle to own who she is and what she really wants may end up landing her on the bench and without the woman of her dreams. (978-1-63555-156-3)

**The Boss of Her: Office Romance Novellas** by Julie Cannon, Aurora Rey, and M. Ullrich. Going to work never felt so good. Three office romance novellas from talented writers Julie Cannon, Aurora Rey, and M. Ullrich. (978-1-63555-145-7)

**The Deep End** by Ellie Hart. When family ties become entangled in murder and deception, it's time to find a way out… (978-1-63555-288-1)

**A Country Girl's Heart** by Dena Blake. When Kat Jackson gets a second chance at love, following her heart will prove the hardest decision of all. (978-1-63555-134-1)

**Dangerous Waters** by Radclyffe. Life, death, and war on the home front. Two women join forces against a powerful opponent, nature itself. (978-1-63555-233-1)

**Fury's Death** by Brey Willows. When all we hold sacred fails, who will be there to save us? (978-1-63555-063-4)

**It's Not a Date** by Heather Blackmore. Kade's desire to keep things with Jen on a professional level is in Jen's best interest. Yet what's in Kade's best interest…is Jen. (978-1-63555-149-5)

**Killer Winter** by Kay Bigelow. Just when she thought things could get no worse, homicide Lieutenant Leah Samuels learns the woman she loves has betrayed her in devastating ways. (978-1-63555-177-8)

**Score** by MJ Williamz. Will an addiction to pain pills destroy Ronda's chance with the woman she loves, or will she come out on top and score a happily ever after? (978-1-62639-807-8)

**Spring's Wake** by Aurora Rey. When wanderer Willa Lange falls for Provincetown B&B owner Nora Calhoun, will past hurts and a fifteen-year age gap keep them from finding love? (978-1-63555-035-1)

**The Northwoods** by Jane Hoppen. When Evelyn Bauer, disguised as her dead husband, George, travels to a Northwoods logging camp to work, she and the camp cook Sarah Bell forge a friendship fraught with both tenderness and turmoil. (978-1-63555-143-3)

**Truth or Dare** by C. Spencer. For a group of six lesbian friends, life changes course after one long snow-filled weekend. (978-1-63555-148-8)

**A Heart to Call Home** by Jeannie Levig. When Jessie Weldon returns to her hometown after thirty years, can she and her childhood crush Dakota Scott heal the tragic past that links them? (978-1-63555-059-7)

**Children of the Healer** by Barbara Ann Wright. Life becomes desperate for ex-soldier Cordelia Ross when the indigenous aliens of her planet are drawn into a civil war and old enemies linger in the shadows. Book Three of the Godfall Series. (978-1-63555-031-3)

**Hearts Like Hers** by Melissa Brayden. Coffee shop owner Autumn Primm is ready to cut loose and live a little, but is the baggage that comes with out-of-towner Kate Carpenter too heavy for anything long term? (978-1-63555-014-6)

**Love at Cooper's Creek** by Missouri Vaun. Shaw Daily flees corporate life to find solace in the rural Blue Ridge Mountains, but escapism eludes her when her attentions are captured by small town beauty Kate Elkins. (978-1-62639-960-0)

**Twice in a Lifetime** by PJ Trebelhorn. Detective Callie Burke can't deny the growing attraction to her late friend's widow, Taylor Fletcher, who also happens to own the bar where Callie's sister works. (978-1-63555-033-7)

**Undiscovered Affinity** by Jane Hardee. Will a no-strings-attached affair be enough to break Olivia's control and convince Cardic that love does exist? (978-1-63555-061-0)

**Between Sand and Stardust** by Tina Michele. Are the lifelong bonds of love strong enough to conquer time, distance, and heartache when Haven Thorne and Willa Bennette are given another chance at forever? (978-1-62639-940-2)

**Charming the Vicar** by Jenny Frame. When magician and atheist Finn Kane seeks refuge in an English village after a spiritual crisis, can local vicar Bridget Claremont restore her faith in life and love? (978-1-63555-029-0)

Bold Strokes Books
Quality and Diversity in LGBTQ Literature